VALENTINE'S DAY

by

April Kelly

Flight
Risk
Books

Published September 2015

ISBN: 978-0692477977

Library of Congress: TXu 1-947-5551

For additional information about this or any other
Flight Risk Books fiction, or to contact one of our
authors, please visit
http://www.flightriskbooks.com

Valentine's Day

"The wonderfully easy first-person voice seems drawn from the golden age of detective stories. ...plays fair with the mystery elements, weaving clues into the engaging central tale via smoothly blended storylines. Murder, greed and betrayal remain constants throughout, making this trip through the Hollywood Hills an example of first-rate escapist reading."

—Kirkus Reviews

"A clever plot, engaging characters, and a solid dose of self-deprecating humor make this unique detective mystery a highly entertaining read."

—Chanticleer Book Reviews

"A character driven novel with a great plot. Keeps the story moving at an easy pace, never losing its readers, while keeping them turning the pages. Filled with drama, humor and the required bumps on the head. For a great read, I highly recommend this to mystery lovers."

Tom Johnson
The Pulp Den

Valentine's Day was named one of the notable books of 2015 by Shelf Unbound Magazine.

Also by April Kelly

Winged

By April Kelly and Marsha Lyons

Murder In One Take
Murder: Take Two
Murder: Take Three

For Dave

Upend every Medieval Times restaurant in America, shake out the employees in one location and you'll have something that looks a lot like the Los Angeles County Renaissance Faire. At the insistence of my high school girlfriend I had gone once ten years earlier, after which I swore I would chug antifreeze before ever stepping foot again in that bogus Camelot.

But a job's a job and the check had cleared. I waited for my client beneath the awning of Squire Landingham's victuals booth, staying out of the direct glare of the hot noonday sun. The squire, exclusive purveyor of soft pretzels to the queen according to his sign, accepted credit cards, so I ate a pretzel and held a pewter flagon of ginger beer. I say held, rather than drank, as one taste confirmed I had not ordered a beverage in the beer phylum, but something in the carbonated urine family.

I hadn't wanted to look too eager or too casual for my very first paying client, so I had ruled out both a business suit and a getup like all the passing Knerds of the Round Table were wearing, opting to roll with working-guy cool: ye olde khaki pants, loosened tie and an open-collar Oxford shirt with the sleeves rolled up to my elbows.

The texts had all come from somebody calling herself Lady Hale. She claimed her sister was being stalked by an ex-BF, and feared he would violate the restraining order while disguised as a participant in the Faire. My client's sister was playing lady-in-waiting to the visiting French queen that day. As I swallowed the last gummy pretzel gob, a short, buxom wench beelined toward me through the crowd of friars, farriers and fire-eaters.

"Richard Valentine?"

"Lady Hale."

Her exploded mane of blonde could have been ripped from the scalp of any eighties' hair-band drummer, and improbably large breasts challenged the load limit of her peasant blouse above a tightly laced...jerkin? Doublet?

"Follow me, please, Mr. Valentine," she said, in a pronounced southern drawl.

I dumped the contents of my flagon and handed it back to the squire, then hurried after a swirl of petticoats and a cumulus cloud of hair. Lady Hale ducked through the flap of a small tent, so I did the same.

The nine by nine space was empty of all but a strong smell of horse manure and a shiny black suit of armor laid out on a rough-hewn wood bench. As I pushed through the human-sized cat flap, she handed me a photograph of a fortyish woman with a kindly face and a plain hair style. Her sister, she informed me.

"Quick, put on the armor."

"Say what?"

"He'll make his move in the confusion after the jousting tournament when the king and queen return to the royal pavilion with their retinue. You need to be inside before they arrive, but no one is allowed entry unless they're wearing period garb."

It seemed to me a stuffed falcon tied to my forearm would have been garb enough, but I tucked the photo into my shirt pocket and sussed out the armor. Lady Hale offered to hold my cell phone and wallet while I wedged myself into Galahad's skinny jeans.

"Here," she said, handing back my things after I was completely armored. "Drop them down the neck opening before you put on the helmet and they'll stay put until you get back."

I creaked along behind her, sweating like an armadillo on a grill as she led me through a maze that included tethered goats and hooded executioners. When a triumphant roar erupted somewhere ahead of us, milady stopped.

"The tournament's ending," she said, looking up at me. "My sister's wearing a forest green gown with a yellow girdle and she has on a white wimple." Pointing, she added, "The royal pavilion is right around the corner from that catapult. Any questions?"

"What's a wimple?"

She reached up to snap my visor shut before assuring me she would find her sister and me after the royal party dispersed and the danger was past.

Because my instructions were to provide a looming, protective presence, not to get physical, I'd left my Smith & Wesson locked in the glove box of my car. I was steel-plated down to my fingertips, though, so if the jerk got pushy with my client's sister I was prepared to go all medieval on his ass.

Moving with the grace of a rusted C3PO, I approached the rear entrance of the purple-striped pavilion. That's when I heard two loud pops, then screams, so I lumbered through the hanging canvas door. In the chaos, costumed folk poured into the tent through the front entrance, while those inside who had already shed their sweltering outfits tried to run out that same opening to see what had happened. As I scanned the interior through the visor's slits, afraid I had failed my client by not finding her sister in time, a man in a suit of black armor like the one I wore shouldered me aside with a clang in his rush to the rear exit. Stumbling in my weighty exoskeleton, I turned to flip him the metal finger, but the dark knight with the bundled-up Santa Claus suit he inexplicably carried disappeared without looking back.

Amidst a crush of frantic courtiers, I forced my way through the front, stepping into the nightmare I'd half-expected to find. On the ground a couple yards away lay a woman in a green gown, the yellow lace-up around her middle soaked with blood. The pointy white hat near her head was still loosely connected by a filmy scarf.

Yanking off my left gauntlet, I crossed to her while the crowd fell back in shock, twenty people pulling cell phones from the folds of clothes that predated this event by five hundred years. When I clumsily knelt to check her carotid, someone yelled, "That's him! He shot her!"

Rudely tackled by three pages and a jester, I crashed face-first in the dirt, pinned under the weight of my armor and a foot clad in a curly-toed slipper with a bell on it until the cops arrived and hauled me vertical.

On the long march to the patrol car they allowed me to remove my helmet, but the rest of my body felt like stew meat in a Crock-Pot as the sun's blistering rays absorbed into the hot couture. I knew it would be fruitless to defend myself to the officers who drove me to the police station a few miles away. They had no interest in my story, so I saved it for someone who counted.

Having shucked my shell and been relieved of wallet, phone and pocket contents, I was left alone in an interrogation room to muse about how stupidly I'd walked into a frame-up. My former boss might be a jerk and a cheapskate, but he would have sniffed out the con from a mile away. I wrote up a description of Lady Hale and a timeline of events on a yellow pad left on the table for badder asses than me.

Eventually someone who counted entered the room, dropping a file folder and my belongings onto the surface in front of me.

"How you holding up there, dick?"

"It's Rick."

"I wasn't referring to your name," he said, pulling out the chair across from me and sitting down. "I was commenting on the fact that you've only been a PI for seventeen minutes and you're already on the hook for a homicide. Most hired eyeballs take at least a year to step into *this* kind of doo-doo."

I'd had my license for nearly three weeks, but chose not to quibble with Det. Bao over his assessment of my professional virginity, as more important issues loomed large. Normally the presence of a hundred other guys walking around in heavy metal would have cast doubt on my culpability, but the photo they'd taken from my pocket was of the dead woman and it had a description of her costume written on the back.

"So, who paid you to make the hit?"

I explained it had been a bodyguard gig, not a contract killing, and assured him multiple texts from Lady Hale would confirm my claim. Det. Bao nodded thoughtfully. "Yeah? Show me."

He slid my phone across the table and I soon discovered the texts had been deleted, obviously by her ladyship while I shimmied into the tin overalls. Again, I explained; again, he nodded amiably. "What about the cash in your wallet?"

I snorted. "Thirty-one dollars? That's less than the going rate for a hit on a cockroach. Seriously, check with Orkin."

Det. Bao opened my wallet, removed a wad of bills, then fanned out more hundreds than I'd seen my whole life.

"Aw, crap."

"And plenty of it. Why'd you ditch your metal glove?"

"It's a gauntlet and I took it off to check for a pulse on the vic.'

"We gonna find gunshot residue when we process it?"

"I'm sure you will, since they thought of everything else."

He pulled the yellow pad to his side of the table and silently read through my handwritten statement, asking for minor clarifications here and there. When he finished he passed it to me, open to the last page. "How about you put your John Hancock there to make it official."

"I already signed it."

"Statements have to be witnessed to be allowed in as evidence."

Suddenly things were getting a little too real. Picking up the pen, I asked, "Do I need to lawyer up?"

"No, but you *do* need to stop getting your lines from TV cop shows."

"Okay, let me rephrase. Am I under arrest?"

"Nah," he said, standing. "Too pat. And that Sigma we found in your car looks like it's never been fired."

"It hasn't." From the weary shake of his head, I could guess what Det. Bao thought about civilian investigators. I *had* fired guns before and I'm a pretty fair marksman, but those weapons were the property of my previous employer and were locked away from me after I gave two-weeks' notice. My own pistol was brand spanking new and hadn't made it to a shooting range yet.

"You're free to go while we look at other suspects."

I hated to leave with him believing I was a total loser, so I peppered him with the questions I thought a pro would ask. "Was she married? Husband having an affair? Money problems?"

"Get serious, I'm not discussing it with you. And remember, I may be cutting you loose, but you're still, shall I say, of interest, so tool on back to your office and let the grown-ups do the investigating on this."

Since my car *was* my office at the time, I had only to tool on over to impound to retrieve it. In trying to make creative lemonade out of my financial lemons, I had printed up business cards that said, in addition to my phone and email contact information: Richard Valentine, MI. Below that line were the words *Mobile Investigator—I come to you*. In LA, where even the shortest drive is a trial, I hoped my willingness to travel to the client would be a plus.

Det. Bao had treated me very decently, but if I thought it was because of my obvious innocence I was disabused of that notion when my cell rang and I saw it was Dako Farona calling.

"You owe me, Valentine."

"How do you figure that when I'm still waiting for my final paycheck?"

"I just phone-shtupped some out-county lawman into cutting you loose on a murder rap."

Dako liked to play that rough-edged P I stereotype to the hilt, but I'd watched him testify in court enough times to know he could be forthright, unshakable, and that he was begrudgingly respected by cops all over southern California.

"I don't suppose your magnanimity would extend to helping me find the real killer."

"Happy to. I'll send someone over for fifty bucks an hour."

"Jesus, Dako, you only paid me *fifteen* an hour."

"And that's what I'll pay the guy I send to help you clear your name. Look, kid, fifty's the friends and family discount; regular chump clients pay sixty."

I passed. No wonder "Lady Hale" had selected me. At twenty per, I must have been the cheapest detective she called. And here I was pleased with having given myself a five-an-hour raise.

On the drive back to my room in the Santa Monica home of Kitty and Bitsy Sutterman, I mapped out my investigation. First I'd call every costume rental place in the area until I knew who had rented two black suits of armor, one for me and the one the killer wore. Beo seemed like a competent detective, but this was personal. The perps had made me look like a fool and I had no intention of being warned off.

I pulled in at Casa de Sutterman after ten and all the lights were out except the one at the front door. My twin octogenarian landladies like to get their beauty sleep underway early, so evenings here are always quiet. Not that I'm complaining. My room is large, private and has its own bathroom, but the best thing about it is the rent: nada. All I have to do is carry the garbage cans down to the curb, drive the Suttermans to the grocery store on Saturday morning and kill spiders for them. That last one is my biggest responsibility. The girls' eyesight is going, so every dust bunny or raisin looks like a possible brown recluse.

As on-site arachnid euthanizer, I receive home-cooked meals from Kitty and Bitsy. Sure enough, I found a pan of Swiss steak, mashed potatoes and green beans in the fridge with a set of warming instructions. The only thing my stomach had pro-cessed all day was an Elizabethan-era pretzel, so I skipped the nuking and inhaled my dinner standing at the sink.

I was the unnamed person of interest held briefly and released, as reported the next morning, merely a footnote, while the main coverage focused on the brazen, daylight shooting of Marie Winters, inheritor of her father's profitable chain of pizza restaurants. Mrs. Winters had no siblings and was herself childless, so unless she'd been one of those cray-crays who wills everything to their cat, her husband stood to gain it all.

Not one of the costume shops I contacted said they'd rented out two suits of black armor to the same person, but that only suggested the killer and his accomplice acquired them separately, most likely using aliases and paying cash. I didn't totally wash out, though, as during my inquiries I learned I was not the first to call. Det. Bao, hot on the trail.

My buddy Cal, who freelances for Dako on hack-ins and cyber identity theft cases, tinkered with my phone for an hour before pronouncing Lady Hale's texts irretrievable.

Next I contacted the senior people at the LA Renaissance Faire, asking for a list of participants in the jousting tournament and royal entourage. The response I got was what I would have expected if I'd been a sleazy lawyer pressuring an MD to hand over confidential patient files in a personal injury lawsuit. The huffy woman I spoke with told me they'd already fully cooperated with law enforcement and referred me to—who else?—Det. James Bao.

Her shutout had been unequivocal, so I was surprised to see the list of names coming through on my fax machine around lunch time. Could Bao be sharing? My phone rang and I heard a grating, but familiar voice. "You owe me, Valentine."

"*You* sent the list?"

"It took me an hour to get it, but I'm only going to deduct twenty-five bucks from that paycheck you say you've got coming. You're welcome."

He hung up before I could respond, and I spent some time interpreting the Dako-speak. If he said it took an hour, you can bet it was more like fifteen minutes, although I had no doubt he would deduct a half-hour's worth of his time from my check. How had he gotten the information when I couldn't? And how had he known I was even trying to get it?

What I should have learned working long enough at Farona Investigations to qualify for my own license, is that you don't always gain entrance to the party through the front door. Sometimes you have to find an unlocked window or, failing there, a crawlspace with access to the ducting.

My mistake, I realized, had been starting with people at the top, the ones Det. Bao could lean on legally, but with whom I had absolutely no juice.

Dako had most likely talked to the least important person in the Renaissance Faire hierarchy—some underpaid flunky or teenage intern—claiming to be a reporter doing a splashy spread on the event for an upscale magazine. Kissed some butt, scheduled a photo shoot, effusively flattered his contact and then, as if it were merely an afterthought, asked to have the list of participants to print in the article. The out-maneuvered dogsbody would have happily sent it. Disturbing as the idea was, I had to start thinking more like Dako Farona.

The king of France gave me my first solid lead, but the interview had not begun well. When I handed him my business card, he glanced at it, then looked at me. "You're from Michigan?"

"No, the MI stands for mobile investigator. See?" I pointed. "The line in italics under my name." It was shorter than the average tweet and he couldn't be bothered to read it?

"What can I do for you?"

"First, thanks for agreeing to talk to me. No one else in the royal party would."

"That's because they're all still working at the Renaissance Faire."

"And you're not?"

"They fired me."

Turns out the players have to provide their own wardrobe and the kingly ensemble had vanished during the uproar following the shooting.

"Not only am I out a paying gig, I'm out of pocket for a cheesy crown and velvet cloak."

A niggling suspicion inspired me to ask for a description of the missing cloak. Sure enough, his ex-majesty said it was bright red with white "ermine" trim, and I realized that's what I had mistaken for a Santa suit in the arms of my doppelgänger, the knight who shoved me aside in his rush to flee the pavilion.

It made sense. Getting out of the armor would have eaten time, as I knew from personal experience. By throwing a floor-length cloak around himself and trading his helmet for a crown, the killer would have passed anonymously through the crowd as he escaped. Had the shooter known King Mike would be among the earliest to return to the pavilion? Had he counted on his highness being one of the first to shed his costume in the extreme heat?

My $200 retainer check traced back to a company housed in a mailbox at an iffy copy place with a slack-jawed proprietor who claimed not to know nothin' about nothin', so I turned my attention to the victim's husband.

Brad Winters anchored a live, half-hour news, weather and sports program on a small cable-access channel I had never heard of, and the website for Channel 81 said their news shows aired at noon and 5:00 P.M. Marie Winters had been killed around 12:15, so if Brad was on the air until 12:30 that day, I would have to rule him out as the shooter. After confirming the grieving widower was taking a few days off, I made an appointment to visit Channel 81 the next morning.

I had expected a large studio, but the entire operation fit in the three-car garage of a man named Chet Anderson and consisted of only two small sets. The first one, a tired, fussy seating arrangement that belonged in your great-aunt's living room, was where Chet or his wife interviewed spelling bee winners, garden club ladies and local business owners who couldn't afford real advertising. The second set was a cross between a compact kitchen and a science lab. This was where Darla Anderson hosted a cooking show and where Chet, a retired teacher, did a Bill Nye rip-off for kids. The rest of Channel 81's schedule featured pre-recorded programming that trickled down from PBS, college stations and larger independents. As long as he aired four hours of live, local product a day, Chet kept his grant money and state funding. The two newscasts made up a quarter of that requirement, but I didn't see a news desk anywhere. I asked him about it.

"Brad's set is at his house in the Palisades and he shoots me a live feed twice a day, Monday through Friday."

I haven't yet mastered the Farona poker face, and I must have looked frustrated, because Chet Anderson suddenly gave me the once-over.

"Hey, how come you're not taking notes?"

I had gained entry by claiming to be a post-grad student researching the unsung heros of indie television, but I'd forgotten to bring the appropriate support material: a notepad or a small recorder.

Waving a hand in the general direction of my breast pocket, I said, "Micro recorder. It's picking up everything." Sure, technology has been shrinking equipment for decades, but I must not have a poker voice, either, as Anderson gave my pocket a suspicious look before turning wary eyes on my face.

"All right, honesty time," I said, handing him a business card.

"Myocardial infarct?" he asked, puzzlement in his voice.

Jeez Ruiz. "Mobile investigator. See? The italics right under my name." I said I was looking into the

death of his news anchor's wife and needed to know if
the mid-day show had aired as usual on Wednesday.
While clucking about the tragedy, Chet produced
documentation even dinky independents are required
to keep for the FCC. Brad had been live on camera
until 12:29:59, at which time Dining with Darla had
signed on from Channel 81's garage/studio.

I couldn't trace the two suits of armor or my
retainer check. I didn't have a clue who the shooter
was, since Brad Winters had been anchoring the news
when his wife was killed, and it looked like I was
going to have to rethink my business cards, so by the
time I pulled up to the house in Santa Monica at the
end of the day, I felt defeated.

Entering, I smelled Bitsy's lasagne, the Italian
generic of Abilify, and my spirits lifted. In her prime
Bitsy Sutterman worked crafts services on movie sets,
so she had cooked food for demanding celebrities long
enough to hone her natural talent into five-star chef
cred. Kitty, herself a former makeup artist, added a
third plate to the table, happy I was home early and
could join them for dinner.

While plowing through the restorative pasta, I
recounted my tale of failure to the only two people who
might be interested in hearing it. There was nothing
wrong with the Sutterman sisters' minds and they
asked intelligent questions about the murder and my
unproductive investigation. Bitsy expressed surprise
I hadn't been able to track the source of the matching
suits of armor.

"I contacted every costume rental business in a
hundred-mile radius."

"Did you call the prop shops?"

"The what?"

"A suit of armor is much more likely to be used as a prop than a wardrobe piece. Museum sets, spooky houses, eccentric collector's mansion, they often feature rows of empty armor or a single focal point suit."

I didn't stick around for the tiramisu, so anxious was I to compile a list of property houses to call in the morning. An online search showed me there were far fewer of them than costume rental places, so I paid a visit the next day to the biggest one, a three-story building on East Sunset where you can rent anything from a full-scale, working guillotine to a replica of a Ming Dynasty tea service.

I showed my license to the Saturday clerk, not willing to put my business card to the test again. For once I'd gotten somewhere before Det. Bao and was rewarded with the information that two identical suits of black armor had been rented out to a company called Big League Productions. The clerk checked the lease agreement and said the suits weren't scheduled to be returned for another month, as Big League was shooting a sword and dragon epic somewhere north of San Francisco.

I spent the rest of the weekend tracking down every movie being shot south of Vancouver, but not one of them fit the clerk's description. The name Big League also turned out to be a dead end and I knew, even if the prop house didn't, they would never see their metal suits again.

Well, maybe they'd see *one* of them. On Monday I placed a call.

"Bao here."

"Detective, this is Rick Valentine. I'm the guy who—"

"I remember. What can I do for you?"

I told him where the armor had come from and how to prove it. According to the clerk I'd spoken to, prop houses etch their names inside the lower left greave of every suit of armor in order to get the correct ones back from film companies renting at multiple suppliers.

I also suggested he run prints from the helmet. Lady Hale, I reminded him, had closed my visor when she issued my final instructions. Considering her diminutive stature and the weight of the armor, I figured her male accomplice must have been the one to wrangle the knightly garb into the tent and lay it out on the bench. Maybe he hadn't thought to wear gloves and had left prints himself.

Bao neither confirmed nor denied he had already dusted for prints, but I could tell the identification mark on the armor was new to him. With a half-hearted growl warning me to stay the hell out of his case, Det. Bao disconnected the call.

I tuned in to Channel 81 just in time to catch Dining With Darla, where Chet Anderson's wife was preparing Beef Burgundy. Bitsy, sharing the couch with me, looked up from her book of Sudokus a couple times and made dismissive clicks with her tongue.

"She doing something wrong?" I asked, after the third click.

"Sweet Pea, she hasn't done anything *right*. I mean, who makes lardons out of salt pork without first simmering it long enough to desalinate it?"

She had me there.

"And she dredged the meat in *flour*, for crying out loud. What does she think she's making, chicken-fried steak?"

With some final pithy snark, Bitsy left the room,

presumably to do her Japanese puzzlers where the culinary arts weren't being dissed. I continued to watch, and was eventually rewarded with an announcement at the end of the half hour saying Brad Winters would be back on the air that evening with the news. Amazingly, Mr. Winters had processed all five stages of grief in less than a week.

He *had* to be guilty; *had* to have hired the pair who killed his wife. I hoped Det. Bao was examining their bank statements for large, unexplained cash withdrawals and looking at insurance policies that might have had recent coverage bump-ups on Marie, things I couldn't do because I was not official law enforcement.

To kill time between then and the Channel 81 evening newscast, I went out to have new business cards printed, keeping the line saying I was a mobile investigator, but deleting the MI after my name. Perhaps reacting to Darla's insult to the ghost of Julia Child, Bitsy had given me a list of groceries to pick up so she could make Beef Burgundy, only she called it Boeuf Bourguignon.

When I commented on how good it smelled later that afternoon, Bitsy claimed it had been Marlon Brando's favorite. Impressed, I asked, "Which Brando movie did you work on?"

"None, but Kitty boinked him for a while in the sixties."

"Blabber-yap," Kitty shot back.

It was almost time for the news, so I excused myself before any more revelations surfaced about my landladies' past.

Brad Winters embodied all a news anchor could hope to be: square-jawed, handsome and in possession of a compelling baritone voice. I watched him as he commandingly delivered the good, the bad and the ugly without a hint of having suffered a recent bereavement. There were no segments from far-flung locations, but that was understandable. Channel 81 could barely afford eggs for Darla's soufflés, much less field reporters.

Once all the grim events of the day had been covered, Brad put on a lighter face to introduce the sports guy, who looked like he *might* be all of a year out of twelfth grade. With locker room pep-talk verve, the kid blazed through the previous Friday night's local high school games, airing footage of plays he had recorded on his cell phone and post-game interviews he had done himself. I got the feeling every broadcast was an audition in the mind of Tyler Benedict. After he did a fast recap of weekend scores in national sports, he turned it over to Winters.

"That's it for Jock Wrap. Back to you, Brad."

Once again the anchor's perfect visage filled the screen while he reported on one of those makes-your-heart-smile stories of a kitten up a tree being rescued by fire fighters. Then, following broadcast tradition, Brad intro'd the weather.

"And now, to tell us if we'll need our umbrellas in the morning, here's Channel 81's lovely meteorologist, Stormy Knight."

It was all very low-tech compared to Al Roker or that bald guy from The Weather Channel, just a big dry-erase map of the USA and a pixie-like woman with different colored markers for cold fronts, high pressure and precipitation.

"Don't worry, Brad, your hair gel is safe from rain tomorrow," she said with a playful wink in what I assumed was the direction of the anchor desk. But it wasn't the perky personality that caught my attention;

it was her voice. I'd heard it before and I knew where.

Stormy Knight's hair was cut in a short, face-framing style, but if I squinted my eyes I could picture that face half-buried in a blonde avalanche. My eyes dropped to her high-riding, but modestly sized breasts and I knew a wig had not been the only fakery "Lady Hale" had employed on the day of the murder. As she forecast the inevitable perfect beach weather, Ms. Knight manifested no trace of the southern accent my phony client had troweled on.

"Thank you, Stormy. And now to our Making Some Differences story of the day."

I didn't stay tuned for Brad's take on the NBC staple. I pulled out my cell and called Chet Anderson.

"Did last Wednesday's mid-day news program feature all the regulars?" I asked, after identifying myself.

"Sure. Brad at the anchor desk, Tyler on sports, Stormy with the weather. Hey, gotta go. He's about to throw to me and I have to make a paper-mache volcano erupt."

If Stormy Knight had been at the Renaissance Faire and simultaneously "live" on Channel 81, Brad could have done the same. All I had to do was figure out how.

Tyler Benedict believed I was a producer from ESPN scouting talent for a late-night sports show when he met me for coffee the following morning. He betrayed no sign of recognizing my face, and was too short to have been the dark knight, so I eliminated him as a partner in the crime. He handed over a resumé and head shots—which have a totally different connotation in my line of work—then boasted about his sports reporting experience. When I directed the

focus to his job at Channel 81, he claimed it was only
a stepping stone to bigger and better, but didn't provide me with anything I could use. That is, until he
checked his watch.

"I hate to cut this short, but I have class in forty
minutes and traffic's a bitch."

Tyler tried to impress me with the fact that he
was in his second year of college and working toward
a degree in broadcasting, then hastily volunteered he
would drop out yesterday if he got a network offer.
Something didn't make sense to me.

"It's almost 10:00 o'clock. When do you get out of
class?"

"Today? Not till 2:30."

"So how will you do your noon sports segment?"

"Oh, I recorded Jock Wrap two hours ago. My
computer gets a heads-up from Brad's computer and
they automatically synch for a clean segue going in
and coming out. No humans involved."

As I reconsidered the concept of "live" TV, I
realized that if Tyler could do that with Brad, then
Brad could do that to Chet Anderson. Chet's funding
was predicated on Channel 81's delivering of four live
hours a day, though, so maybe he didn't realize he
might be getting a canned response when he counted
down for Brad to begin. And I wondered if Det. Bao
was tech savvy enough to know there was a gaping
hole in Brad's alibi.

To tie a festive bow onto the package before
presenting it to Bao, I called the prop house and said
I worked for Big League Productions and would be
returning the two suits of armor that day. I asked to
speak to the clerk who'd written the contract, and
when he came on the line I conned him with Dako

Farona flare.

"I want to send the same gal to deliver them who signed them out, but both my assistants are at lunch and I can't recall which one rented them for me. Was it the petite brunette or the blonde with all the hair?"

"It was *definitely* the blonde with the big, uh...hair."

I chuckled in a way I hoped made me sound like a middle-aged letch. "Yeah, that's Bitsy all right. And now I remember Kitty was scouting locations with me that day." TMI. Dako always says to shut up once you have what you came for.

And I had it: a witness who could give Bao a description of Lady Hale that matched mine, although I suspected she'd used some other weather-related alias when she rented the armor. Misty Morn, perhaps. Or Lorraine E. Day.

All I had to do was advise Det. Bao to compare the prints on my visor with those of Stormy Knight. I still had no idea if Brad was scheming to get his wife's money and pizza restaurants using Stormy as a hired accomplice, or having a torrid affair that needed wifey out of the way so he and the weather girl could share both bed *and* cash, but Bao could figure it out. I'd already done the hard work of loosening the lid on the jar; he could take credit for unscrewing it that final inch.

Before I could call him, though, my fax machine beeped awake and spat out a single sheet of paper with no identifying source. The only printing on it was a series of letters and numbers: CID4614K59-V. I waited for a delayed cover sheet or a second page, but that was it. Figuring the transmission had been in error, I crumpled the fax and tossed it as my cell rang.

"Rick Valentine, mobile investigator."

"This is Det. Bao. We just arrested Brad Winters and Stormy Knight for the murder of Mrs. Winters, so you can extract your nose from my business now. The only role you'll play in this case from here on out is testifying in court   Got it? Good-bye."

"Wait! Before you hang up, how good *were* they?"

"Good enough to fire the murder weapon ahead of time while holding it in the metal glove you were later duped into wearing. And Brad dropped the gun in a trash barrel not fifteen feet away from the royal tent, knowing my guys would find it and match it to the slugs in the victim."

"But if you had the weapon, the matching bullets and my gauntlet covered in residue, how did you know I *wasn't* the killer?"

"Because they weren't good enough to leave the residue on the correct glove. You're left-handed."

"How did—?"

Suddenly I understood why Bao had asked for a second signature on my unofficial record of the crime. His guys at the scene had previously collected a left gauntlet, the one I had taken off to check for a pulse, and he wanted to see which hand I used to sign my name.

"Cagey, Det. Bao, but how do you know I'm not ambidextrous?"

I could hear him sigh before he answered. "That's the *second* question I asked your former employer. Now, if you don't mind, I've got crimes to solve, so collect your reward and go find somebody's missing dog."

Reward? I didn't know what he was talking about, but Dako Farona says never reveal your own ignorance, so I merely grunted a thank-you that didn't make it under the wire before the prickly detective hung up on me.

Okay, so there was still a lot for me to learn about the PI biz, but the fact remained that I had come to the same conclusion as Det. Bao, only I'd gone on the scenic route, while he'd taken the express. And as you-can-guess-who always likes to say, time equals *ka-ching*.

I jumped online to see what had been happening while I was off chasing a loophole in the perfect alibi. I skipped right through the what—an arrest of murderous lovers—and went directly to the how. According to reports, a phone tip had led police to a shed on Brad's property where, hidden behind a pile of tires and a riding mower, they found black armor. Prints on it matched the ones from a second metal suit already in evidence, and stuffed inside was a red velvet cloak, a cheesy crown and a block of wood containing a bullet fired from the gun that killed Marie Winters.

Six days of hard work on my part to put the pieces together and it fell into Det. Bao's lap on a telephone tip? He apparently thought I was the one who called it in, and I wished I had. When I read further I learned the tipster qualified for a $5000 reward put up by the employees of Gianni's Pizza in memory of their deceased boss.

To collect the reward, the anonymous source had only to give authorities the confidential ID number he had been issued when he passed along his tip. I retrieved the crumpled fax page from my trash can. Was it possible? And who would do this? Might Bao be a benefactor as well as a reluctant teacher? Law enforcement is prohibited from claiming rewards, so maybe he liked me and had decided to pay it forward.

Then my cell phone rang and a familiar voice snarled in my ear.

"You owe me, Valentine."

The reward money bought me a small office resting on concrete rather than Michelins—or at least the first four months' rent for that space. It wasn't much compared to the Beverly Hills home of Farona Investigations, but I figured Dako probably started out in much less luxurious digs himself back before Methuselah's bar mizvah.

The two-story building, unofficially called the Gingerbread House, was tucked onto a Sherman Oaks side street and looked as if the architect couldn't decide between Tudor or Hansel and Gretel. Six utilitarian twelve-by-twelves made up the top level, while four pricier thirteen-by-fourteens shared ground floor space with an insipidly decorated reception area. Occupancy wasn't yet at a hundred percent and the realtor said I could have my pick, so I went with the northwest corner office upstairs, the one whose only window looked out into the dense branches of an avocado tree. If things got tight I could always survive on guacamole.

The land line and a one-tenth share of the front desk person's time were included in the rent, although Lloyd, the actor-slash-receptionist, made it clear the quality of that time would be substantially improved by a gratuity at the end of each month.

The makeshift desk in the corner of my room at the Suttermans' house didn't have the gravitas my new professional quarters required, so I made a trip over the hill to the strip of used furniture stores on Western south of Melrose. After looking at three different desks on which Gone With The Wind had been typed, I settled on the scarred oak workhorse that had more likely been the platform for the writing up of B&E reports at some outlying police precinct half a century earlier. Since the inflated price tag reflected the fake pedigree, I insisted they throw in Margaret Mitchell's leather office chair. My framed diploma went on the wall along with a pair of clipper ship paintings I discovered at a nearby yard sale and Valentine Investigations was up and running.

Well, up and waiting. Business did not drop into my lap simply because I finally had a stationary lap for it to land in, and weeks went by without a call. Bitsy Sutterman's friend Mia hired me to find the sapphire-and-diamond ring she suspected had been stolen by a member of her household staff, but in less than a day I located it at the jeweler's where she had left it to be sized-up to slide over a knuckle swollen with arthritis. The lady was losing her memory as well as the use of her hands, so I didn't have the heart to charge her for anything other than gas. With all the crime in LA, you'd think a go-getter like me could catch a taste of it.

At the end of that first dry month, Lloyd smiled expectantly and I slipped him two twenties, although the only service he'd performed was handing me one piece of mail. The envelope had been from Dako Farona and contained my final paycheck, a check with more deductions than Jim Bob Duggar's tax return.

I joined the Chamber of Commerce, attended a couple networking breakfasts and expanded my online advertising without getting a nibble. Recalling that Dako sometimes turned away smaller, less profitable cases, I decided if things didn't pick up soon I'd ask him to vector a few of those my way. I knew his cut would leave me at break-even or in the red, but I needed some referrals and word of mouth if I was going to survive. Lost dogs, pilfered petty cash, I was willing to take anything, not suspecting that right around the corner there lurked a murder-for-hire and political corruption case destined to violently reconfigure everything in my life.

Unaware I was about to sail into Typhoon Feces, I filled time by introducing myself to the other tenants, leaving each of them a business card in case they, or one of their acquaintances, ever needed help of a discreet sleuthing nature. Three of the other five offices on my floor were occupied, two by would-be screenwriters—guys around forty-five who recently had aged out of lucrative TV writing jobs—and a gray-haired music producer shaped a lot like SpongeBob who bragged she hadn't missed a Dykes on Bikes Parade since Cher was in pre-K. Jason, Justin, "call me Pat" and I formed the plebe contingent at the Gingerbread House, acknowledged, but not actually embraced by the peerage in the larger offices down-stairs.

Directly below me was Moonbeam Fink, the masseuse whose noxious incense and post-Aquarian flute fugues wafted upward, jarring two senses at a time. An occasional deep-voiced moan rising from that den of chakras and crystals suggested Moonbeam was either playing whale-song CDs or topping off the shiatsu with a happy ending.

An independent talent agent occupied another of the downstairs spaces and, except for my first day there, when he eye-raped me before asking if I'd ever considered giving acting a try, I never saw his door open.

The other two offices downstairs remained empty,

as did the final pair on my floor. At the end of the second month, when Lloyd gave me his lean and hungry look, I handed him a twenty. He managed to act believably insulted, so I inquired how much the masseuse and the agent gave him. He declined to quantify their generosity, but Justin told me Lloyd took it out in trade with Moonbeam and was a member of the agent's stable of acting talent.

"Burbank Danny Rose has never gotten Lloyd so much as a walk-on part, but every couple months he sends him out on a cattle call and blows flowers up his butt about grooming him for the next pilot season. Lloyd wouldn't take a dime from him."

With only enough ready cash to cover two more months at the Gingerbread House, I had no choice but to beg for Dako Farona's leftovers.

I pulled into the underground parking lot, rode up to the tenth floor and stepped out onto plush maroon carpeting that added drama to the reception room. Laurel sat on the Queen Bee throne behind a desk large enough to host a table tennis tournament.

"He in?"

"Who's asking?" She used her tough-girl voice, the one that intimidates the riff-raff and it took me a second to realize she was yanking my chain.

"Bite me, Laurel."

"You wish."

Formalities complete, she gave me a welcoming smile and told me I should have called first. Dako had already left for a lunch meeting. "Some studio veep had a tchotchke stolen right off a shelf in her office."

"Isn't that kind of minor spuds for Dako to handle personally?"

"The tchotchke's worth a couple hundred grand."

"Judas on a joystick, what kind of salary do those execs get?"

"Not enough to afford kinetic sculptures by Calder, but once upon a time this particular lady executive married up, old and rich. Can I tell Dako why you stopped by?"

Preferring not to broadcast my failure to launch any more widely than I had to, I said I'd give him a call later in the afternoon. She put her hand out, palm up, surprising me. I pulled my parking chit from my pocket as she rummaged around in a drawer for the seldom-used sheet of stamps that covered the building's exorbitant fee for visiting one of its tenants.

"You ever tell him I validated a non-client, I'll hunt you down and garrote you while you're taking a dump."

The vividness of the threat more than offset the impossibility of getting behind someone on the can and strangling them, so I solemnly nodded my intention to keep the secret.

Laurel was a mystery to me, and I thought about her as I reclaimed my Jeep and drove back over the hill. When I started working for Dako almost four years ago—and, for the record, he recruited me, not vice-versa—she had already been employed there for at least ten years and, although I never saw any actual PDA between them, I always got the feeling there was at least a frisson of attraction going in both directions.

I worked closely with Dako at first, going out with him to client meetings, learning the subtle tricks of the trade. Then, shortly after pronouncing me ready to do simple surveillance on my own, he said Laurel would be joining me for a couple of the all-nighters. When I bristled at the idea of a baby-sitter checking my every move, Dako confided to me that Laurel aspired to be an investigator.

"Show her the ropes and let me know if you think she's got the right stuff."

Of the three pathways to acquiring a private investigator's license in California, Laurel would be taking the longest and hardest. My own way had been made easier the year before I separated from the Los Angeles County foster care system, when a lawyer turned up and notified me that a portion of my father's death benefits had been set aside and would be available to put me through college. That was a surprise, as my mother had never mentioned it, nor had any of the numerous boys in blue uniforms who stepped in after one of their own was killed in the line of duty, taking a suddenly fatherless five year old to Dodgers games, beach outings, movies and Chuck E. Cheese. I have no memory of their names, those cops who showed me such kindness, but I wish I could thank them. They provided a multi-cultural paternal presence during the three years it took my mother to ride the bottle to a resting place alongside my dad. As a teenager I romanticized their deaths into some kind of *Romeo and Juliet* tragedy, young love too strong to be broken by mere death, but, like most teens, I didn't know a whole hell of a lot about my own parents.

I have no foster care sob story, because, aside from that whole parents-dying thing, my life has been charmed. The first place they put me was temporary, and I recall nothing more than bunkbeds and a boy named Randy, but within a short time I was placed permanently with Babs and Tommy Carmichael, a welcoming couple who never differentiated between their biological three and the two younger foster siblings. In fact, after their own kids left for trade school, marriage and the military, Shane and I moved up in the pecking order, becoming "mentors" for the next pair of children the Carmichaels brought into their home. In one sense I had a perfectly normal childhood, older sibs to tease, teach and torment me, younger ones to tease, teach and torment in turn.

Babs and Tommy have long since moved back to the Boston neighborhood where they grew up. We connect by phone or email every couple weeks and my "brother" Chris still sends me the occasional mail-order brides catalog, joking reminders of the Chinese girl I crushed on when I was eleven. Once Ling hit puberty, she blossomed into a hentai anime fantasy and I was left in the dust with no underarm hair and no chance.

The Carmichaels were as surprised as I was to learn about the bequest that would enable me to continue my education. My high school grades were okay, but not scholarshipworthy, and Tommy and Babs were a one-income, blue-collar couple with no money (or obligation) to send their many strays to college. The lawyer made it easy, setting up tuition payments and stipend checks so I didn't have to think about those things my five years at UCLA. Now, though, it seems strange I never once looked more deeply into my orphan's windfall.

When I first met Laurel, she was nearing forty and didn't think sitting in a classroom surrounded by cute young coeds would do her ego any good. And so, she resigned herself to the long process of work-study apprenticeship at Farona Investigations that would eventually earn her a license. At least that's how things looked to me at the time.

While we did those low-level stakeouts, mostly cheating husbands and custody-motivated witch hunts against single moms, we sat in the car and exchanged biographical information. It didn't occur to me then to wonder at how little she volunteered about herself during those protracted periods of paid spying, or how much she asked about me. Even at twenty-three I knew women often flattered a man by pretending to be interested in all things him.

I enjoyed Laurel's company those few weeks we shared surveillance and I showed her some of the little tricks Dako had taught me. Tricks like putting a hand on the hood of a car before going into a meeting with someone in order to see if they'd lie about how long they'd been waiting.

Dako told me a story once about being set up as a murderer's alibi at a time when cell phones hadn't been born and closed-circuit cameras weren't staring out from every house, business and traffic light. The man scheduled an evening consultation with Dako, ostensibly to discuss having his ex-wife followed. The day of the appointment, Dako had dinner at the place around the corner from his apartment where he ate every night. When he came out he found one of his tires had been slashed. He tried calling the guy to say he'd be late, but the line was busy, so Dako changed the bad tire for his spare and raced to the office of his potential client. When Dako pulled in next to the only other car in the small lot, a light was on in the office window, but it went off a moment later. As Dako approached the building, the guy came out like he was leaving, then acted all pissed-off about being kept waiting an hour. Dako already knew from laying a hand on the hood of the other car that it had pulled into the lot no more than ten minutes earlier.

Not knowing why he was being lied to, but reluctant to lose the gig, Dako endured the berating and followed the man back inside for a delayed confab. Only later, when the killer tried to use Dako and the original time of their meeting as an alibi, did Dako reveal the truth.

When I repeated that story to Laurel, full of self-importance at providing a "teachable moment," she turned the table and taught me something.

"It seems to me," she said, "that the boss was showing you a mistake he made, in addition to the technique about checking the temperature of the car's hood."

"What mistake?"

"Well, he was too predictable, wasn't he? If the killer hadn't known Mr. Farona ate at the same place every night, it would have been a lot harder to delay him an hour."

Dako had not come right out and said to avoid patterns that could make me vulnerable, so I had only absorbed the more obvious lesson, while Laurel had picked up on it immediately, proving she had the potential to be an intuitive investigator as well as an attentive student.

Maybe that's why I was disappointed when she abandoned her aspirations a few weeks later and went back to being nothing more than the receptionist at Farona Investigations.

"Don't take this too personally, Rick, but those stakeouts are boring as hell. The idea of another 3000 hours of them makes me want to enter a convent just for the excitement."

When I finally spoke with Dako by phone, he agreed to toss a few bones my way as long as I didn't tell anyone where the work had originated, protecting his hard-ass rep, I assumed. The jobs were small and uncomplicated, but they gave me the chance to hone my skills in preparation for the day I'd start landing those big-time cases that filled crime novels and Hollywood thrillers. Today a lost cat, tomorrow the kidnapped heir to a European throne.

As if my former boss's throwaways had primed some cosmic pump, work started to pick up. By the end of my third month in the Gingerbread House, Lloyd was fielding three or four calls a week for me, with one usually panning out, so I gave him seventy-five bucks to ensure his continued sensitive handling of the sometimes distraught callers.

In an effort to establish professional courtesy, as well as wanting to stay on the fringe of his good graces, I invited Dako Farona out to lunch. I knew he would anticipate my asking another favor, so I intended to deal with him pro to pro, impressing him with my independence *and* picking up the tab.

Riding to his office in the elevator, I went over my short list of small-talk topics to carry me through the meal, the first one I'd have with Dako as a non-employee. I realized I knew almost nothing about the man's past or personal life, so I resolved to get him talking, per Kitty Sutterman's advice. Of course, she had been coaching me on how to approach a woman.

"Ask questions, Rick. Get her talking about herself. Everybody feels valued when someone listens to them, and they always gravitate to the people who make them feel valued."

I hadn't yet tested her theory on the romantic front—business wasn't the only area of my life that had undergone a dry spell—but I figured it was a universal, common sense approach that might put me on a more even footing with Dako.

Through the glass door I saw a stranger at the

reception desk, a quite attractive stranger whose thumbs skipped over the screen of a cell phone. She stopped and looked up when I pushed open the door and stepped inside.

"Good morning. May I help you?"

She was a year or two past the cute-as-a-button stage, but had not yet transited into stop-your-heart-beautiful, so I guessed her to be nineteen or twenty.

"I hope so. Where's Laurel?"

"Oh, you know Ms. Briley? I'm Rexanne, her replacement."

Here I was trying to make myself like Dako, and he dumps his most loyal employee in favor of eye candy with a hooker's name. It wasn't the girl's fault she'd gone to work for a jackass, but I couldn't keep the attitude out of my voice when I said, "How nice for you. Tell Dako Rick Valentine's here to take him to lunch."

I was already formulating the harsh words I would hurl at him in the restaurant, my withering indictment of his sense of honor, when the Disney princess behind the desk spoke again.

"Uh, Mr. Farona was suddenly called away."

And there it was, the last freakin' straw. "When he gets back, tell your boss he's a total dick," I barked. "No, you know what? Give me a piece of paper and I'll tell him myself!"

She froze like a bunny in a flashlight beam, too fresh-off-the-turnip-truck to qualify as a deer in the headlights, so I reached down to snatch a pen and the pink While You Were Out pad. She recoiled and, as I scribbled my final communication to Dako-shitheel-Farona, she picked up the phone and punched one of the buttons.

"Laurel? We've got a man in the lobby causing

problems."

I stopped writing. *Laurel?* "Wait a minute, she still works here?"

"You're joking, right? Of course, she's still here. Who do you think—"

She never got a chance to complete that sentence, as Laurel swung into the open doorway that led to the inner offices, one mother of a .45 leveled at my head. Rexanne yelped and dropped to the floor, while I nearly crapped my pants in the two seconds it took Laurel to recognize me and lower the Colt.

"Jesus, Rick! You scared me."

"How? I only have a pen in *my* hand."

"I'm sorry," she said, making the gun disappear.

Rexanne tentatively raised her head above the desk, looking at Laurel with no small measure of fear.

"It's all right, Rexanne, I thought it might be somebody else. Mr. Valentine is a fr... a former employee," she said, correcting herself midway. "And Rick, I see you've made a great first impression on Dako's daughter."

Stood-up, aimed-at and gobsmacked in under a minute. Before I could reassess Rexanne, searching for signs of the second-rate DNA that had formed Dako Farona, Laurel grabbed my arm. "Come back to my office; we need to talk."

She strode away down the hall before I could respond, so I followed her to the last door, stepping inside in time to catch her slipping the gun into the top drawer of the desk. Nobody ever called the Combat Commander a girly weapon, and Laurel handled it like someone comfortable with a firearm. What the hell was going on? "Since when have you had your own office here?"

"Since the agency opened sixteen years ago."

As I sat down in the client's chair, I shook my head in bewilderment. "How did I not know that?"

"Maybe you're not quite as astute a detective as you think," she said, a flash of her usual playfulness shining through.

While I was on Dako's payroll I had normally operated out of the Sutterman sisters' house, only going into BH on Monday morning to pick up my assignments and turn in reports on the prior week's work, and then again every other Friday afternoon to collect my check from Laurel at the front desk. Had I mentally extrapolated a full-time existence for her as a receptionist, with only those two small signifiers?

She opened another drawer, but instead of a gun, she pulled out a large manila envelope, dropping it onto the desk top with a thud.

"I'd like to hire you to hold onto this until it's needed."

"What's in it?"

"Nothing that can hurt you as long as nobody knows you have it."

"That's *so-o-o* reassuring," I said, picking up the envelope and examining it. The only thing that differentiated it from every other manila envelope in the world was a yellow label with www.2regni.net written in large block letters. Intriguing. "Why me? As I recall, Dako has a safe in his office."

"And if someone comes a-looking, that'll be their first stop."

"But not their last if they don't find this," I said, hefting the bulging envelope on my palm.

Laurel rested her elbows on the desk and leaned in, face as serious as I'd ever seen it. "Oh, they'll find an envelope that's a look-alike for the one you're holding. And if they think they've recovered the evidence against them, I will have bought Dako enough time to finish his investigation."

"And all I have to do is hold onto the copies."

"The originals. What's in the safe is a collection of quite convincing facsimiles."

"Okay, I'll do it," I said, standing.

"One more thing. Don't come here; don't even call here. Until this is over I want nothing connecting you to this agency."

"Are you sure that isn't only to keep me from flirting with Dako's sexy daughter," I asked, aiming for some of our old levity.

"Either way, I'm trying to keep you from getting killed." Laurel stood up, signaling the end of our meeting, but I had one more piece of business.

"May I duck into Dako's office to leave him a note about rescheduling our lunch?"

She hesitated for a second, then nodded. I might not have known Dako was a father, and somehow I had missed the fact that Laurel Briley was much more than a receptionist, but I could tell from her slight hesitation any note I left would be destroyed as soon as I walked out the door. That was all right with me, because the note was only cover. I slipped into Dako's office, going straight for the bottom drawer where he kept extra office keys and the magnetic cards that got his people into the building. As soon as I'd pocketed one of each, I scribbled the note Laurel would come looking for and went back into the lobby, where Little Miss Sunshine had resumed her texting.

"Miss Farona, I apologize for being obnoxious earlier, and I hope that won't prevent the two of us from becoming friends." Her fingers quit flying and she looked at me warily.

"Uh, sure."

I had no desire to get more closely acquainted with Dako's spawn, but I wanted to yank Laurel's chain and, by extension, Dako's. I would have bet money she was listening from the hallway. I put the envelope on the desk while I searched my pockets for my parking stub. finally producing it and placing it on top of the manila-wrapped evidence.

"What's that for?" Rexanne asked.

"If you'll check in the top right drawer you'll find some—"

"We don't validate parking, Rexanne," Laurel said, her sudden appearance in the doorway confirming my suspicion she was watching my every move. The only thing that surprised me was the coldness of her voice when she said, "Good-bye, Mr. Valentine."

Having delivered her warning to me about not lingering, Laurel turned and disappeared down the hall. Taking the cue, Rexanne picked up both my parking ticket and the manila envelope, handing them to me. I could tell she didn't know what was going on, but then, neither did I.

A few tunes would have been welcome on the drive back up to The Valley, but my CD player had been dead for a week, refusing to play Engelbert Humperdinck, but refusing to release him either. My taste in music has been strongly influenced by the eclectic selections in the Wurlitzer jukebox that graces the Sutterman twins' living room. I may be the only male on Earth who knows all the lyrics to "Walkin' On Sunshine" by Katrina and The Waves, a fact best hidden until the day I'm forced, at knife point, to save the world by singing it at a karaoke bar.

The radio stations I tried were improving their

bottom line by airing as many political ads as possible. Without an incumbent standing for re-election, two wannabes duked it out loudly, relentlessly and below-the-beltily in LA's mayoral race. I hit the off button and tried to deconstruct my unnerving visit to Farona Investigations.

As Dako had taught me to do, I made mental lists: What I Know and What I *Think* I Know. Everything else fell into the What I Don't Know category and, as always at the start of a case, was the largest of the three. The idea is to break down the first two into the most basic, one-beat concepts, like single Scrabble tiles that mean little on their own. Collect a group of "tiles" until they make sense, then move them from the holding rack to the board, where they fit in with the rest of the What I Knows. All the face-down Scrabble tiles represent the What I Don't Knows and remain mysteries until they are turned over one or two at a time.

WIK: Dako has a daughter. WIDK: where she lives, if Dako's married to her mother, why she's working at the agency and if she was attracted to me even a little bit. The most important thing when going through the list of WIDKs is sensing when you're about to slide down a rabbit hole that takes you some distance but gets you nowhere. Thinking about Rexanne Farona risked an unproductive slide, pretty brown eyes notwithstanding.

WIK: Laurel had expected to confront someone other than me when Rexanne reported trouble in the lobby. Could it be connected to the envelope on the seat beside me? Did it have anything to do with why Dako had left before I got there? I slid those ideas into the What I *Think* I Know category as I pulled into a parking space at the Gingerbread House.

Realizing there was no secure hiding place in my spartan office, I considered finding a spot for the envelope amongst the movie memorabilia and odd bric-a-brac that filled the Sutterman sisters' house, but since one of the things I did *not* know was how dangerous its contents were, I opted out of putting Kitty and Bitsy at risk. I would have to get creative.

Lloyd looked up from the reception desk when I entered. "The landlord called. Your door plaque will be ready next week."

Tenants who stayed more than three months were entitled to put a brass name plaque on their door, the catch being that it had to be purchased from the building's owner at a morbidly obese price. The one-man talent agency and sketchy masseuse had sprung for nameplates, but upstairs nobody cared. The two writers on my floor didn't need anyone to be able to find them during business hours, and the producer taped a CD to her door when she was expecting a musician, but I had to project a professional image if I hoped to impress future clients. "Thanks. Any calls?"

His apologetic shrug conveyed disappointment, more about the potential reduction of his end-of-month baksheesh, I surmised, than the security of my livelihood. As I got to the top of the stairs, I heard laughter coming from Justin's office at the southwest corner of the second floor. His door stood open, so I walked the short way past Pat's recording studio and looked in.

"Hey, Rick, come join the party," Jason called out when he saw me.

"I don't want to intrude," I said, although the sight of a bagel platter loaded with all the usual accoutrements reminded me that I had missed my scheduled lunch with Dako.

"Get in here and help me celebrate," Justin said.

I almost put my foot in my mouth by asking if he had sold a script, but luckily, Jason spoke first. "Yeah, Justin's turning forty."

"Third time's the charm," SpongePat added.

Far from insulting Justin, Pat's reminder of television's lack of interest in high-mileage humans made Jason and him crack up.

For the next half hour I inhaled bagels, lox, cream cheese and tomatoes, while Justin gave me a photo tour of his career. He had spent his final seven staff years on a juggernaut cop show, so his office walls featured mementos of those glory days: the cast, posing in the uniforms of their fictional police force, staged crime scene photos, an honorary detective's certification and a framed letter from Elmore Leonard. I took it all in, but stayed aware of the envelope I had left on the credenza by the door.

Somewhere between a poppy seed bagel and my plate of potato salad, I figured out where to hide my mysterious package, so I left Justin's party to swing by an office supply store.

I didn't return to the Gingerbread House until after 6:00, as I preferred not having any witnesses while I worked. Once the envelope situation was handled—and in a way I thought would have impressed even Dako Farona—I began trolling the internet.

I may not possess hacker-level chops, but like everyone else under thirty, I was born into a world where computers serve as almost a sixth sense, and I know my way around a search engine. So I was puzzled when I came up blank on www.2regni.net. Whatever the site represented, it was enough to scare

the hell out of Laurel. After having seen nothing more
threatening in her hand than my paycheck for three
years, the image of her in that doorway aiming a
badboy Colt at me was tough to shake. I wanted to
know what she and Dako had gotten themselves into.

Nothing squared. I quickly found Dual Registry
Norwegian Importers located in New York City at
www.2regni.com, but even if they were smuggling
narwhal tusks through customs—and I have no idea
if narwhals live in Norway, or if their tusks are
banned like elephant ivory—it would be a stretch to
connect them to a medium-sized investigative agency
on the West Coast.

I found Reginald Nicholson II Antiques out of St.
Louis at www.regni2an.com, a specialty shop dealing
in old marionettes that were about as threatening as
Sesame Street's Elmo.

There was a www.2reg-n/i.gov I considered for a
minute, as it was geographically the closest to Los
Angeles, but, again, I had trouble making the link
between Laurel's über-caution and a two-lane roadway
elevations guide for Nevada and Idaho.

The domain name www.2regni.net showed as
unused and available, so I bought it for three years.
A small investment, but my thinking was that it
might come in handy. As things turned out, it almost
got me killed, but I guess that can be viewed as a
learning experience.

I pushed the mysterious envelope out of my
mind, but was less successful in banishing thoughts of
Dako's lovely daughter. I honored Laurel's request
that I make no contact and continued my work for a
new client, an independent retailer who suspected
some of her employees were stealing merchandise.

The surveillance was boring, but I soon found the real culprit, the delivery man for one of the store's regular suppliers. While the owner was busy checking the delivered goods against an accompanying manifest, the supplier's guy helped himself to expensive shirts, slacks and blazers from the storeroom, boxing them up and rolling them out to the van on the delivery dolly before returning to collect the signed receipt from her. Mr. Velcro Fingers wasn't happy to find me waiting when he darted through the store's rear door to hide the pilfered goods, but he didn't put up a fight.

Once he was arrested and taken away, I advised the owner to notify her supplier and request a driver be sent to move the van. Not wanting to deal with any more unpleasantness, she handed me her phone and asked me to do it. I told the appalled supplier about the thefts and volunteered that apart from pressing charges against the driver, we wouldn't post any online complaints about his company's ethics, *if* he offered my client a deep discount on her next dozen orders. He did.

Happy with the outcome, the client said she would recommend my services at the next meeting of her neighborhood business association. I left her a dozen of my cards and drove back to the Gingerbread House. It was the end of the day, but I wanted to bang out an invoice and email it to her while she was still basking in the afterglow of my successful investigation.

"I took it down verbatim," Lloyd said archly, as he handed me the phone message from Laurel. When I read the slip I saw why.

Don't call me, but turn on your fucking phone so I can reach you.

I had turned it off around noon so as not to give a Cyndi Lauper ring-tone warning to my quarry as I watched him load a box with designer clothes in the storeroom, then forgot to turn it back on. I found five missed calls from Laurel and was about to miss the sixth by the time I turned the phone on again.

"Laurel, sorry about the missed—"

"Forget it. Is the envelope secure?"

"Poirot couldn't find it with a psychic and a sniffer dog. Why?"

"Somebody broke into the office last night."

"They take the decoy?"

She told me the intruders hit the safe first, then once they believed they were in possession of the damaging documents, they systematically went through the suite, smashing anything they could and walking off with the computers.

"Is Rexanne okay?" Stupid. I should have asked if *everyone* was okay. Leaping headfirst into the pause that followed my gaffe, I said, "I only ask because I know you and Dako can take care of yourselves, but she seemed a little naive and—"

"Rick," Laurel interrupted sharply. "You can delete Ms. Farona from your hard drive. As soon as Dako realized how intense things are likely to get, he hustled her out of town."

"Oh, good," I said, trying to sound like I wasn't disappointed. "Then she's safe and out of the picture." Another pause. Laurel can do more with a pause than most people can with a full interrogation, and I could sense her slicing and dicing my phony relief.

"Yes, this morning I drove her to the Greyhound station, the lowest-profile and, therefore, safest transportation I could think of." She sounded like a teacher giving extra emphasis to the lesson. "Waved at her till the bus pulled out. Rexanne's on her way back to her mother, which is where she belongs."

I can do a little slicing and dicing myself, and I noted Laurel did *not* say where the bus was headed. Boy, Dako Farona really didn't want his daughter associating with the likes of me. To change the topic, I asked what the police had said about the break-in. Her voice was tight when she told me it wasn't a police matter and they hadn't reported it, then she said they'd need another week or so to work their case, and that she'd call me when she wanted to retrieve the envelope.

After we hung up, I couldn't help but wonder if Dako was on the wrong side of the law on this one. Why wasn't the break-in a police matter? Could the envelope I was holding contain blackmail material?

While considering the possibility of my unintentional participation in a felony, I wrote and sent the invoice, made two follow-up calls to people I had met with earlier in the week, then phoned Bitsy Sutterman to see if she needed me to bring anything from the store on the way home.

"We're getting low on Dewar's, but don't bother unless you're picking up something for yourself."

When I moved in with the Sutterman twins right after college, I had this image of older ladies drinking tea out of frou-frou little cups in a living room filled with sepia-toned photos and hand-crocheted doilies. My foster-dad's grandmother, Lillian Carmichael, had lived up to that movie-influenced concept of the way women past seventy spent their lives, and was my only previous model.

Bitsy and Kitty expunged that misconception from my mind with all the gentle finesse of Darth Vader chopping off Luke Skywalker's hand. The

throbbing bass of "In-A-Gadda-Da-Vida" drew me from
my computer that first night in their home, but Iron
Butterfly wasn't the only culture shock awaiting me in
their living room. The changing colored lights of the
Wurlitzer Bubbler shone on a scene that was part
1950's Fellini, part 1960's flower power.

Bitsy Sutterman, wearing a headband and a long,
flowing dress, swayed in the arms of an elderly man in
bell-bottom jeans and a shirt that would have been
equally at home on Sir Walter Raleigh or your average
pirate. I learned later he had been a bit-part actor
through the several decades after World War Two
before moving into a successful career as a realtor.

Kitty had on a *really* short skirt and a fringed
suede vest that didn't appear to have anything under
it except Kitty. Her partner was more observer than
participant, as he sat on the couch with one hand on
his parked aluminum walker, the other grazing Kitty's
hip affectionately every time her slow-speed grind
brought her within his reach.

A third couple twirled out of the corner of the
room into the glow of the juke box and I realized the
dance partner held closely by the silver-haired
gentleman in the white dinner jacket was Carlos, the
full-scale medical skeleton who normally reclined in
one of the Eames chairs with a martini glass wired to
the bones of his right hand, one leg crossed jauntily
over the other.

That night I was introduced to Joe Cocker, Janis
Joplin and sitar music. I did not smell anything
unusual perfuming the air, but I suspected intoxicants
other than alcohol were in play. My image of senior
citizens as sedentary bingo players took a hit that
night, supplanted by the truth: growing old may be
inevitable, but growing up is a choice. Also, 'shrooms

be bitchin'.

Four years later, the Sutterman sisters still like to listen to music ranging from Frank Sinatra to The Everly Brothers, and Jimi Hendrix to Lady Gaga, but their gentlemen friends have passed away, moved in with children or gone into nursing homes, so those psychedelic evenings are now memory, rather than reality. Carlos Santana rarely leaves his Eames chair anymore, although he never lets go of his bone-dry martini. Every once in a while, when the Wurlitzer bubbles and glows, singing "Crying" in Roy Orbison's voice, I take Carlos in my arms and waltz him around the room to make my landladies smile. They love it when I deeply dip my Hollywood-thin partner on the big, falsetto finish, and that's reason enough for me to play the dork for a few minutes.

These days the Suttermans' hell-raising is limited to one nightly post-prandial scotch apiece, and I stopped at Rocco's Liquor for a bottle of Dewar's. I also grabbed a six-pack of Bud Lite so Bitsy wouldn't fuss about my having made a special trip for her and her twin. After so much time living with the ladies, I was confident they had no more surprises left for me, but it turned out I was big-ass wrong.

Since I needed to drop off the Dewar's, I didn't enter through the door in the back that led to my own room, but went in the front entrance. When I heard laughter from the living room I headed that way, wondering if the sisters had found another elderly man to amuse and entertain them, but after I rounded the corner, I stopped dead.

"Oh, Rick, there you are," Kitty said. "And I think you've already met Ms. Farona."

"Yes," Bitsy tossed in. "Rexanne's going to stay in the guest room for a few nights. Isn't that nice?"

I had only bought the Budweiser as cover for the scotch, but when Rexanne Farona smiled up at me from under a thick fringe of dark lashes, my heart went thump and I suddenly needed a beer.

Forty-five minutes past their usual bedtime and half-hammered from a second drink each, Bitsy and Kitty announced they were retiring for the night.

"If you need something, sweetheart, ask Rick. He knows where everything is around here," Bitsy told Rexanne, before unsteadily rising from the couch.

"And don't be afraid to knock on his door during the night if you find any spiders in your room. We do it all the time," added Kitty.

"That's okay. If I find a spider I'll just eat it."

Rexanne's delivery was deadpan and the sisters rocked with a combo of laughter and alcohol as they tottered from the room.

Finally alone with Dako's daughter and able to ask what had been on my mind since I walked into the house, I inarticulately blurted out, "What the hell, Rexanne? I mean, what the hell?"

"Well, *obviously* I had no intention of staying here when I showed up, but those two are very persuasive and it does save me the trouble of finding a motel to hide in."

She didn't seem nearly as mousy as she had been when Laurel and I played out our stand-off at Farona Investigations. In fact, her self-confidence rattled my cage. It was like she was paying me back for invading her turf and intimidating her by storming my own turf and taking my lunch money.

"How did you find this address?"

"As soon as Dad said I was being shipped back to Texas and told me to gather my stuff, I went into the personnel files to find out where you live."

"But why me?"

"I've been here a total of ten days, so you're the only other person I know in LA besides Laurel and my father. I thought you might be able to tell me what's going on and if either of them is in danger."

"Look, your old man and I are not BFFs, so he doesn't confide in me about his cases. The only reason I came by the other day was to take him to lunch to solidify our professional relationship."

"To suck up to him, you mean."

Rexanne Farona was becoming less attractive and more annoying by the minute, but before I could mount a defense against her insult, she went on the attack again.

"Let's face it, my father's a successful, respected investigator and you're a guy relying on him to toss you a client every now and then."

"Is *that* what he said about me?"

"He's never even mentioned your name, but after you left the office I checked you out in our computer system."

"Why?"

"What?"

"Why'd you go checking me out after we met?" Her blush told me I'd taken the high ground for the first time in our conversation. Little Ms. Farona was apparently jonesing for some Valentine, so, with a shocking lack of maturity, I went for the jugular. "Forget it, doll. You're much too young for me." If there's one thing I'd learned from Rexanne's father, it's how to sound like a sexist, hard-boiled gumshoe, so I was not expecting unladylike snorts to wilt my metaphorical fedora.

"Oh, cripes, you think I *like* you?! You're even

more shallow than you look!"

I was half past pissed-off when I retorted, "Hey, who went looking for *who*, missy?" I was pretty sure that second who should have had an m at the end and there might be some law prohibiting men under fifty from calling women "missy," but I bluffed with a steely glare.

Her return eyeballing was equally metallic and, for a moment, neither of us had the advantage. Then she leaned forward with an unnerving grin, probably the same one those poor spiders see right before her tongue snaps out and seals their fate. "What's in the envelope?"

Uh-oh. "What envelope?" I widened my eyes and lifted my eyebrows to sell innocent as best I could, but Rexanne Farona was not in a buying mood.

"The one you laid on my desk while you searched for your parking ticket. The one Laurel gave you only days before somebody broke into Dad's office and trashed the place."

It was careless to have dropped the envelope on the desk, as she obviously shared her father's observational skill and memory for detail. We were suddenly at what I have been told is the "come to Jesus" moment, so I stopped playing games and started treating her like the intelligent young woman she was proving to be, if only by convincing Laurel she was on her way to Texas. When I asked Rexanne later how she'd pulled that off, she said she stayed on the dogmobile till the first stop, then disembarked and purchased a ticket back to Los Angeles. Observant *and* resourceful.

Coming clean, I told her I had no clue about the envelope's contents, and had only been tasked with keeping it hidden until her father needed it.

"So, what do you think is in it?"

I did not voice any suspicion that Dako was blackmailing someone, telling her instead I thought it was evidence for an upcoming court case, evidence strong enough to make the bad guys try to steal it.

"But if they came away empty from the office, aren't they going to keep looking?"

Backed into a corner, I had to tell her about the duplicate envelope, then watched as her eyes scanned our surroundings. "Where'd you hide it?"

"Oh, please. You think I'd jeopardize Kitty and Bitsy by stashing it in their *home*?"

She stared hard for a moment, then flashed that creepy grin again. "Sure you would, because *you'd* bet someone *else* would assume you wouldn't put the Suttermans at risk. *That's* reverse psychology, dude." Her eyes swept the room, evaluating potential hidey-holes and, for all I know, looking for webby nooks that might harbor snacks.

"Look," I said, standing abruptly. "I've had a long day, so I'm going to bed. Feel free to toss this place."

"Rick, wait." She rose, blocking my exit. "I need to ask you a favor."

"Well, you sure know how to put a guy in the mood to help you. *That* is sarcasm, dude."

I juked to go around her, but she reached out and put her hand on my arm. "Okay, okay, I get that I can sometimes be annoying. At least that's what my dad says."

Wow. Something Dako Farona and I could finally agree on.

"But, here's the thing. I need to borrow your car for a few days. And before you say no, you can use a rental while I'm driving yours."

"Why don't you rent one yourself?"

She looked embarrassed. "I tried, but you have to be twenty-one."

"Tough garbanzos for you, because at the moment I don't have the extra funds to rent a—"

"No, I'll pay for it," she interrupted.

"With what? Your baby-sitting money?" I enjoyed watching her squirm, as she hovered between the desire to tell me to drop dead and her need to convince me to help her. Coming to a decision, she spoke without rancor. Without groveling, either, and I had been looking forward to the groveling. Letting go of my arm, she sat down again.

"According to easily accessed public records, I am the seventh-richest twenty year old in Texas. I could charge a private jet for you with no problem, so the rentable Ferrari or Maserati of your choice is well within my budget."

The girl was not boasting; if anything, her body language conveyed discomfort. I could see this wasn't a topic she had intended to broach unless she absolutely had to and it was only the first of many things to surprise me over the course of the following hour. I sank down onto the couch as Dako's daughter told me about herself.

Rexanne's mother's maiden name is Amanda Richfield, as in billionaire Harmon Richfield's only child after Amanda's older brother died in an accident on one of his father's oil rigs. Harmon's obsessive need to protect his remaining child caused him to push Amanda into an early marriage with the "right" kind of man, but she scandalously dumped the dad-approved husband two years later. Refusing to buckle under her father's threat to disinherit her, she walked out of her marriage with her head held high, declining a settlement or a penny in alimony.

"She even gave back her engagement ring and wedding band, and I've heard rumors they were worth close to three million dollars," Rexanne said.

"So how did Dako come into the picture?"

"Classic scenario. Little rich girl wants to stick it to her father, so she runs off to Los Angeles and looks for the scruffiest poor boy she can find. A broke young private investigator was perfect."

I didn't have to stretch my imagination to believe Dako capable of taking advantage of a vulnerable heiress, marrying her for the money.

"They went to a courthouse and made it official six days after they met, and Mom says they really thought they were in love. A few months later, when Amanda got pregnant, Harmon moved off his hard-line stand on disinheriting his daughter and after I was born, my grandfather pushed to get my parents to move to Dallas. Offered to set Dad up in cushy offices and direct high-end clientele his way."

"Sounds like Amanda had made her point and Dako could've used the help, so why didn't they do it?"

"Because before I was a year old, they both knew they had gotten married for the wrong reasons. She'd only done it, like I said, to rub her father's nose in it and—"

"Dako was after the money," I interjected.

Rexanne looked surprised. "What? No. Mom told me he was on the rebound after some girl broke his heart."

If Rexanne was to be believed, Amanda and Dako had parted as friends, divorcing quietly and amicably before Amanda returned to her Dallas home with the baby.

"They've never asked me to pick sides, and my mother sends me here whenever I want to visit my dad."

"Then how come I never met you while I was working for your father?"

She'd enrolled at Texas State University right after graduating from high school. Between studying and a busy social life, there had been little opportunity to get home to see her mother, much less make a trip to Los Angeles.

"I decided to take a year off and spend some time with Dad before I go back to get my degree, and he said I could temp at the agency until I found a job."

"But you don't *need* to work."

"So? What am I supposed to do with my life, parade around in designer clothes with a Pomeranian in my purse? Look, can I borrow your car or not?"

When she brought the conversation back to her original request, I asked why she couldn't hire a limousine or buy a new car for herself, but Rexanne dryly pointed out that a limo didn't sync with the low profile she wanted to maintain while she kept an eye on her father. And California is particularly insistent about requiring a driver's license from the Golden State if you purchase a vehicle within its borders, treating an official license from Texas or any of those other lesser states like a medical degree from East Crapistan.

At least she had stopped harping about the envelope. After two beers and a troubling day, I was fried, so I gave in and told the seventh-richest twenty year old in Texas she could use my Jeep.

Bitsy laid out a spectacular breakfast the next morning, but I would have preferred dry cereal. I didn't want our guest getting too comfortable in the house.

After showing her the quirks of my twelve-year-old Wrangler and verifying she could drive a stick, I rocketed away from the rental car place in a sleek, black Corvette. I finally had a working CD player. Unfortunately, I'd left all my discs in the Jeep, so I was forced to search the airwaves for music, once again finding mostly political ads trash-talking or supporting one of the two mayoral candidates. The big real estate developer ran with a "political outsider" theme, crowing about the large number of jobs his construction projects had created in LA county. His accusers called him out for greed, governmental inexperience and alleged hiring of illegals. The other candidate, a former Chief of Police, capitalized on the pervasive, big-city fear of terror attacks by playing up his many years in law enforcement. The ads against him charged that cronyism and corruption had tarnished his journey from cop to would-be mayor.

Bored to the brink of a stroke, I found a Spanish station. The music wasn't exactly my taste, but at least the attack ads assaulted me in a language I didn't understand.

Lloyd stood, breathy and excited, when I entered the Gingerbread House, and for a nanosecond I thought maybe a VIP client might be waiting for me. But no, he only wanted to hand me a flyer for *Desire Trumps Will*, an English-manners play, he explained, in which young Will, son of Sir Chauncey Larkwhit, loves an innocent tavern maid named....

That's when I interrupted. "My finely honed detective skills tell me you are in this play and would like me to come to a performance."

"Oh, *would* you, Mr. Valentine?"

His neediness was almost palpable, so I quickly calculated that enduring two hours of bad British accents might be worth some future barter with Lloyd. "Sure, I'll come," I said, glancing at the flyer. "You're playing Will?"

He pulled himself up, as if insulted. "No, I am sketching the much meatier role of Sir Larkwhit's trusted second under-valet. Fewer lines, but *so* much more nuance."

If the meaningful look he gave me on the word nuance was an indication of Lloyd's acting ability, his performance promised to be excruciating.

Upstairs, I saw Justin coming out of the other corner office at the back while I opened the door of mine.

"Did Lloyd collar you?" he asked, walking toward me.

I held up the flyer to show he had. "This going to be any good?"

"A talking hemorrhoid. But it's the kid's first play, so Jason and Pat and I bit the bullet and said we'd go Friday night. You in?"

"I got nothing else to do."

"Exactly the enthusiasm the play deserves. And don't worry, Pat says she can score us some black tar heroin. A pinch between the cheek and gum, and *Desire Trumps Will* is going to look like *King Lear* at the Old Vic."

I sat at my desk, flipping through the stack of mail Lloyd had handed me with his flyer—purveyors of junk mail having tracked down me and my alter ego Occupant—when I found a messengered envelope. My client from the day before had sent payment and a thank-you note offering to give me a reference if I ever needed one.

It felt good driving home in the flashy Corvette, but when I parked at the curb shortly after sunset, I was relieved to see my Jeep in the driveway with no apparent dings or scrapes. I grabbed a dozen CDs out of the console and tossed them into the rental ride, but couldn't find my Dodgers cap in the glove box where I kept it when I didn't need the bill to keep the sun out of my eyes. That's because it was on the head of Rexanne Farona, her long ponytail dangling out over the size-adjustment band as she stood at the stove with her back to me when I entered the kitchen.

"Hi, Rick," Bitsy trilled cheerfully. "Rexanne's showing us how to make Tex-Mex chili." The wink she gave me was a heads-up not to reveal she already knew how to make Tex-Mex chili, as well as about a dozen other varieties, with a lot more skill than the girl who hadn't yet turned around from the pot she stirred.

Kitty perched on a stool at the counter and threw Bitsy a conspiratorial look before saying, "Aren't you going to say hello, Rexanne?"

The girl in my Dodgers cap turned slowly, first presenting her perfect profile, then cold-cocking me with the complete view.

The other side of her face was a scarred, melted nightmare: a bloody hole in her cheek, a tattered lid failing to cover the smashed, out-of-socket eyeball and the once pouty and inviting lips reduced to charred shreds. My sharp intake of breath triggered shrieks of laughter from the twins and a zombie's half-grin from Rexanne.

"Did you know Kitty used to work as a makeup artist in the movies?" she asked.

"Yeah," Kitty proudly said, "I've got more alien/monster/flesh-eater juju in my little finger than those kids on Face Off have in their whole body."

Trying to recover my dignity, I had to admit Kitty

had done an amazing job, but it was rapidly becoming apparent Rexanne's ability to annoy me was on the verge of infecting my landladies. Attempting to sound like the only grown-up in the room, I said, "I see you three have had a productive afternoon."

"Don't be a buzzkill," Kitty admonished. "When Rexanne found out what I used to do for a living, she asked for a makeover."

"I was way tempted by Maggot-riddled Civil War Corpse and Bloaty Drowning Victim, but Mutilated Undead made my heart go pitter-pat."

I recognized the captions from Kitty's scrapbook of horror. She also kept a book of glamour photos, leading ladies she had transformed into luminous beauties with her magical makeup kit, but she was much prouder of the work she had done in thrillers and monster flicks from the mid-1950s to the late 1960s.

"My Twitter followers *love* the makeover," said Rexanne, leaning away from the stove to avoid shedding bits of faux rotting flesh into the simmering chili.

"Yeah, while I did her totally awesome new look, she streamed it live on Meerkat," Kitty told me.

My landladies, who I didn't know were aware of the concept of tweeting, had already joined Rexanne's followers.

"That brings me to eleven hundred and twenty-seven," said Rexanne. "I am *so* crushing May-Ann Harris!"

"May-Ann," Bitsy said dismissively.

"Ho," added Kitty.

Apparently, some meangirl bonding had gone on during the afternoon.

The Tex-Mex tasted okay, but Bitsy's cornbread

and salad were better, and the dinner conversation was as normal as it can be among four people when one of them looks like something a grave puked up.

After Bitsy and Kitty went to bed, Rexanne told me she had spent the morning surveilling her father's office building. I wondered if the red Jeep had been a bit obvious sitting at a meter on the short block where Dako's office is, but Rexanne revealed a surprising bit of ingenuity. "There's a five-story parking structure right across the street, so I found a spot on the side facing Dad's building and watched without ever being seen. You didn't think I was going to risk having him or Laurel recognize your wheels, did you?"

"Kudos for resourcefulness. Did you see anything unusual?"

"Not with the goings-in and comings-out, but I *did* notice I wasn't the only one watching the place."

That piqued my interest. Rexanne handed me a piece of paper with a make, model, tag number and a description of the vehicle's two occupants.

"I bought a pair of killer binoculars this morning, so I could almost count the hairs sprouting out of the driver's ears."

We were in agreement on one thing: the watchers were most likely not interested in one of the dentists, attorneys or accountants that filled the building, and I promised to find out who owned the car.

The conversation was not as charged or adversarial as the one the night before, and I almost felt like Rexanne and I were teammates, though what the game we were playing was, I couldn't tell you. As we said our good-nights and headed to our separate rooms, I gestured toward her decimated face.

"It's a good look for you."

"Isn't it though? I only wish Kitty had been there

to do me for that gawd-awful debutante ball Mom forced me to go to when I turned eighteen. My white satin gown would've looked sick rocking a little blood spatter and a few gobbets of brain." With a distorted grin, Rexanne Farona disappeared down the hall.

The seventh-richest twenty year old in Texas had grown up surrounded by luxuries—including two loving parents—and, as I went to my own room, I thought about how different our backgrounds were. Maybe it was that whole opposites-attract thing that drew me to her, made me feel protective. Either that or the tease in the sparkling brown eye that had *not* dangled down onto her ravaged cheekbone.

I prevailed on my tenuous connection with Det. Bao to get the name of the car's owner, then went to work. A dirtbag in and out of penal facilities since he was fourteen, Zeke Martin didn't appear to have permanent employment with any one particular criminal enterprise; he was more of a freelance guy, beating up people, wrecking places and doing time over the years for arson, theft and extortion. Zeke always managed to get exonerated or slapped with the shortest amount of time for the crime, and his high-dollar lawyers didn't jibe with his lowlife persona, so I assumed he was a crime-on-consignment bum doing the dirty work for powerful someone elses. His usual associate was a bottom-feeder he had celled with at Chino, a real piece of work named Bobby Chalk. Zeke's one-year stint for breaking the legs of a man who was ninety days past-due on his bookie's bill corresponded with Bobby's tenth and final year for a murder which had patently been contract, but which was pled down to manslaughter to save the state the cost of a trial. California's budget can't afford to give *every* killer the deluxe O.J. package.

If they were the ones who had wrecked Dako's office and stolen the computers, their surveillance the day before suggested they weren't finished yet.

***Desire Trumps Will* was not as bad** as I had expected, mainly because it was a spoof of an English-manners play, rather than an attempt at the real thing, a subtlety that passed right over Lloyd's head as he sold his five lines with the intensity of Hamlet gazing into Yorick's empty eye sockets, inadvertently adding to the tongue-in-cheekiness of the production.

A cracker, cheese and cheap wine mixer followed onstage after the final curtain fell in the munchkin-sized theater, with about half the audience staying to mingle with the actors. Jason told me the half who left were casting people, producers and talent agents who hadn't seen anyone in *Desire Trumps Will* who stood out as even the roughest of diamonds, while the half who stayed were spouses, parents, friends or guilted co-workers like us.

With his dippy young wife hanging on his every word, Lloyd shared the minutia of a childhood back story he had fabricated for the second under-valet, including his name: Bartholomew Canterbury. This prompted Pat to mutter the word "actors" with disdain. Luckily, the glowing, puffed-up thespian was deaf to all but his own words, so he didn't hear the slight. After having wrung every possible drop of attention out of our small group, Lloyd and his ditzy missus moved on to the next gaggle of unlucky ears, but not before advising me that the landlord had delivered my door plaque at the end of the workday.

"I proofed it twice to make sure your name was correct before I sent the installer up to your office, even at the risk of being late for my premiere."

He made it sound as though he'd been looking out for me, but I knew it was Lloyd's way of hinting he expected a little something extra at the end of the month.

The woman playing Sir Larkwhit's daughter was a hella fine blonde named Piper Lang who wouldn't give me her phone number, but agreed to take one of my cards and "think about" calling me after I charmed her by offering a third alternative to the cheapie red and even cheapier white available at the makeshift bar. When I heard her disappointed sigh on learning there was no white zinfandel, I filled a clear plastic cup with "shardonnay" and splashed in enough red to replicate the pale blush of a white zin. Gallantly introducing myself as world-renowned wino-ologist Rico Valenti, I was rewarded with a smile and a ten-minute chat thrumming with erotic potential.

The plate of cheddar cubes emptied quickly and Justin whispered to me that he and the others were going out for a real drink. I had no shot at Piper that night, so I joined Jason, Justin and Pat at a nearby Italian restaurant featuring Chianti that cost more per glass than a half-gallon box o' red at our previous venue.

We all turned our phones back on, having been admonished by Sir Larkwhit to shut them the hell off in the second scene of *Desire Trumps Will*, when a soliloquy on the king's gouty leg was interrupted by a loud and bouncy *it's all about the bass, 'bout the bass, 'bout the bass, no treble*. I saw a missed call from Cal Cooper, but I decided not to return it until after our impromptu gathering dispersed.

Since Pat's studio was in the only other office above Moonbeam Fink's, I asked if the New Age music drifting up to the second floor bothered her. "I'm fully soundproofed for my recording sessions," she said, "so I never hear it. I smell that gaggy patchouli, though."

After small talk and one round we broke up, so I zoomed off in the 'Vette, dialing Cal's number as I merged onto the 405 South.

"Jesus, Rick, what kind of shit have you gotten yourself into?!"

When a phone conversation starts that way, you know it isn't going anywhere good. Cal told me two knuckle-draggers had shown up at his place earlier and forced him to search online for the owner of the domain name www.2regni.net.

"I about died when your name popped up. And before you ask, the one with breath like rotting fish was leaning over my shoulder watching the screen, so there was no way I could fudge to protect you."

Cal's highly specialized skills make him popular with law enforcement *and* criminals, so he regularly does business with a wide spectrum of clients. He prefers criminals because they pay cash up front and never quibble about his rates, while cops require legitimate invoices and have a payment lag-time of up to four months. I had been introduced to him by Dako—who floated somewhere between the polar opposites of Cal's normal range of customers—and knew him to be a chill guy who never rattled. Until that night.

"Tell me what happened."

"They demanded everything, addresses for home and office, phone numbers, but when I saw it was you I diddled the keys like I was searching my ass off and kept throwing screens that said access denied."

They had made Cal pull up the site and, when they saw it wasn't active, put a gun to his head.

"Mackerel-breath gave me until the count of ten to produce something they could use and I caved. I'm sorry, but I really thought he was going to shoot my brain."

"Cal, it's okay. What did you have to give up?"

"Hide your Jeep and get a rental car for a couple weeks."

He had given them my license plate and a description of my aging, cherry red Wrangler, the vehicle in which Dako Farona's daughter was now tooling around Los Angeles.

The next call I made was to Rexanne. When it went straight to voicemail I called Bitsy, who woke up long enough to check the guest room and tell me it was empty. At my request she also walked to the front door to see if the Jeep was in the driveway. It wasn't.

What I Knew: Rexanne Farona didn't have any friends in LA she could be out with at 11:30 at night. What I Thought I Knew: she had been followed and grabbed by two felons who were under the delusion they were following me. What I Didn't Know? Why? Everything boomeranged back to the envelope I was safekeeping. Somebody believed the contents were important, if not downright dangerous, and had been willing to vandalize an office and maybe snatch a girl in an effort to lay hands on that envelope. They'd put a gun to Cal's head, but hadn't otherwise physically hurt him. I did not know if I should take that as reassurance Rexanne wouldn't be harmed once she'd convinced them she didn't know the envelope's whereabouts, or to assume the direct, scary threat to Cal had been an escalation of the "search" of Dako's office and might preface an escalation of violence, this time against Rexanne.

WIDK: would she have the sense not to tell them she was Dako's daughter and become a bargaining chip? Suddenly I was afraid for the mouthy little rich girl, but wasn't sure what I could do. If I called Dako and told him I'd been harboring his kid under my own roof when he thought she was safe with her mother, he'd kill me. If Rexanne was only off catching a movie and I ratted her out to her dad, *she'd* kill me. I could call the police with an anonymous tip about a possible kidnapping, giving them the alleged 'nappers names, but that point became moot as I turned the corner onto the Suttermans' block and saw my Jeep in the driveway.

I didn't need to put my hand on the hood to know it had pulled in only minutes earlier. As I rushed past it on my way to the front of the house, noting the smashed-in driver's side door, I heard settling, crackling noises indicative of a rough ride and rapid cooling. The Jeep had been run off the road and driven hard. The only question was who would be waiting for me inside, so I had the Sigma in my hand when I quietly entered the dark foyer, and crossed the living room.

Weak light filtered into the hallway, but when I moved toward it I could see it was not coming from the guest room where Rexanne was staying, and Kitty's and Bitsy's doors were shut. Whoever had grabbed Rexanne must be searching my room, I thought, so I raised the S&W beside my left ear and inched forward along the wall.

I spun around the door frame, dropping the gun into firing position, then jerking it up when I realized it was Rexanne sitting on my bed. She startled, then threw herself at me. I was at a disadvantage for a hug of relief, so I thumbed the safety before tossing my gun onto the spread and wrapping both arms around her.

"Are you okay?" we asked simultaneously, her voice half-muffled as her face pressed against my shoulder. Barely were the words spoken, when we pulled apart.

"Wait," I said, "why would you think *I* wouldn't be okay?"

"Because two butt-munches are out looking for you. What they *should* be looking for is industrial strength mouthwash."

"Did they hurt you? Threaten you?"

"I've handled drunk frat boys more threatening then those two."

I declined to share the homicidal bona fides of Bobby Chalk, but I assumed she was still shaken from her encounter, so I pretended to believe she was fine.

"How'd you get away from them?"

"Easy peas. I said I didn't know who owned the Jeep, that I'd boosted it from a parking lot."

"And they bought that?" I asked, skeptically.

"They did after I proved I could hotwire a random car on the street."

I had to admit the girl knew her stuff. The descriptions she gave me matched what I'd pulled on Zeke Martin and Bobby Chalk, and after she had confirmed they were the same two guys sitting on Dako's building, she wanted to talk about the "case," meaning the envelope, but it was after midnight, so I suggested we each get some sleep and tackle everything fresh in the morning. Surprisingly, she agreed it was a good idea.

I waited until I saw the light go off under Rexanne's door before slipping out of the house. I intended to find out what Dako Farona was mixed up in before somebody got killed.

I used the "borrowed" mag card to gain entry to the Beverly Hills office building's underground parking facility, pulling in next to the unmanned valet station. The sleepy clerk on duty in the lobby didn't bother to check my signature. If he worked graveyard he wouldn't recognize the day people anyway, so I flashed my key card and said I worked for the CPA firm on eight. After getting off the elevator at that floor, I walked up two flights to Farona Investigations and let myself in.

Everything had been put back where it belonged and new computers had replaced the stolen ones. Dako always said if you want to hide something, put it where no one ever thinks to look. He had shown me all the places narcotics cops check for drugs, from the very obvious freezer compartment to the more subtle wall pockets behind light switches. Plastic-wrapped inside toilet tanks. In hollowed-out books or fake cans of vegetable soup. All amateur choices, according to Dako, and all easily discovered.

The best spots, he told me, were the places where someone could stare at what you had stashed and never see it. With that in mind I skipped anywhere that seemed like it might be a hiding place and went right to spots where nobody would be dumb enough to leave anything important. Tomorrow I would examine the contents of the envelope Laurel had placed in my care, but if she and Dako were blackmailing somebody, it would only contain incriminating material on their target. My goal that night was to find any evidence linking Dako to whatever had triggered the hiring of Martin and Chalk.

I razored open the end seams of a couple dozen

innocuously labeled manila envelopes in a file cabinet drawer that purportedly held tax return back-ups for the years 2006 through 2013, examining contents that had nothing to do with taxes, eventually coming to one marked: *2009 gas receipts/mileage records.* The file inside, however, bore the notation May 16, 1994, a date I was very familiar with.

That was the night of the botched raid in which my father had been killed.

I had no inkling why Dako would have the police file from that event, and it didn't connect to the problem at hand—or so I thought—but before I could decide whether to return it to the metal cabinet or take pictures of the contents for later perusal, I heard voices from the lobby. There was no place to hide in the small space, so I clicked off my flashlight and froze where I was: seated on the floor alongside an open file drawer.

The voices belonged to Dako and Laurel, who passed within six feet of me as they moved down the dark hallway. I was relieved to know that in the event I was discovered, I would not be facing two prison-hardened felons, but after seeing the competence with which Laurel had handled the Colt Commander, I knew I still might wind up shot.

I didn't dare move closer to the doorway to eavesdrop on the conversation coming from Dako's office, but enough of it drifted out for me to get the gist. They had been on surveillance, though they never mentioned who or what they'd been watching. Laurel made the case that they now had enough and could make their move, but Dako said he wanted a few more days to gather intel before striking. Timing had to be perfect, according to him.

They talked for another ten minutes, but I heard nothing that could help me figure out what they were involved in. If the envelope I was keeping held enough incriminating material to drive his target to steal computers and put low-end gangsters into play, why would Dako waste his time and risk people's lives to get more?

As my paranoia ran free, I constructed a model in which that night's surveillance was part of a *second* blackmail scheme. From there I began to think back on my years at Farona Investigations. Had there actually been enough lucrative work to support the lease in this upscale building? I had mostly been a legman, assigned to ferret out bits and pieces of information, but rarely involved in the big picture of each case. Could my small contributions have factored into an ongoing illegal enterprise?

WIDK: what the heck was going on at Farona Investigations. WIK: all conversation had suddenly stopped in Dako's office. Had I given myself away somehow? Were they poised with weapons in hand, listening for a creak or a footstep? Slowing my breathing, remaining motionless, I strained to catch hints of a stealthy approach. Only silence for several minutes, then, the unmistakable sounds of a couple making love. Unable to leave without the possibility of being discovered, unable to do what I really wanted—which is to put a finger in each ear and sing *la-la-la-la-la* loud enough to block all incoming—I was forced to have all doubt erased about the nature of the relationship between Dako and Laurel.

The squeaking of the leather couch in his office eventually stopped, the post-coital whispering too soft for me to catch, thank God, and the two dressed and left. I waited several minutes after hearing the suite

door lock before checking the time. Almost five and
I wasn't sure when the parking valet came on duty,
but I didn't want my presence known, so I closed the
cabinet drawer, keeping the file I had discovered right
before the lovebirds arrived.

On the drive home, perhaps in response to my
role as aural audience for a live sex show, my thoughts
waxed amorous and Piper Lang's long, shapely legs
sashayed into my mind, legs that had been demurely
covered while she played Lord Larkwhit's daughter,
but flagrantly flaunted in the miniest of minis in her
real-life role as star-to-be. I briefly wondered why my
mind didn't stray to Rexanne Farona, especially since
she had hurled herself at me and hung on tightly with
relief earlier that night, while Piper had coquettishly
deigned only to accept my card, but then one of the
slender legs stamped its high-heeled foot to regain my
attention and that was the end of Dako's pretty
daughter.

It was almost daylight when I pulled into the
Suttermans' driveway and I desperately needed to
shower and get a couple hours' sleep. All the bedroom
doors were still closed, so I slipped in unnoticed and
did the former, but postponed the latter to examine
the contents of the file I'd pulled out of that drawer at
Farona Investigations—the police documents per-
taining to the incident in which my father died.

The official report said two detectives and four
uniformed officers converged on a warehouse owned
by Hamid Khavazhi, a Chechnyan mobster who had
avoided prosecution for years, even though the LAPD
had carried out multiple raids and stings. Violence
had not been anticipated, as the facility was supposed
to be unguarded, but something went sideways and
when the shooting stopped a half-dozen people were

dead: Khavazhi, his right-hand man Yusup Belkhan, two of their enforcers, one of the lead detectives on the case and thirty-four-year-old Officer John Valentine.

I have only the haziest memories of my father's funeral, but I know it was a ceremony honoring a fallen hero. He was credited with shooting Belkhan, who had already killed one of the lead detectives. Belkhan's boss, Khavazhi, then fatally shot my father before being killed by the second detective on the case, a man who went on to rise through the ranks and eventually become Chief of Police. His name was Grant Tenninger and he was one of the candidates currently duking it out in the mayoral race.

I recognized Tenninger's name from the political ads I'd been hearing for a month, but his wasn't the name that rattled me. Of the six police officers on the premises that night, five discharged their weapons at least once. The remaining officer apparently never even pulled his gun, but was one of only two surviving witnesses to my father's murder.

That young officer was Dako Farona.

A lack of sleep, combined with that vivid memory of bagpipe music which always makes me choke up closed my eyes for a moment as I got to the end of the report. Of necessity, foster kids travel light. The system is hard-pressed to keep its charges safe until they're grown, and would be stretched beyond capacity in also trying to protect their few mementos. The Carmichaels had carefully kept for me the small collection of items passed on to them from the family that had sheltered me the first five weeks after my mother died and, presumably, that original family had handed over everything they had received—along with the skinny, buck-toothed eight-year old—from Child

Protective Services. Tommy Carmichael had replaced the flimsy cardboard box with a more permanent cookie tin from a defunct company called Wigmore's Wafers, even painting my name on the front in chunky blue letters. That cookie tin became the permanent receptacle for my treasure, but it was a paltry lot. My father's badge—so very heavy when it was placed in my hands at the funeral by his partner, Victor Ramirez—became lighter as I grew, as if diminishing in weight at a rate similar to the diminishment of my ability to recall the man who tousled my hair when he came through the door, right before he lifted my mother off the ground and spun her around. I impatiently waited my turn to be lifted and spun, listening to their laughter and averting my eyes during the inevitable kiss.

My mother's engagement ring and four photographs rounded out the sparse physical evidence of a childhood that had taken two sharp left turns. The tiny chip of diamond in the ring represented all a young cop could afford at the time, but I remember seeing my mother kiss that ring on several occasions after my father was gone, always when she thought I was asleep.

Along with the badge and the ring, the box held their wedding picture, my father's official police photograph, my kindergarten class picture with a hand-drawn arrow pointing to me in the second row, and a snapshot of my mom and me eating ice cream cones in the shade of a lifeguard tower at the beach, presumably taken by my dad.

I jolted awake at the sound of knocking on my door, which was immediately followed by Rexanne's voice. "Rise and shine, Sherlock. We've got leads to follow."

I groggily recalled my promise the night before to include her in the unraveling of the hidden envelope mystery, but finding that file in Dako's office had shifted my attention in another direction. WIK: Farona Investigations recruited me straight out of college. WIDK: Why? Was it a coincidence that one of the two surviving witnesses to my father's murder became my first employer? Or, could a darker issue be in play? Maybe guilt over something he did or didn't do during that warehouse shoot-out. I needed to lay some questions to rest about my former boss before I cozied up any further to his daughter, so the hidden envelope would have to wait a few hours.

"I'm going to shower first," I shouted at my door. "I'll meet you at breakfast in fifteen."

"Well, don't gripe to me if all the bacon's gone by the time you show up," Rexanne shot back.

In two minutes I had the phone number of Victor Ramirez; in four, I had his Long Beach address and an invitation to drive down and talk to him; in seven, I was out the back door and in the Corvette. Rexanne could eat bacon until the pig union put her on its hit list, but I needed to hear everything my father's partner could tell me about the op gone wrong and Dako Farona's part in it.

The view from Victor's condo was a million-dollar oceanfront vista, although the place itself was minuscule. Or, as he put it, the best you could buy on a cop's retirement less alimony. He was big and beefy, but hadn't gone to fat, despite his assurance he did nothing more these days than daub amateurish seascapes and watch the sun set every night with a beer in his hand. The stunning paintings on the walls and the half-finished one on an easel belied his claim of amateurishness as much as the ropy muscles of his legs did the claim of a sedentary existence.

The last time I'd seen Victor, he had been in uniform, so the flip-flops, Bermuda shorts and toucan-print camp shirt threw me for a moment as reality shoved memory aside.

"Ricky Valentine! Look at you, all grown up," he said when he opened the door, extending his hand for a shake, then pulling me in for a back-thumping hug. "Come in, come in. Mi casa and all that happy shit."

The first few minutes were mostly catch-up and apologies. I felt I shouldn't have waited until I needed something from him to seek him out, and he had his own regrets. "Look, I'm sorry I didn't stay more in touch. Me and the other guys did everything we could to fill in for your dad those years before your mother passed—"

Passed was a euphemism for putting your dead husband's service pistol in your mouth and blowing your alcohol-saturated brains out, and I respected Victor's sensitivity.

"—but once you went into the system, it got harder to keep tabs on you. CPS moved you right about the time we found out where you had initially landed, but we were all starting families of our own, and I guess I didn't try as hard as I should have."

"Uncle Vic," I said, surprising myself. Up until that moment I hadn't remembered my childhood name for him was so familial. But it had been. He and my father were more like brothers than partners, and for the first time I considered the tremendous loss he must have felt back then. "I have only good memories of what you and those other officers did for me. Don't beat yourself up because you think you could have done something more."

I told him about the Carmichaels, even pulling out my phone to show him pictures of Babs, Tommy and the rest of the clan to reassure Victor I had grown up as part of a loving family.

"Well, if you aren't here to offer me ten grand for one of my tacky paintings, what can I do for you, muchacho?"

And there it was, another piece of my past. When my mother used to bring me to the station to see my dad, Victor always acted like I was a suspect, marching me into an interrogation room to question me about whether I had robbed such-and-such a bank or burned down some building for the insurance. I now understand it was his way of keeping me occupied while my parents had a few minutes alone, but back then I was thrilled to be under the intense focus of a police investigation. After I giggled my denials in response to his allegations, Victor would tell me he was letting me walk *this time*. "But you better keep your nose clean, muchacho, 'cause I am watching you like a hawk." He'd point to his eyes with two fingers, then whip them around to point at me, and I felt protected, safe. Full, too, as Uncle Vic always brought me a glazed doughnut and a glass of milk before grilling me about my criminal deeds.

I told Victor I needed to know about the day my father died during the operation that had gone so tragically wrong. "And before you think about sugar-coating anything, you should know three things: I'm a grown-ass man, that was a long time ago and I've already read the official police report."

He rubbed the stubble on his chin before asking very neutrally, "And what did you think about that report?"

"I got a faint whiff of rotten egg as I turned the

pages. Could've been mildew from sitting around in a drawer so long. Or?"

"Or," he affirmed, nodding in resignation. "Well, you certainly inherited your dad's gut instincts. That report was fabricated to cover a lot of rear ends, all the way up to the commissioner's."

"Tell me the story. And please don't leave out anything, no matter how gruesome it is."

He refilled our coffees and dived into the tale. "We were idiots, your dad and me. We'd been cops for ten years and were itching to move up, you know? Somehow we got it into our heads that if we single-handedly brought in a *really* big fish, detective badges would be forthcoming. The two biggest fish around were Hamid Khavazhi and his asshole-buddy, Yusup Belkhan. You hear a lot about how ruthless those Russian mobsters were when they shouldered aside the homegrown gangs starting in the late seventies, but the Chechnyans, who moved in a few years later, made the Ivans look like Boy Scouts."

Vic outlined Khavazhi's criminal history, saying he'd earned the sobriquet Nostradamus for always knowing ahead of time when law enforcement would come knocking. Everything the cops found would be clean, legal and up to date on required import fees and taxes.

Grant Tenninger and Jermaine Rowan, the two detectives who spearheaded the fruitless pursuit of Khavazhi and Belkhan for years, suspected a leak from within the department, but they were never able to pin down anyone working under the table for the Chechnyans.

"So, anyway, your dad and me figured if we kept our plans off the official grid, cutting out Khavazhi's in-house rat, we could catch Nostradamus with his dick in his hand. For months we spent our lunch hours and a lot of all-nighters sitting on his warehouse locations, making charts of when they were active and when they were dormant. Turned out even violent, Eastern European douchebags crave routine."

Victor and my father had finally selected their target, intending to break in, document any illegal contents, then take the proof to the two lead guys. The detectives would quickly aquire a search warrant on the down low and the four would return to the warehouse that same night to obtain the evidence legally. My father had even constructed a ruse to keep the original evidence from becoming fruit of the poisoned tree. He and Victor would grab some small piece of contraband from inside the warehouse, hide it half-under a Dumpster by the rear loading gate, then claim to have been on a foot pursuit of a suspicious character when they accidentally stumbled upon the fallen piece of Kavazhi's most recent illegal delivery.

"It looked airtight to us, and we were sure the place would be unguarded, but one of us would have to stand lookout up front while the other broke in the back door. A cop alone, middle of the night, entering a mobster's storage facility is more than a target, he's an engraved invitation, so we decided to bring in two other people to give us a team at both ends of the building."

They had chosen officers with only a few years on the force, knowing the leaks to Nostradamus dated to back before their time. Gayle Chandler would go with Victor to break in at the loading dock, while my father and Dako Farona guarded the front.

"We only asked them the day before, giving them five minutes to make their decision, but we promised they'd get some trickle-down accolades and they were eager to team up with more experienced officers for a headline-making career boost. At midnight, the four of us met a few blocks away, intending to approach on foot."

"Wait, the official report says all six of you went in together."

He hesitated before saying, "A lot of that police file won't jibe with what I'm about to tell you."

"Gayle was a little slip of a thing, maybe five-one, but all she had to do was watch the alley while I picked the padlock, so I didn't feel I'd drawn the short straw. We left your dad and Dako up front and eased around the side of the building. It took me a couple minutes to open the lock, because I was doing it blind. Didn't want to risk even the smallest flashlight beam drawing any attention to us. After we entered the cavernous warehouse, Gayle and I threw only the illumination required to take pictures and look for something small enough to tuck under the Dumpster.

"We were about a third of the way through the interior when we heard a shot from up front. Knowing it would take more time to retrace our steps out the rear door and run around the building than to go forward and look for another door, we drew our weapons and went straight up the center aisle. Turns out we weren't the only ones inside, though, and two sleeping guards came up off their cots at the sound of that first blast. Gayle and I rushed at them, so they didn't pause to pick up the Kalashnikovs under their makeshift beds. They dived behind opposite rows of packed shelving with the handguns they must've kept under their pillows.

"We were sitting ducks out in the aisle, so we followed their lead and leapt behind shelving two rows back from where they had disappeared. It was like a Wild West shootout for a few minutes there, and while Gayle and I exchanged fire with the Chechnyan goons, I heard more shots from up front."

"How many?"

"Hard to say, but not nearly as many as there were back by me. The first two shots in front came fairly close together, but then there was a long break—say thirty seconds—before I heard three more shots almost on top of each other. By then Gayle had squeezed herself up over the stacked stock boxes and come up behind one of the guards. She got him, but took a slug in the thigh and went down howling. That brought the second one out in the open, so I burned him and ran to Gayle. She was bleeding like a son of a bitch, but the bullet hadn't hit bone and she told me to keep going while she called for backup.

"The steel door to the office wouldn't budge and after trying twice and nearly breaking my shoulder, I retraced my steps to the exit, then out and around the warehouse. When I rushed in the front with my gun drawn, your father was already down, along with Khavazhi, Belkhan and Det. Rowan. Det. Tenninger stood over Khavazhi's body and Officer Farona was radioing in our location."

It didn't sound like the end of the story and I watched Victor get up and go to the sliding glass door that opened onto a little balcony. He looked out at the ocean, but I got the feeling he was seeing something less serene than rolling whitecaps licking the sand.

"Why were Tenninger and Rowan at the warehouse? You said you didn't tell anybody but Dako and Gayle what you were planning."

"That's the big question, isn't it? Tenninger *said* he and his partner were running their own off-the-books deal in an effort to finally trap Nostradamus, before we stumbled in and cocked it up."

"Sounds like you didn't believe him."

"What I did or didn't believe became irrelevant pretty quickly. First, Gayle pounded on the door and we let her in. Backup was still a minute or two out, so Tenninger connected the dots for us."

The detective had told the three younger officers that getting caught in a failed, unofficial action with fatalities, no matter how noble the motive, would normally end in everyone being busted down a pay grade and getting a permanent stain on their record, but since two of the dead were cops, the fallout would be much worse, possibly resulting in dismissal from the force and criminal charges.

"*That* sure as shit put the fear of God in us. We all knew Tenninger was the darling of the top brass, thanks to his quick burial of a coke bust involving the commissioner's son, so we believed him when he said he could get us out of the jackpot we were in. Told us he could persuade the bosses to claim we had been on a sanctioned raid."

Since an official police operation would provide more of a firewall against lawsuits from survivors, while protecting the careers of the four cops who were walking out alive, Victor, Gayle and Dako agreed to swear they had been working all along under the direction of Detectives Tenninger and Rowan.

"Deuce was right. The higher-ups backed the lie to protect the department and then made sure everything went on the books retroactively."

"Deuce?"

"Tenninger's nickname. He dated a rich Beverly Hills divorcee a few years older than him about the time a movie called *Deuce Bigelow, Male Gigolo* came out, and we all started calling him that. Not to his face, but cops can't resist a nickname, you know?"

I figured I'd gotten all I was going to get out of Victor, so I joined him in turning the conversation to a lighter topic. "What was yours?" I asked.

"Mine was I'll-shoot-you-in-the-balls-if-you-call-me-anything-other-than-Vic-or-Victor."

"Catchy."

"Your dad's, by the way, was Tino."

"Why?"

"It was common knowledge your grandfather changed his name from Valentino to Valentine before he joined the force. I guess wops were a little touchier than us beaners when diversity shoved itself down the throat of the LAPD. We all kept our final Zs and Os."

What was common knowledge among the officers my father worked with was news to me and it really drove home what a Swiss cheese my past was. I never knew my grandfather had been a cop, much less that the family name was originally Valentino. So many holes to be filled in.

Maybe that's why I lingered at Victor's after I'd gotten what I came for. By the time our unofficial business was over, it had warmed up enough for us to move out onto the balcony, so we each settled into an aluminum-frame chair, the worn plastic webbing stretching enough to provide comfort.

"What was my mother like?"

"Hell, she was something else, muchacho," he said, face lighting up at the memory. "And so damn gorgeous. There wasn't a straight guy in the unit who didn't envy your dad going home to her every night. No disrespect, you understand."

"Oh, I've seen her picture; I know she was beautiful."

"But she wasn't only a looker, Rick. She was, I don't know, more alive than other people, brimming with energy and fire. That's why we were all so gutted when she...."

Victor stopped, realizing what he was about to say and who he was talking to. He pulled up short and took it off in an obfuscating direction. "Anyway. Hey, you remember your uniform?"

My blank expression fueled his barrel-ahead, putting distance between us and my mother's suicide.

"She'd dress you in this little police uniform before bringing you down to the station every Wednesday. All you could talk about from the time you were three was growing up to be a cop like your dad, so we had a mini badge made for you. You may have grown up to be ugly as sin, but you were a cute kid in those baby blues," he said, punching my shoulder playfully.

I had no memories of the outfit, nor of ever consciously wanting to be a police officer when I was little, but I suddenly felt a pressing need to terminate this walk down a long-forgotten path.

"Uncle Vic, thank you for filling in some of the blanks for me about my dad's death," I said, standing.

He insisted I take one of his paintings as a gift, so I selected one with a moody sky and a churning sea, a picture that said to me there isn't so much a lull before the storm as a barely contained warning.

I slid some classic Brubeck into the Corvette's CD player for the drive home, no lyrics to distract me while I mulled over WIK. There were two versions of the raid on Hamid Khavazhi's warehouse, but neither gave me a settling clarity about my father's death. If anything, I was more unsettled about the disparity between the official version and Victor's recounting of events.

In the police report, Det. Tenninger said my dad had the drop on Khavazhi, but took his eyes off him for a split-second, during which Nostradamus had fired, a claim supported by Officer Farona. Absent from the report was any mention of either man being questioned about what had pulled my dad's focus off an armed killer.

When I ran the curious omission by Victor, he had been unequivocal: his partner didn't make mistakes like that.

Before it was over, I would hear two more versions of John Valentine's murder and see Dako Farona lying in a pool of blood on my office floor.

The scowl Rexanne gave me when I arrived home that afternoon was scarier than her ravaged zombie look. At least she'd had the sense not to go anywhere in my Jeep, stashing it, instead, in the garage and parking Kitty's antique blue Chrysler in the driveway. I assured her I had taken no action on the mysterious envelope without her and agreed to drive her somewhere to replace the cell phone Zeke Martin had stomped on before he bought her story about the car-jacking.

There was a Verizon store not too far away and, as I drove, Rexanne interrogated me about where I'd been all day and why I had sneaked out the way I had.

"Another case. Nothing to do with your father." A half-truth at best, but that's what I went with.

"Ri-i-ght." Skepticism drew out the one-syllable response to three, but before I mounted a defense or Rexanne could probe for more, my cell phone rang. Unknown caller.

"Hello." I don't identify myself to strangers.

"Is this Rico Valenti, winologist extraordinaire?"

Piper Lang's throaty purr popped all my tired senses to boing, although her timing could not have been worse.

"I am he, although you should know that's only my CIA cover legend."

I was rewarded with a soft laugh from Piper and a hard look from Rexanne, making me doubt I had the skill to hold one woman's attention while throwing the second off the scent.

"I'm free this evening after the performance and wondered if you'd like to buy me a *real* glass of wine."

"That will fit into my schedule with no problem." There was a hesitation while she considered my response. It hadn't been totally robotic, but it fell way short of the pressing charm of the night before.

"Ah, you're with someone right now. A female someone?"

"Not what you're thinking, but yes."

"Dog." It was spoken like an observation, not an indictment, but I feared I was losing Piper while sending Rexanne into DEFCON-1. Time for a Hail Mary.

"My landladies are a pair of eighty-two-year-old spinsters and most Saturdays I drive them to the grocery store."

Before I could judge if that information had scored any points with the desirable Ms. Lang, Rexanne mouthed off: "Not today, though." Sadly, she had locked the passenger door, so shoving her out wasn't an option.

"She sounds younger than eighty-two." The purr now had an arch edge, and I suspected I had blown it.

"I'll be there when the curtain falls."

"And *maybe* I'll be waiting."

With that she disengaged. "Very mature," I said, glancing at Rexanne.

"You could have just told me you were out getting your beans baked this morning, instead of making up a case. And how rude is it to talk on the phone when someone else is trapped in the car with you?"

"I can slow to thirty-five, if you'd like to exit." What was it about her that brought out the snotty kid in me? I hadn't acted so petty since the verbal scraps with my almost-siblings in the Carmichael house.

Another call came in, but letting it go to voicemail would be ceding a point, so I answered immediately.

"Rick? Jason Ludeman. How fast can you get to the Gingerbread House?"

"Why? What happened?"

"We've got cops here and you'd better come check your office."

"Fifteen minutes." To Rexanne I said, "Phone's going to have to wait. Something's happened at my office building."

"Is that where you hid the envelope?"

I nodded solemnly, although I was certain it couldn't have been discovered. More disturbing was the fact that Zeke Martin and Bobby Chalk had found me—or at least my office address—so quickly. I had to ask. "Are you *sure* you didn't give those two jerks anything they could use to trace me?" The withering look Rexanne shot me was answer enough, so I put in a call to Cal Cooper to ask if he'd had another visit from Freak and Frack.

"Jesus, no! Why? Do you think they're coming back?"

I assured him he was safely out of that particular loop and inquired as to how they could have leapt from my automobile information to my place of business so fast. I already knew my pre-emptive purchase of the domain name www.2regni.net had put my name up for grabs, and that Cal had, under threat, supplied my Jeep details.

"If they got into the DMV records they'd come up with your home address," Cal said. "But that's tough without law enforcement connections. Have you done any recent online advertising?"

And there it was, the way in. My advertising included an email address, of course, but most people who find themselves in need of unofficial surveillance or investigating want to hear a live voice on the telephone before revealing even the sketchiest details about their problem, so I had also posted my phone numbers. My cell wouldn't link to an address, but the land line at the Gingerbread House could be run through the reverse phone directory.

The parking lot was nearly full: Pat's F-150, two BMWs belonging to Justin and Jason, the agent's pretentious Humvee and a Prius with a bumper sticker that read *Hinduism: Recycling our followers since the Big Bang.* Moonietunes the masseuse, no doubt. Lloyd's dented old Civic and a police black and white completed the vehicular presence.

"Tenants only, sir," said the young officer in the lobby, although the look of appraisal he gave Rexanne told me he'd be willing to make an exception for her.

Flipping open my ID, I gave my name and he stepped aside. I moved forward, checking out Lloyd's desk, where he dramatically huffed into a small paper bag while a female officer patted him on the back. Rexanne was busy returning the other cop's bold eye contact with a flirtatious smile, so I had to go back and take her arm to get her moving.

"My secretary, Madge," I explained to Officer Hard-on, pulling Rexanne along.

"Hey, he was kinda cute," she said, twisting her arm out of my grasp. "And what do you mean by *secretary?* How about partner. Or boss."

Jason approached me at the top of the stairs. "Better check your office. Justin's got ransacked last night."

As I turned and walked toward my door I heard Rexanne introducing herself. "Hi, I'm Rick's partner, Svetlana."

"Jason. Nice to meet you. I didn't know he had a partner."

"Oh, I'm with our Dallas office. I'm only here to help him with a big case. *Mondo* biggo."

Eager to check my office, I didn't glance over my shoulder to see if Jason was buying into her bull. My door opened onto a scene identical to the one I had left yesterday afternoon. A look around convinced me no one had been inside since then, so I went back to the hallway where Rexanne regaled Jason with the tale of a case we had supposedly worked together.

"—and the entry wound was right between the Pit Bull's eyes. I could tell from the position of the dog's body that it had been shot mid-leap while trying to stop the intruder, so I knew our perp had brass balls and dead aim. The missing ruby necklace—"

"Excuse me, *Svetlana*, but should you be revealing that confidential information while Slick Mickey's appeal is pending?"

Jason looked at me, made a mouth-zipping gesture, then headed down the stairs.

"*Slick Mickey?!*" Rexanne hissed disdainfully.

"*Svetlana?!*"

"Hey, Rick, come take a look," Pat called from the end of the hall. As I passed her recording studio, I peeked in and saw the mixing board and the glass enclosure with its microphone, stool and two music stands. Nothing appeared to have been touched.

Justin's office, however, had been trashed. Pat and I helped him right his heavy desk, but we could only stare helplessly at the sea of paper on his floor.

"Old scripts. They're backed on hard drive, so I'll recycle all this," he said, gesturing at the tree-based mess.

"I don't see your computer," I said.

"They took it, but everything's on my home set-up, and I've already changed passwords and alerted my server."

He didn't seem as upset as he might have been, but I suppose a writer rarely sees danger or action other than on the page, so the break-in might have been kind of a rush for him. When Pat confirmed none of the remaining offices had been touched, I considered the possibility that the incident was unrelated to my possession of the bad-luck manila envelope. Only briefly, though, because while Justin and Pat and I talked, Rexanne wandered out into the hallway and made a discovery.

In the early 1900s an Ohio fire took the lives of 174 children when they were unable to escape from a burning school building. The massive front doors opened inward and, as two teachers tried to pull them back so the students could get out, frantic throngs of children pushed forward, sealing the doors even more tightly with the press of their own bodies. The flames herded more kids toward the doors, exacerbating the disaster, so the ones who weren't crushed to death in the stampede burned alive within yards of safety.

After that, municipalities around the country passed laws mandating doors on public buildings must open outward in the event of a need for rapid, mass escape. Those laws never filtered down to the private sector, although enlightened architects and builders often took it upon themselves to do the smart thing.

The main entrance of the Gingerbread House, as well as all interior office doors, opened outward, and when Pat had shown up for her mixing session that Saturday, she found the lock at the entrance broken and the door of Justin's office standing wide open, doorknob touching the hallway wall. Rexanne was the first to look behind the door and spot what the investigating officers had missed.

While she snooped, I asked Justin, "Do you have any idea who might have done this?"

"No clue. I mean, once an ex-NFL player pulled a gun on me in my office on the Warner Brothers lot, but that was because he didn't like one of the lines I'd written for him in that week's show."

"Actors," Pat muttered.

"Hey, Rick, maybe I should hire *you* to solve the mystery," Justin said brightly.

Before I could respond, Rexanne called from the hallway. "We'll take it. A hundred bucks, flat-fee, and we'll tell you why you were targeted."

We all turned to the doorway, where Rexanne waved us over to see something. Once Justin and Pat had followed me out into the hall, Dako's daughter closed the door and pointed at my new nameplate: Richard M. Valentine, Private Investigator. "Ta-da!"

Then it came back to me that between the chardonnesque beverage at the play and the robust red at the Italian restaurant, Lloyd had mentioned the earlier delivery of my door plaque. When I'd gone to my own office I hadn't registered that it was not there.

"I'm so sorry, Justin," I said. "I think whoever did this was looking for me."

An annoying voice interrupted us. "Case closed. That'll be one hundred dollars."

I gave Rexanne a hard look and she responded defensively. "So kill me for trying to drum up a little work for you."

Tempting as her offer was, I needed to talk to Lloyd. First I wanted to square things with Justin, so I asked Pat to accompany Rexanne to the reception area, then turned to him.

"I know you've got to be bummed about this, but I'll pay for every bit of the damage and clean-up."

"Forget it. That's why I have insurance."

"Are you sure?"

"Absolutely."

Given my financial situation, I was relieved by his generosity and felt I should explain Rexanne. "Oh, and the delusional chickadee is in no way my partner. She's not even a detective."

"Yeah, I figured that out when I overheard her talking to Jason. She was describing a case I wrote for an episode of CSI a few years ago."

He was eager to know why someone would wreck the office they thought was mine, and I could see from the intensity of his expression that the adrenaline bump of a real crime out-jolted anything he'd ever put in a script. I didn't want to discuss my toxic envelope, but I did "pitch" with him for a minute. We concluded that his office full of crime show memorabilia looked a lot more like the digs of an authentic private investigator than my bland space with nothing more than two clipper ship paintings and a diploma on the wall. Justin was as curious as I was about how the nameplate wound up on his door instead of mine, so we went downstairs to talk to Lloyd.

He still sat at the reception desk, but his attack of the vapors had passed. Lloyd no longer huffed into the paper bag, although it remained within easy reach on the desk top. The two police officers, having taken everyone's information and documented the zero-priority crime, left to protect the streets of The San Fernando Valley. Rexanne was deep in conversation with Moonbeam Fink at the doorway of our in-house massage parlor, thankfully out of my way while I questioned Lloyd about the nameplate. He claimed the installer had arrived with the brass plaque a few minutes before five the previous day.

"Everyone else had already gone and I needed to report to makeup for the premiere of *Desire Trumps Will*, so I sent him straight upstairs."

"Only after you proofread the engraving, right?"

"Oh, yes," he affirmed, suddenly remembering the fib he'd told me to pad his end-of-the-month handout. "Twice," he lily-gilded.

When I inquired if he had gone upstairs with the installer, Lloyd said he'd been too busy making sure all phone messages for the tenants were in the correct cubbyholes for Monday. With that, he flashed a tip-trolling smile at Justin and Pat. I asked him to recall exactly what he had told the guy when he sent him up to my office.

"I said to take a left at the top of the stairs and go to the corner office." Once he heard himself say that, he got a panicky look on his face. "OMG! I was thinking *stage* left, which is the total opposite!"

Stage left? I had no idea what he was talking about, but Lloyd helpfully plunged ahead to explain.

"See, actors like myself have to reposition at the

director's suggestion during rehearsals and since we're
facing each other, our lefts and rights are reversed. So
stage left for an actor like myself is actually to the
right. I am *so* sorry, Mr. Valentine." Lloyd's apology
strained the limits of his thespian cred, but he was
trying to hold onto the possibility of any gratuity at all
from me. I didn't really care how the nameplate mix-
up had occurred only that it hadn't been intentional.
The receptionist's carelessness was believable, even if
his acting wasn't.

The landlord's locksmith arrived at that moment,
so Lloyd went to supervise the repairs. Jason had
already gone and Pat checked her watch, saying she
needed to leave for an early dinner.

"I'm eating at the Y tonight." The bounce of her
unibrow implied a double-entendre, but it went over
my head. As she exited, I turned to Justin with a
questioning look, but he only shook his head and
placed a hand on my shoulder.

"Ah, to be young and naive again."

Not wanting to look clueless, I punted. "Yeah, I
got what she meant. I was only wondering if all that
stage-left, stage-right stuff was on the level."

"Predictably, Lloyd got it wrong. Stage lefts and
rights are oriented to the actor, not the director. It's
on multi-camera TV shows where the directions are
reversed for the benefit of the camera crew. Actors
have lots of time to memorize their positions, but the
cameras only come in for blocking the day before the
shoot, so you want to keep things clear and simple."

"The bottom line here being what?"

"Lloyd sent the installer to my office instead of
yours."

He then told me he had to leave, but wanted to
take me to lunch on Monday and hear why someone

would target me. Rexanne emerged from Moonbeam's lair and walked toward me, while the masseuse stuck her head out and aimed a wink in my direction before ducking inside and closing her door.

"When's your birthday?" Rexanne asked.

"What? Why?"

"I bought you a one-hour massage. She does Shiatsu, Swedish, ampuku and a smidge of Rolfing."

"I suspect she might also do a smidge of hand-jobbing."

Rexanne tucked Moon-Unit's business card into my jacket pocket. "Take the freebie or not, I don't care. I only bought it to win her confidence so I could find out what she saw during the break-in."

"Jason said she told the police she wasn't here last night."

Rexanne subjected me to the eye-roll of a fifteen year old. "I'm guessing she also told them she doesn't give tuggers."

As we walked to the parking lot Rexanne said Moonbeam had been working the tight quads of a wealthy bar owner around 1:00 A.M. when she heard a loud metallic snap at the front of the building, the sound of the lock breaking. She quickly turned down her music and opened her door far enough to see two men enter the Gingerbread House.

"Her description was a dead-on match for the jackwads I met earlier in the evening. Anyway, she saw them reading the nameplate on the agent's door, then checking out the two blank slots on the vacant offices. She closed her own door and listened as they approached."

Moonbeam had suspected they were vice cops, Rexanne explained, so she flipped a towel over her client's incriminatingly engorged member and put a finger to his lips to let him know to be quiet. Luckily, the guy's fear that he was about to be busted cooled his ardor and the tented towel flattened.

"She gave you all those details?" I asked with surprise.

"Why? You think it was a violation of masseuse-client privilege? She's a chatty person and I have a face people trust. The important thing is those guys went upstairs and she heard them banging around for thirty minutes. Did you check to make sure the envelope's still safe?"

I assured her Zeke and Bobby hadn't found it. When she wanted to stay there and examine the contents, I told her not while Lloyd and the locksmith were still on scene. We'd have to come back later.

We killed time by securing a new cell phone for Rexanne, as it was too early for dinner and too late for lunch. She called her mother in Dallas to give her the new number and find out if Dako had been asking for her. He had, but Mom had covered.

"Where does she think you are?" I asked.

"Cabo San Lucas, with a guy Dad doesn't care for. She remembers what that's like, so she's on my side. And, anyway, it isn't all that far from the truth." She deliberately batted her eyes at me in a parody of actual flirting. "I *am* with a guy, and you are *not* my father's favorite person."

I didn't like where she was heading, so I changed the subject, suggesting it was probably safe to return to the Gingerbread House. While I drove, Rexanne checked her Twitter account.

"Eleven twenty-eight," she announced.

"You got another follower?"

"Affirmative."

"Who?"

"Andy, the cute cop." Her fingers flew over the keys. "Suck on *that*, May-Ann."

The lot stood empty—normal for a Saturday evening—so I pulled in and parked, telling Rexanne to wait in the car until I made sure the coast was clear. What I really wanted to do was open the envelope in private to scan through the contents. If there was evidence of illegal behavior by Dako, I could slip it into a drawer before the poor kid found out what kind of father she had.

"See that window behind the tree branches?" I asked, pointing. "That's my office. Once I check all the interior doors and make sure the place is empty, I'll turn my light on-off-on to let you know it's safe to come up." I was relieved when she did not challenge me, since I wanted to put my hands on the envelope without revealing its location. The less she knew, the safer she'd be.

I figured I had ten minutes at best before Nancy Drew got tired of waiting for my signal and came in without it, so I didn't bother checking for intruders. I quickly retrieved the envelope in the dark, then I carried it into the upstairs hallway and flipped the light switch. The only windows on the second floor were inside the closed offices, ensuring Rexanne couldn't see any light from where she waited. I tore open the envelope and poked around inside. Micro cassettes, flash drive, a bundle of 8X10 photos and at least fifty printed pages. No way could I even skim the material in time. I turned off the hallway light, entered my office and did the on-off-on signal.

The immediate, answering rap at my window surprised me, but not nearly as much as seeing Rexanne looking in from outside. She jabbed a finger

at the lock, so I hurried over to unlatch it and slide up
the pane, after which she scrambled off the avocado
tree limb on which she'd been perched and tumbled
into my office.

"What the hell, Rexanne?"

"I thought you might be going through the stuff in
the envelope without me," she said, brushing leaves
from her jeans. I decided not to tell her about the one
in her hair.

"No, you were trying to see where it was hidden,
weren't you?"

The angry flash of her eyes told me I was right,
but—surprise, surprise—Rexanne wasn't admitting
anything. She silkily said, "I was only worried you'd
been ambushed and needed my help."

"Ri-i-ight," I said, replaying her earlier response
to me.

"Oh, give it a rest and let me see." She made a
grab for the envelope, but I snatched it out of her
reach. If she saw it was already open, she'd know her
instincts about me had been right, so with my back
toward her, I noisily ripped a strip from the flap I had
previously torn.

As I dumped the contents on my desk, her eyes
searched them, giving me the opportunity to crumple
and pocket the thin strip of guilt. She went for the
photos first, as they would give the fastest overview.
Rexanne flipped through the stack, handing me each
one after glancing at it.

"It's the same two guys in every picture," she
observed. "Who are they?"

She hadn't been in town long enough to recognize
the mayoral candidates, two men who claimed to be
mortal enemies. From the relaxed body language and
the bottle of champagne on the table between them in

one of the shots, you might have mistaken them for a groom and his best man.

I told Rexanne who they were, but declined to speculate as to why her father might be interested in either man. We split up the pages and started reading transcripts of conversations between two people identified as Grant Tenninger and Hank Bledsoe. I told Rexanne to scan for the word "regni," thinking it might be an acronym for something, but neither word nor website turned up on any of the pages.

Two hours later we knew Tenninger and Bledsoe were partners on a huge land deal. What we didn't know was why they were pretending to hate each other as they competed for the same powerful political slot. Rubbing my eyes, which were feeling the effects of my having had so little sleep in the last few days, I tried to focus on my watch to check the time.

"Damn it! We have to get out of here."

"Why? What's wrong?" Rexanne went on alert.

"Nothing, but I need to be somewhere at 10:30," I said, grabbing all the scattered material and stuffing it back in the envelope. "We'll continue this in the morning."

Over her objections, and feeling the heat of her suspicion, I hustled us out of the Gingerbread House, then red-lined the Corvette all the way to Santa Monica.

With no time for a shower and change, I dropped Rexanne off at the house and raced to the theater where *Desire Trumps Will* was playing, still wearing the clothes I'd thrown on that morning to visit Victor Ramirez. I would have liked to be fresher for drinks with Piper, but after Rexanne's little stunt in the car while I'd been on the phone with the sexy actress, I figured showing up late would kill any chance I had with her.

Cars were already exiting the lot when I arrived, with some human stragglers still leaving the theater, so I lost another five minutes dodging slow-moving pedestrians and waiting for cars to back out.

By the time I went inside, Piper had changed from her costume and was sitting on the edge of the vacant stage in a dress short enough to show ninety percent of the shapely right leg crossed over her left. A red high heel dangled precariously from her toes as her foot moved in provocative little circles.

"I was beginning to think you were a no-show." The purr of her voice somehow maintained intimacy while projecting to the back of the empty theater where I stood.

I walked down the middle aisle, taking in the seductive picture she made with her palms flat on the stage behind her, torso tilted back far enough to give her breasts an extra bit of projection. "Sorry. Your second under-valet buttonholed me in the parking lot to tell me about tonight's performance."

"Lloyd? Did he mention that a piece of flown scenery crashed onto the stage near Sir Larkwhit during his soliloquy?"

Even in the dim lighting, I was able to see the red gloss on her lips and hoped her open body language was an invitation. "Yes, he told me it was the highlight of the evening," I vamped, watching for a clear signal to move in for the kiss.

A signal came, but it wasn't the green light I'd hoped for. Her right foot stopped rotating abruptly enough to send the dangling high heel pinwheeling to the concrete floor.

"No scenery fell during the performance." Her

tone wasn't accusatory, only weary, and I realized a beautiful woman like Piper Lang must have been listening to men lie since puberty.

I had failed a very simple test and could only hope for a do-over. Never taking my eyes off hers, I dropped to my knees, picked up the tantalizing ruby slip-on, cradled her ankle in my left hand and—like a defective Prince Charming trying to redeem himself in the eyes of Cinderella—I gently slipped it onto her foot. Still holding her slender ankle, I said, "Okay, I did not run into Lloyd, but I foolishly thought that would sound better to you than the fact that I was working, lost track of time and almost didn't get here."

I'm not sure if it was the genuflection or my sincerity that did it, but her face softened. "If it's all the same to you, Rick, I'd rather have honesty."

I stood, coming to attention in more ways than one. "Okay, right now I *honestly* want to kiss you."

Piper uncrossed her legs, enabling me to step between her knees, so I put my arms around her and transferred as much of that red gloss as I could from her lips to mine during a grinding, minute-long kiss. As if we were reading from the same script, she wrapped her legs around my waist at the precise moment I slipped both hands under the taut, silky fabric of her skirt and lifted her up against me. One of her hands slid down along my spine, fingernails blazing a trail of little shocks to my nerve endings, while the other burrowed into my hair, encouraging me to continue the kiss.

She was an excellent director and, although it was my first time onstage, I turned in a strong performance.

The other side of the bed was empty when I

woke, but I smelled coffee and got up. My clothes weren't in the immediate vicinity and I had a memory of us frantically undressing each other on our way to the bedroom, leaving a trail of unzipped, yanked-down and ripped-off garments in our wake.

On the drive to Piper's apartment the night before, I had picked up a chilled bottle of white zinfandel, and the two of us finished it during the hour of conversation between performances, so my brain was muzzy as I went looking for my abandoned clothes.

Stepping from the bedroom, I saw her lounging against the counter in her compact kitchen, both hands snugged around a mug of coffee. She wore a short, black wraparound thing that covered her body and arms, but left those amazing legs on full display. Neither her clothes nor mine were still on the floor, but when I scanned the room I saw mine had been neatly placed on a hanger hooked over the knob of her front door.

"Coffee?" she asked, as I walked to her, naked as the proverbial jaybird and already at half-salute.

"God, yes."

She turned to put her cup on the counter and get one for me, the hem of her black wrap rising enough to reveal an inch of tight convexity as she reached up for a second mug. I stepped over to press myself against her back, my chin resting on her shoulder while she poured the coffee. "Every muscle in my body aches," I murmured into her ear, intending it as a tribute to her skills and stamina.

"Really?" Piper turned around, which put the hot cup between us. I took a step back, unwilling to let a careless spill scald anything I might want to use later. "Then maybe what you need is a massage."

Far from being an offer, it was a declaration of discovery. Damn Rexanne and her stupid gift. The manifestation of my ardor unmanifested.

"Don't worry, I didn't go through your pockets. The card fell out when I picked up your jacket to hang it with the rest of your clothes."

Although I explained Moonbeam was a witness withholding information from the police in a case I was working, and although she seemed to believe me, I once again felt I had fallen short of her expectations. Last night it was a flimsy excuse, this morning a dicy masseuse.

We were silent while I finished my coffee and got dressed, but I promised I'd call her later. She smiled when I kissed her chastely on the forehead before leaving, but sadness was in her eyes, hope dashed.

On the way to the car I reached into my pocket for Moonie's opportunity-killing card, which I looked at for the first time. Below the words *Moonbeam's Massage* was the line: *Come and put yourself in my hands.* I suppose I should have been grateful she had not gone with: *Put yourself in my hands and come.*

I searched for an open florist shop on my drive home, but my phone informed me Sunday morning is not the best time to buy an I-swear-I'm-not-a-horndog arrangement. First thing the next day, I'd send Piper a dozen roses.

Rexanne was so eager to resume examining the envelope's contents that she only half-heartedly ragged on me about being AWOL for the night, wryly noting I had a "cranberry juice stain" on my collar and smelled like Obsession. She told me she had gone out early to buy a cassette player so we could listen to the micro cassettes.

"And I wasn't dumb enough to take your Jeep. Kitty let me borrow the Chrysler."

She complained that she could have gotten a jump on the work if I had trusted her enough to hold onto the envelope while I'd been out at my meeting—a word she punctuated with air quotes—but I had kept it locked in the Corvette, worried what she might learn about her father. I still hoped to intercept and hide anything indicating Dako was a blackmailer.

As we hunkered down for a long afternoon of sifting through the cache of information, a picture slowly emerged.

The flash drive contained all the same images from meetings between Grant Tenninger and Hank Bledsoe that were printed out in hard copies, along with a surveyor's plat map of a sixty-acre parcel in Playa del Rey. The land was listed as owned by an off-shore corporation, but we came to a quick dead-end trying to trace it. I'd have to put Cal Cooper on that one. If he'd still take my calls, that is. There was also a set of reduced-size architectural plans for two high-rise buildings—one condominiums, the other office space—and a three-story shopping mall, each presumably to be situated on the surveyed land. No prospective builder was listed on the plans, but we didn't think it was a coincidence that Hank Bledsoe helmed a large and successful construction business.

Going through other papers, we learned the Playa del Rey land was priced at twenty million dollars, although it was not being marketed aggressively. In fact, it looked as though someone very specifically wanted to keep its availability low profile.

The copy of a petition by a group of tree-huggers revealed they were advocating for a consortium of conservation-minded one-percenters to purchase the property for wetlands restoration and preservation, but another document, from an environmental assessment company, certified the long California drought had already killed the wetlands and that no examples of either flora or fauna required to be protected under federal law still survived there.

"So, what do you think's going on?" Rexanne asked me, rubbing her eyes after hours poring over the material.

My response was predicated on the information contained on a single sheet in the envelope, a page from Volume One of the Los Angeles City Charter, with a provision circled in red. Article III—Finance, Budget and Contracts—outlined a provision which allowed the mayor to move preemptively on certain issues without the prior approval of anyone else in the governmental hierarchy. One of those issues cited was the purchase of land for the future benefit of Los Angeles, and the condition under which the mayor could do it was if another offer were about to be made, especially if the other buyer had deep enough pockets to run up the bid until it was out of financial reach. The tree-hugger's appeal to billionaires looked like it could do exactly that.

"The cozy photos suggest Tenninger and Bledsoe are in on this together," I said. "Although we won't know for sure until we listen to those micro cassettes. It appears to be a plan to sell that parcel to LA without anyone learning about it until the deal is done."

"You think the two of them are behind the off-shore corporation?"

I had no doubt they were. Bledsoe would make a fortune from the construction alone, and then he and Tenninger would control the leases on every office suite or mall shop. The condos they could sell outright or hold paper on, giving them even more profit. But the mayor who approved a land purchase of this size would need to justify it after the fact to the taxpayers and city council by showing it would bring in much-needed revenue.

"The amount would have to be large enough to reassure the municipal government and calm the electorate," I speculated. Two things did not make sense in my theory. First, if the off-shore corporation already owned the property, why would they sell it only to turn around and pay mega-bucks to lease it back for their project construction? And second, while whoever was mayor would have to collude on this to pull it off, that still didn't explain why *both* men were running.

When Rexanne's phone chimed she glanced at it and said, "It's my mom."

"Take it; we need the break." I stood to stretch as Rexanne picked up the call and left the room, Cyndi Lauper singing from my own cell almost instantly. I saw it was Laurel, so I answered in a reassuring voice. "Not to worry. The envelope's snug as a—"

"Dako's been shot."

"What?! When?"

"About an hour ago. He was trying to lay hands on a final piece of proof he needs to optimize the value of that envelope."

"Where are you now? And are *you* safe?"

"I'm at Cedars, and who knows? They're rolling him in to surgery and I need you to come so he has someone here when he gets out of recovery."

"Where will you be?"

"I'm heading to Cabo San Lucas to find Rexanne. She's his next of kin and they won't let me sign any paperwork in case...in case...."

Struggling to get her voice under control, she told me she had tried Rexanne's number only to get an out-of-service message. She then called Dako's ex in Dallas, but Amanda said her daughter was in Cabo. She didn't know where, so Laurel was planning to hop a private jet to find Rexanne and bring her back to LA.

"No! Stay where you are. And call some of your guys for protection. I'll track down Rexanne and bring her to you."

"Rick, Dako doesn't want—"

"I know, I know," I interrupted. "He doesn't want me anywhere near his precious daughter. Tell him it's strictly business and I'm going to bill him for every minute of escort and bodyguard service."

"You two only met for ten seconds, so why would she trust you enough to come back with you?"

"Have a little faith in the old Valentine charm. Besides, who's Dako going to want to see when he wakes up, me or you?"

There was a hesitation, and she didn't answer the question, finally saying, "Okay, go look for her. If Amanda reaches her in the meantime and gets a location, she'll tell me and I'll pass that on to you. The plane's at Santa Monica Airport. It's all pre-paid and I'll text you the hangar number and pilot's name."

Laurel disconnected and I turned to see Rexanne standing in the doorway.

"My dad has been shot," she choked out, before hurling herself into my arms. I held her while she sobbed against my shoulder for a minute, but then I took her firmly by the arms and moved her far enough away to make eye contact.

"That's enough. It's time to step into your big-girl knickers. Your father needs you." My tone was harsh, but it snapped her out of any temptation to fall apart, so we strategized on the way to Cedars Sinai Hospital.

Our first decision was to keep Amanda out of the loop for the time being. Rexanne had told her mother on the earlier call that she would leave Cabo at once to get to Dako's side. Now she made a second call to her mother asking her not to talk to Laurel again, fielding Amanda's questions with a promise to explain later, then saying she was about to go into a tunnel and lose contact. "Bye, Mom," she said, providing a voiced hiss before disconnecting, fake proof of the tunnel's impact on reception.

Laurel would not be so easily manipulated. We couldn't delay our arrival long enough to pretend I'd accompanied Rexanne back from Cabo, so we'd have to come up with some innocuous version of the truth. We decided to go with her having stuck around to keep an eye on her father, but we'd omit the fact that we were temporarily living under the same roof. With any luck at all, Laurel would be too distracted to ask for specifics like where Rexanne was staying.

I suppressed my aversion to the disinfected hospital smell with its bottom notes of vomit, blood and worse while Rexanne queried a receptionist in the lobby and then a desk nurse on the fifth floor before being directed to a waiting room.

Laurel sat alone looking desolate, although her face registered relief when she saw Rexanne. They came together in the center of the room, hugging each other for support. That lasted maybe three seconds before the questions started, Rexanne's about her father's condition and Laurel's about how we had gotten there so fast.

We blew through our cover story as quickly and

with as little detail as possible, and only Laurel's concern for Dako prevented her from seeing through our flimsy construct. Rexanne asked about her father, but Laurel had no information beyond that he was still in surgery.

"Since I'm not a family member, they won't even let me hold his effects."

"Where are they?" Rexanne asked.

"Locked away. You'll have to sign for them and get the key at the nurses' desk."

"While I'm doing that I'll see if they know any more about his condition," Rexanne said, before she hurried out of the waiting room.

Once she was clear of the doorway, I turned to Laurel. "How about you tell me exactly what's going on." She stiffened, whether from guilt or knee-jerk defensiveness I couldn't tell, but before she could try stonewalling me, I described the rough treatment Cal Cooper had received at the hands of Bobby Chalk and Zeke Martin, then Rexanne's little run-in with the same two pricks. "And now Dako's been shot. You gonna wait until somebody dies before letting me in on the game?"

"First tell me how they found Cal and Rexanne."

I confessed I'd triggered everything by searching for information on that web address.

"What web address?"

I couldn't believe she chose to play dumb with so much at stake. "The one printed on the yellow label stuck to the world's most dangerous envelope."

She started to say something, then set her mouth in a hard line, as if clamping her teeth shut would keep her from spilling the frijoles. While I still had the advantage, I leaned in closely, making sure my words would not be heard by anyone passing outside in the corridor.

"Dako's blackmailing someone, isn't he?"

Laurel looked convincingly shocked, before asking how I'd come to that moronic—her word—conclusion. I told her I had sifted through the envelope's contents, leading me to infer Dako had stumbled on a shady, multi-million dollar deal and was angling for a piece of it in return for his silence. What else could explain his refusal to call in the police when his office got trashed by his targets' henchmen?

Laurel shook her head sadly. "Why would you automatically assume the worst about him? When has he ever been anything but generous and fair with you?"

I snorted derisively and it was as if I had dropped a lit match into a gasoline can. She came at me with the sharp nail of her index finger, tattooing anger and indignation onto my sternum, causing me to take a step back.

"Who offered you a job at *double* minimum wage while the ink was still drying on your diploma? You graduated from UCLA in the middle of this country's worst economic crisis since the Great Depression, and a lot of your classmates wound up wearing paper hats and asking if the fries were for here or to go!"

Another hard jab; another step back.

"And *who* took you under his wing and spent three fucking years teaching you every trick of the trade, modeling perfect witness-stand testimony for you and introducing you to guys like Cal Cooper who he knew would be valuable to you when you went out on your own?"

Jab, jab; step, step.

"*Who* talked Jimmy Bao into cutting you loose when you blindly walked into a murder frame-up?

And then worked his ass off to find the *real* killer so you wouldn't even be looked at again?"

The next jab and retreat put me flat against the wall. If she wasn't close to being done, that fingernail was going to shiv my lung.

"And *who* set you up to collect the reward on that deal? Dako Farona, the man you think is committing a felony!!"

"What's going on?" We both turned at the sound of Rexanne's voice, but Laurel recovered first and deflected her interest in the argument.

"Nothing worthwhile. How's your father?"

Rexanne's eyes darted to mine for a second, but I plastered on a bland expression that sent her back to Laurel, while I furtively rubbed my bruised sternum.

"Still no word, but they let me sign for his things. All but his gun. The police have to clear that before it can be released."

She held Dako's wallet in one hand, a sheaf of papers in the other, and had a familiar brown leather jacket over one arm.

"Ms. Farona?" A thin woman in surgical scrubs appeared in the doorway and introduced herself as Dr. Reece. "Your father's on his way to the recovery room and I'd like to discuss his condition. If you'll come with me, please."

"Rick, hold this stuff till I get back," Rexanne said, dumping everything she held so fast I almost didn't catch it all, then grabbing Laurel's hand. "You should hear this, too."

The doc turned and headed down the corridor with Rexanne and Laurel following her. I sat down, putting the paperwork on the chair next to mine and placing Dako's wallet and medical insurance card on top. I started to drape the bomber jacket over my lap, but stopped and held it up for inspection.

The two bullet holes told a tale that could not promise a happy ending. One blood-rimmed entry was eight inches down from the left shoulder seam and three inches away from the zipper, right where Dako's heart would have been. Since he hadn't been killed instantly, I assumed the slug had angled off enough to give the surgeons a slender chance of saving him. A quick look at the back confirmed the shot had been a through-and-through.

The second bullet had pierced the jacket on the lower right side all the way down by the knit ribbing. There was no exit wound, so I figured the doctors had poked around in Dako's liver for the brass after doing what they could to patch-up his heart. The man was a freakin' grizzly bear, but I couldn't see any way he'd survive injuries like those. I was glad Laurel would be with Rexanne as she got the news.

After draping the jacket over the chair to my left, I glanced at the wallet and papers on the other side, bending to retrieve Dako's Blue Shield card, which had slipped onto the floor. Since Rexanne would return a grieving mess in a minute, I decided to put the card back in the wallet to keep it from getting lost, but not before looking at it and learning Dako's full name: Dakota Lee Farona.

Upon opening the worn leather necessity, I saw an empty glassine sleeve behind the one containing Dako's driver's license. As I wiggled the card into the tight space, my eye caught a photo in the next consecutive sleeve, a picture of Rexanne, maybe twelve or thirteen years old. She was smack in the middle of that awkward stage, all goofy grin, braces and a baseball-sized pink pompom pinned in her dark hair.

When I moved into the Carmichaels' home at the

age of eight, nine-year-old Shane and I mercilessly teased Ruthie Carmichael for being the freckled, gawky pre-teen she was. Four years later, though, the ugly caterpillar had morphed into a hot, sixteen-year-old butterfly, and Shane and I spent pained nights in our bunk beds fantasizing about our not-sister, wishing we'd been a little nicer to her when she'd been a bug.

I knew it was not a good time to give Rexanne any crap about the embarrassing photo, but I thought I'd file the specifics as ammunition for some future stand-off with her, so I slipped the picture out of its clear plastic housing for closer examination. When I did, I noticed a second photograph had been tucked out of sight in the same sleeve, behind the unflattering one of Rexanne.

The folded snapshot showed a beautiful woman in a bathing suit. She stood on a beach in the shadow of a lifeguard tower, holding an ice cream cone.

With shaking hands I tried to fumble the photo of my mother out of the glassine sleeve, but while pulling it free I heard voices in the corridor. Rexanne and Laurel were thanking the doctor, so I had only seconds to slip the folded snapshot into my pocket, return Rexanne's photo to its niche and put the wallet back on top of the hospital forms.

They came in acting more cheerful than they should have been, considering the severity of Dako's injuries, but before I could ask a question, Laurel looked at me with concern.

"Rick? Are you okay?"

She was an astute observer and my face must have reflected the wretched, sinking response I'd had to seeing a picture of my mother in Dako's wallet.

"Hospital smell. It'll pass."

"Dad's going to be fine," Rexanne said, unable to hold in the good news a minute longer.

Later that day, after Laurel got the chance to speak with him, we learned why. Dako had been knocked to the ground from behind. When he pitched forward, rolling onto his back, his jacket had ridden up several inches. The would-be executioner had stood directly over his stunned victim and fired two close-range shots—one to the gut and one to the heart—not realizing the scooching up of the jacket had skewed his estimate of where to aim.

As a result of the shooter's miscalculation, Dako's injuries weren't life threatening: a clean, left-shoulder through-and-through that hadn't nicked bone, and a wound that went deep, but didn't involve the liver. I had jumped to an erroneous conclusion on the basis of misread information. And not for the last time.

Rexanne and Laurel didn't want to be far from Dako when he woke up, but the three of us needed to talk privately, so we located an unoccupied non-denominational chapel down on the Plaza Level where families went for meditation or prayer. I shoved all thoughts of the snapshot to the back of my mind when we sat down.

Laurel confirmed what we had surmised from the envelope's contents, that the next LA mayor would secretly sanction a land purchase, then lease it back to the sellers for an amount large enough to quell any backlash from city council members or the county Board of Supervisors. A massive development would be built on the former wetlands and the corporation leasing the land would make a killing. Dako had proof the off-shore corporation that owned the property was one-hundred percent controlled by Grant Tenninger and Hank Bledsoe.

"*That's* why we couldn't tell the police about the break-in," Laurel said pointedly to me. "We aren't sure how deep Deuce Tenninger's influence runs, but as a former Chief of Police, he most likely has friends high up on the force."

What Rexanne and I did not know until Laurel told us was that two additional off-shores connected to the deal, one owned exclusively by Bledsoe, the other by Tenninger.

"Technically, nothing they're planning is illegal," Laurel said, "unless the new mayor can be linked to the company selling the land to the city. Once Dako found proof of the other two companies he speculated that all the assets of the jointly owned off-shore will be sold for a token fee to one of the other two the minute the mayor's race is over."

This suggested that if Tenninger were elected, Bledsoe's company would swallow up all the holdings of the original corporation, thus erasing Tenninger's fingerprints from the seller's side of the deal before it went through. And vice-versa, should Bledsoe be elected.

"But wouldn't that leave the one who becomes mayor vulnerable to getting ripped off by his partner?" I asked. "Do they trust each other that much?"

"Hell, no. And that's why Dako believes there's a poison-pill document somewhere, proof of the deal that neither man would ever make public."

"Unless he got shafted by his partner," Rexanne interjected.

"Exactly. It would bring down both of them, but the one with nothing left to lose might not care. When Dako was ambushed he was surveilling the office of a notary in East LA. Tenninger went there Friday and stayed for ten minutes and Bledsoe would have done the same thing another time if our theory is true. Those documents could prove collusion, so we have to get our hands on them to make our case."

Everything she said sounded believable, but it still made no sense to me that both of them were running for mayor, when they only needed one man in place to pull off the deal. "Why didn't they flip a coin and have one guy run, instead of spending all that money on two separate campaigns?"

"Yeah, that one threw us for a time, too, but then we figured with only one of them running, there'd be an outside chance another candidate could squeak by and win, sending the whole plan down the toilet."

Two rich, powerful men going at each other tooth and nail provided the electorate with an either/or sensory-overload, leaving them scant incentive to evaluate anyone else in the race.

"Look at how many over-the-top accusations are flying between them," Laurel said. "And, more to the point, how easily disproved each claim is. They're presenting the *appearance* of scorched-earth tactics without actually doing any real damage."

I thought back over the last couple weeks of campaign coverage on the radio and online. "So if one guy says the other has a swastika tattooed on his ass, the other one's going to take a butt-selfie and prove it isn't true."

"Precisely. They're putting on a tabloid-worthy performance to distract us from the fact that other choices are available, virtually guaranteeing one of them will be in position to facilitate the land deal that could make them billionaires."

There were sixteen days left until the election, and Dako still didn't have his last two pieces of proof:

the poison-pill statements—if they existed—and a plausible reason for the land's owner to sell it to LA county, then lease it back for decades. There had to be a profit angle, but could we find it?

"Bledsoe and Tenninger know Dako's been nosing around," Laurel said. "They didn't know how close he was getting until their gun-happy scumbag spotted him watching the notary's place this morning, and the fact that they gave the go-ahead to kill him indicates there's something there worth protecting."

Rexanne excused herself to check on her dad, so Laurel and I had a few minutes alone. She gave me a long look, then spoke with resignation. "Not blackmail, Rick. He's trying to prevent two bad guys from getting in position to do worse."

I should have had the decency to admit I'd been wrong about Dako, but that photo in my pocket was providing new fuel for my distrust of the man and I could not manage so much as an apologetic shrug. Laurel shook her head, wondering about my obstinance, no doubt. "If we can pull all the loose ends together, we'll go to the media five or six days before the election," she said. "Any earlier and their lawyers might offer a plausible-sounding explanation to dilute public outrage. Any later, and not enough voters will hear about it in time."

What Laurel didn't say? That no one was paying Dako to take these risks, but I wasn't in the mood to view him as a white knight. Timing, however, was critical, and Dako was sidelined for the interim. I had been peripherally, if unwittingly, tangled in this hot mess from the moment I'd accepted responsibility for that envelope, so I said, "I'm in."

Before she could respond, the door opened and an elderly man entered, accompanied by a look-alike forty

year old who had to be his son. They'd been crying
and had obviously come for the meditating/prayer use
of the chapel, so Laurel immediately stood.

"Please, come in. We're leaving."

In the corridor we continued our conversation.
With Dako out of commission and the two candidates
getting more and more desperate to keep a lid on their
scam, it was down to me to make sure Rexanne and
Laurel remained safe. The important thing was to
buy a couple days while I came up with a plan. "Do
you have your own men here?"

"Two on him and one at the main entrance."

"Good. Make sure they never interact with Dako,
then convince them he isn't going to make it."

"What?" She looked horrified.

"Let's don't give Tenninger and Bledsoe a reason
to send someone to finish the job. If they think he's
already out of the picture, maybe they'll assume no
one else will risk pursuing them. Make them believe
they're right."

Laurel recognized the gambit's logic. "Rexanne
and I can start a little whisper campaign. Maybe I'll
visit a funeral home to make arrangements, in case
they're keeping tabs on me."

I suggested she and Rexanne wait at the hospital
till Dako woke up, while I did some digging.

Before I slid behind the wheel of the Corvette,
I pulled the snapshot from my pocket, then unfolded
it once the door thunked shut on a presumption of
privacy. As I had feared, the man on the other side of
the vertical crease, his arm draped casually over my
mother's shoulders, was *not* my father.

Dako wore electric yellow surfer baggies and
looked impossibly young and happy. My mother had

on a bikini in her favorite color, a blue she called periwinkle. I recognized it from the photo in my Wigmore's Wafers tin. The chocolate ice cream cone in her hand was the one I perpetually licked in the snapshot of my mother and me standing in that same shadow. The picture I'd always believed was taken by my father.

The only difference between the two photos, other than a change in the cast of characters, was the steeply-raked angle at which this one had been shot, as if the camera were being held by a child.

I turned it over, but the back was blank, unlike the one in my treasure chest. How many times had I studied my mother's flowing cursive—*Ricky (age 4) at the beach with mommy. Santa Monica, 1993*—and tried to conjure up that day? The elusive not-memory had always been one of family, a fantasy day at the beach for the three of us, and it sickened me to realize I was holding virtual proof of an affair between my mother and Dako Farona, proof captured by a camera held in my own ice-cream-sticky hands. The sense of betrayal was sharp, but not as strong as the feeling of revulsion knowing I had mooned away so much time over the years studying the other picture, the one I *thought* my father had taken.

I quashed an urge to tear the thing into pieces and scatter them across the hospital parking lot, deciding to hold it as evidence for my inevitable showdown with Dako. When I started the car I had every intention of driving straight to Cal Cooper's place, but as scenarios of a sordid affair ran through my frontal lobes, a more primitive part of my brain propelled me toward the cemetery where John and Zoë Valentine rested alongside each other.

For the second time that Sunday I was frustrated

by the lack of an open flower shop, finally standing in front of my parents' burial markers with nothing to lay on their graves but questions, blame and anger.

Was Zoë the girl who had broken Dako's heart, sending him into the arms of Rexanne's mom, Amanda Richfield? Had my mother come to her senses after a short fling and kicked Dako to the curb? Had John Valentine known of the affair between his wife and a fellow officer? Those were questions I was unlikely to find answers for, even if I confronted Dako about his sleazy behavior. And maybe those weren't the real questions I needed answered. Maybe they were trivial in the larger scheme of things. My mother was not the first woman to cheat on her husband, and she certainly wouldn't be the last. For all I knew, my father might have had an affair, too. Maybe Zoë found out and did a quid pro quo to get back at John, using Dako as nothing more than an instrument of revenge.

From the outside it was only a soap opera trek through someone else's marital minefield, titillating, perhaps, but ultimately unimportant to anyone not directly involved. The real question was what role, if any, had Dako played in my father's death.

I stood for a long time, looking at the flat squares of polished granite set into the well-tended grass.

John Marco Valentine—born February 10, 1960. Died May 16, 1994—Loving husband and father.

Zoë Mayne Valentine—born July 6, 1965. Died September 7, 1997—Devoted wife and mother.

Just because it's carved in stone doesn't make it true.

Once I'd convinced Cal it was only me at the door, he started unlocking what sounded like the security system for a DeBeers vault. When the final deadbolt slid free, he opened the door a couple inches, peering out at me suspiciously.

"I'm alone and I wasn't followed."

His eyes darted left and right for a quick visual verification before he pulled the door open enough for me to slip through. The visit from Zeke and Bobby last week had made him jumpy and paranoid.

"Look, Rick, if this has anything to do with that domain name you bought, I don't want—"

"It doesn't, I swear. I only want an employment search on somebody. Easy peas and I'll pay cash off the books."

A large part of Cal's income is untraceable and, therefore, untaxable, another reason he likes doing business with criminals, rather than law enforcement. Prior to his encounter with Zeke Martin and Bobby Chalk, however, Cal's exposure to bad guys had been limited to men in suits and ties looking for dirt they could leverage in territorial or financial disputes. The break-your-effing-legs faction favored crowbars over computers.

"Two hundred dollars for a half hour right now," he said.

It was steeper than I had hoped and it would necessitate finding an ATM in the area. Cal noted my hesitation and went on the defensive. "Hey, it's Sunday, you know."

After I agreed to the price, Cal and I went into the second bedroom of his condo, the room he refers to as "WebCommand HQ," where multiple monitors displayed screensaver images ranging from Star Trek's Uhuru to Star Wars' Princess Leia and every Comic-Con geek's fantasy crush in between, including several large-breasted non-humans. I was banking on my guess that Martin and Chalk had not formally introduced themselves when they called on Cal, and I watched for a reaction when I gave him the name. Nothing. So far, so good.

"You have a social?" he asked, fingers already tapping away.

"No." Not true, but I wanted Cal to go in fresh. Also, it helped to stroke his ego and let him think I was helpless without him.

"Well, you'd better give me something. Martin is almost as common as Smith, and Zeke's probably a nickname."

It was time to give up a fragment I'd uncovered myself. "He did a year at Chino back in 2012."

A few more seconds and Ezekial Ward Martin's prison ID photo appeared on the screen.

"Oh, shit!" Carl whirled around to confront me. "You said this had nothing to do with that web address."

I tried to convince him nothing he found on Zeke would come back to him, but fresh in his mind was the memory of how quickly he had given up info with a gun barrel humping his temple, so I dug deep in the Valentine charm arsenal. "Tell you what, if he starts shoving bamboo under my fingernails I'll bite down on the sarin capsule implanted in one of my molars. I'll be dead before he can get your name out of me."

Cal thought about it for a couple seconds before saying, "Double."

I'd have to find *two* ATMs nearby to cough up that much, but I agreed.

"You have twenty-seven minutes left," he said.

I used every one of those minutes, but it was worth it. My own limited skills had turned up the basics on Zeke, but burrowing through all the layers of obfuscation that shielded his connection to the masterminds of the land deal required a level of tech sophistication possessed only by born wonks like Cal.

Once he pulled up the name of the janitorial service from which Martin drew a suspiciously fat weekly paycheck, I knew I could confirm on my own that Bobby Chalk also worked for the company that connected through six degrees of Kevin Bacon to Hank Bledsoe's construction firm.

I gave Cal the hundred dollars I had on me, promising to be back in an hour with the other three. Making use of the drive time, I called Victor Ramirez for contact information on Dako's old partner, who I already knew was no longer with the LAPD. She and her husband owned a bakery out in Pasadena, according to Uncle Vic, and I decided to make that my first stop in the morning.

WIK: my father's murder and Dako's single-minded pursuit of Grant Tenninger were linked in some way, but like a Scrabble rack containing only Ks, Xs, Zs, Js and Fs, the facts at hand refused to be arranged into anything cohesive.

Maybe Gayle Chandler could fill in some blanks tomorrow about the time her former partner and my mother were sleeping together.

Dako had been moved to a private room by the time I returned to Cedars and when I asked the guard on the door—a fellow Farona Investigations legman named Steve I had run into a couple of times over the years—how his boss was doing, he set his mouth in a grim line and shook his head.

"Laurel and Dako's kid inside?"

"Nah, they're down in the chapel, although, from what I hear, prayer ain't going to do a whole helluva lot at this point."

Good. Recovery expectations had been set at the lowest rung. I took the elevator to the mezzanine level and found my way to the chapel. Even before reaching the door I detected the unmistakable aroma of Fatburgers. Far from being on their knees asking for divine intervention on Dako's behalf, Laurel and Rexanne were hunched over spread, waxed-paper wrappers, each devouring one of LA's iconic, dripping Holy Grailburgers.

"Oh, my God, Rick," Rexanne exclaimed when she saw me. "Have you ever eaten one of these?"

"Half my body weight is Fatburger and onion rings."

"How do they make them taste so good?"

Laurel and I figured that out years ago when Fatburger provided our mid-shift sustenance on all-night stakeouts. Serving twenty-four hours a day, three hundred and sixty-five days a year since opening for business, they must never have had time to clean the griddle. Our theory was that by now the cooking surface was so imbued with flavor you could throw an Air Jordan on the thing and have it wind up tasting like heaven.

"If you had called to let me know you were on the way here," Laurel said, "I would have picked one up for you, too."

Suppressing my Pavlovian salivation, I got right to the point, sharing my discovery of a link between Hank Bledsoe's company and Zeke Martin.

"And I'm pretty sure ten minutes online will prove Bobby Chalk collects checks from the same business," I added.

It was another piece of the puzzle, but we all agreed it didn't yet complete the picture. We still needed to figure out how the next mayor would convince everyone acquiring the land in Playa del Ray was financially beneficial for LA and we were running out of time before the election. Also, Dako was being released the following day, so keeping up the ruse that he was dying would be more of a challenge.

On the drive from Cal's place to the hospital I had half-formed a plan to get the heat off Dako, Laurel and Rexanne, but it would mean stepping into the cross-hairs myself. The first thing I had to do was make sure anyone watching stayed convinced Dako was no longer in the picture, so I turned to Laurel as she blotted her fingers and chin with a coarse paper napkin.

"Okay, no wheelchair ride out to the car for Dako when he's released in the morning. Book a private ambulance and have him brought out to it on a gurney, then take him to a hospice facility that can keep him under wraps a few days."

"He isn't going to like that," Rexanne said in a sing-song voice.

"Tough titmice," Laurel told her. "If he goes home those two shitbirds will report to Tenninger and Bledsoe he's going to survive and that'll put all of us in danger. Dako's going to have to park himself at death's door for a little while longer."

I was glad Laurel saw the necessity of keeping Dako semi-dead and felt certain she could convince him to play along, although I suggested she tell him it was her plan, not mine. Rexanne was less sanguine about her own part in my scheme: booking a meeting for me with Hank Bledsoe.

"So, I'm your secretary now?" she bristled.

I explained Hank would be more inclined to come unarmed to a meeting with a sweet young lady—and here Rexanne snorted derisively, dislodging the bit of limp lettuce that had clung to her upper lip and sailing it onto the carpet—than he would with a guy he already suspected was in league with Dako.

"Invent something, find a way in and then I'll show up instead of you. And for criminy's sake, don't use *Svetlana*. Stick to plain American names."

I could see she was ready to challenge me, but Laurel reached out and put a hand on Rexanne's arm. "He's right. First rule of investigating? Don't attract attention to yourself. Blend in and keep a low profile."

"Mary freakin' Jones it is, then," Rexanne said, accepting the wisdom of playing down her natural flair for the dramatic, but not liking it all that much. "And what exactly do you intend to do at this meeting I'm supposed to make happen?"

Laurel and I exchanged a quick look before she turned to Dako's daughter and said, "Rick's going to convince Hank there's a new player in the game."

I was relieved when Rexanne agreed to stay home with Laurel that night, as I needed peace and quiet to figure out an approach that would trip-up Tenninger and Bledsoe without getting me killed. Calling Kitty from the car, I asked if she needed me to stop for anything on my way to the house. She said her blood pressure prescription was ready, so I picked up the refill from a CVS near their Santa Monica home.

When I pulled in around 10:00 the Sutterman sisters were still awake and were surprised Rexanne was not with me. I told them she had made other arrangements for the night and they asked how her father was doing. The question didn't surprise me, as I assumed Rexanne had mentioned the shooting before we left for the hospital all those hours before. Bitsy said she hoped he'd be all right, then the two of them retired to their rooms.

When a long, hot shower failed to revive me I got into bed. I wanted a good night's sleep before I talked to Gayle Chandler about Dako and my mother in the morning, so I decided to lull myself to Slumbertown with warm thoughts of Piper Lang.

Piper! Damn, I'd forgotten to call her like I said I would. I sat up and checked the clock on the night stand. After eleven. I texted an apology, saying I had been working all day and into the night. It sounded lame, even to me, and *I* had the advantage of knowing it was true. Why couldn't I do anything right in my pursuit of the very attractive actress? And how many dozen roses should I send to get back into her good graces? I'd start with three and see how that went.

Not knowing where I stood with her, it felt wrong to mentally replay the previous night's amorous romp in an effort to drift off, so I turned my thoughts to the case. And Rexanne. Nothing even slightly erotic entered my mind when I brought up her image and I wondered why not. There was no denying she was beautiful, though with a more all-American-girl look than the smoldering Piper Lang. Maybe I had not responded to Rexanne's charms because of the way we'd been thrown together by circumstance. Maybe it was the goofy photo of her with the giant pink pompom exploding from her head. Or maybe because she was seven years younger. And annoying. And related to Dako.

At the very edge of sleep, the thought of Dako triggered a question I was too winky to be alarmed by. The last thing Bitsy Sutterman had said to me was, "I hope Mr. Farona will be all right. He's such a sweet man."

How did Bitsy know Dako Farona? With that thought in mind I....

Cream-filled pastry horns were not new to me. On special occasions Babs Carmichael would bring home a box of them from the grocery store and we rugrats would plow through dinner like it was the defensive guard standing between us and dessert. I had always thought they were wicked delicious, but sampling the featherlight, crispy spiral that Gayle Chandler handed me on a small white plate made me realize how ordinary those store-bought treats had been: dense yellow pudding packed into a hollow cone of doughy pie crust.

My initial bite into the croissant-like pastry at Delizioso, a bakery in the middle of the pedestrian-friendly historic district known as Old Pasadena, sent a flurry of golden flakes floating to the table and filled my mouth with the rich taste of sweetened whipped cream—the real thing, not some aerosol pretender.

The petite blonde sitting across from me at the table for two grinned at my response to the rave going on in my mouth. "To die for, huh?" she said.

I swallowed that first heavenly bite and dusted off my shirt front with the paper napkin. "Will you marry me and make these every morning?"

Gayle Chandler laughed. "I only sell and serve them, darlin' If you want to propose to the pastry chef, go in the back and ask for Anthony."

We were alone in the small seating area. When I had identified myself on the phone the day before and said I wanted to ask her about John Valentine, Gayle suggested I come in before the shop opened so we wouldn't be interrupted by customers.

She had been on the job a half dozen years when

my father died, so I figured her to be close to fifty years old, but she still had the sparkle and pep of a high school cheerleader. Also, a slight hitch in her stride which I noticed when she brought our coffees and my cream horn to the table. I wondered if the injury she suffered the night of the calamitous raid was the cause of her limp.

"I barely knew your father," she said, as I devoured the pastry. "So I'm not sure what I can tell you."

I wanted to naturally work the conversation around to Dako and my mother, but Gayle provided the opportunity with her next statement.

"I remember you and your mom, though. She used to bring you to the station in your little cop uniform. Vic Ramirez would parade you around on his shoulders while your folks spent a couple minutes together and you would salute each one of us so seriously it was hard to keep a straight face when we saluted you back."

Though she had only spoken to my mother a few times, Gayle remembered her as friendly, pretty and an obviously devoted wife and mother.

"What kind of relationship did she have with Dako Farona?"

"My partner?" she asked with genuine surprise. "None that I ever knew of. I mean, I'm sure they exchanged pleasantries when she stopped by. We all did. Your mother had a vivacious personality and everyone liked her."

If Gayle was telling the truth, the affair was not known to the other members of the squad, and it was a relief to think my father hadn't been the butt of jokes or an object of pity to his co-workers. Needing more, however, and not wanting to waste time dancing around the subject, I told her I was partnering with Dako on a case and needed to know why he left the LAPD. For the first time since she had unlocked the door and greeted me, Gayle's smile disappeared. She gave her half-gone coffee an unnecessary stir, as if to buy time to choose her words carefully.

"A lot of cops leave the force, but that doesn't mean anything's *off* with them, if that's what you're getting at." Before I could protest I wasn't searching for dirt on her old partner, she went on. "Take me, for example. One of Khavazhi's men put a slug in my leg, and a couple years later only a Kevlar vest stopped another round from killing me. With no desire to roll the dice for my life a third time, I left the LAPD to help my husband open his first bakery."

As if on cue, a good-looking bald man around sixty pushed through the swinging door at the back with a huge metal tray of newborn glazed doughnuts. He nodded at Gayle and me, slid the tray into the glass display case and was back through the door before it had quit swinging from his entrance. Gayle checked her watch and I knew it must be close to opening time, so I matched her suddenly serious demeanor.

"Look, something happened that night you got shot, and all I know is Grant Tenninger and Dako Farona were the only witnesses when my father was gunned down *Any* detail you can remember would be greatly appreciated."

Driving to the Gingerbread House with a box full of doughnuts on the shotgun seat of the Corvette, I mulled over all I had learned from Gayle.

She couldn't say if it was woman's intuition or cop radar, but she knew something wasn't right after she staggered to the front of the warehouse and banged on the door until Victor let her into the office and helped her to a chair.

Gayle had worked alongside Dako for more than four years and the expression on his face was one she had never seen before. "He seemed to be uneasy," she had told me. "As if he had done something terrible he couldn't take back." Since he hadn't fired his weapon, Gayle always assumed he felt partly responsible for the deaths of Det. Rowan and my father. If he had been quicker on the uptake, maybe he could have saved them. At least that was her interpretation; she and Dako never spoke about that night again.

Gayle had described a change in her partner after the Khavazhi incident. At first she thought he was embarrassed to be the only officer involved who had *not* received a commendation—even Rowan and my dad were awarded posthumous medals for valor.

I didn't let on I knew about the unholy pact for survival Grant Tenninger had coerced Victor, Dako and her to make with him, but her obvious bitterness toward the rising-star detective proved it still gnawed at her. She claimed he had systematically undermined Dako at every turn after the raid.

"No outright accusations, you understand," Gayle had said. "But little things whispered into the ears of the bosses, who trusted Deuce like he was Jesus, Moses and Gandhi all rolled into one. Notes began appearing in Dako's file, claims of minor paperwork screw-ups or little miscalculations in the field. *I* never saw them and I worked with him every day, but still, 'evidence' began to show Dako was not a competent officer, and I'm ashamed to say that for my own professional survival I put in a request for a new partner, last rat to jump the sinking ship."

No one else wanted to partner with Dako after
that because, even if he was innocent, if he was being
unfairly hounded by a high-ranking bully, the stench
of failure hung over him like a noxious cloud. A year
after the fatal incident, Dako Farona quit the LAPD.

I left the pink pastry box with Lloyd, saying
the doughnuts were for everyone to share. Because I
had neglected to turn my phone back on after the
meeting with Gayle Chandler, he handed me three
messages: one from our landlord saying the nameplate
would be moved from Justin's door to mine later in the
week, one from Victor Ramirez asking if he could stop
by mid-morning to drop something off, and one from
Piper with only two words: *impressive* and *lunch?*
Three dozen roses had struck just the right balance
between casual interest and stalker creepiness.

Since it was already 10:30 I returned Victor's call
first, catching him as he dropped off some paintings at
a gallery in Encino. He told me he'd be at my office in
half an hour, so I immediately hung his seascape on
the wall opposite the two clipper ships before checking
in with Laurel, who confirmed Dako had gotten
settled—begrudgingly—at a care center way out at the
trash end of Canoga Park. She was fairly certain Zeke
Martin and Bobby Chalk had observed the transfer to
the ambulance from a block away and tailed the rig to
the hospice, so she had paid staffers to give out an
imminently terminal prognosis should any strangers
call or stop by to ask about Dako's health. Two men
were posted 'round-the-clock to make sure the dire
prediction did not come true.

Rexanne brusquely responded, "Working on it,
boss," when I called for a status update on the Hank
Bledsoe meeting. God, she was annoying.

With a few minutes left before Victor's arrival, I dialed Piper Lang's number and was rewarded with an invitation for lunch at her place. Not knowing how long I'd be with my father's old partner, I made our date for 1:00 o'clock.

The burled wood box Victor placed on my desk was thirteen inches by eight, and four inches tall. I opened it and saw a gun in a custom-molded nest.

"That was your dad's," he said when I looked up at him.

"What is it?" I had never seen anything like the blue-steel beauty in the security case.

"A Kimber Custom, made by a company out of New York. Authorized LAPD carry weapon, but, to the best of my knowledge, John was the only cop who used one back then. Everybody else, including me, wanted a Glock or a Smith."

I carefully lifted the gun to examine it, checking to see it was unloaded. Nothing looked skimped-on or assembly-lined, from the beveled shoulders on the slide where it lapped the frame, to the polished bone grips, each held on by a pair of blued hex screws that gleamed more like jewelry than utilitarian fasteners.

"So, my dad had a taste for the bling, huh?"

"Don't let the looks fool you, muchacho. That gun has all the guts of a Colt without any of the draw-backs. Solid aluminum trigger'll drop the hammer at a precise 4.5-pounds every time and that extry-large beavertail makes it handle like a dream."

I hefted the Kimber on my palm. "Not light."

"Almost two and a quarter pounds. I know I should have given this to you years ago, but I didn't even remember I had it until after you showed up on Saturday."

If the gun had been kept in storage all that time, Victor must have painstakingly cleaned and polished it before bringing it to me and I was touched by his thoughtfulness. "Thanks. This means a lot."

"A month after your father died, your mother handed me this and said to get rid of it, but I decided to hold onto it, although I've never fired it since your dad and I tried out each other's weapon at a shooting range. I transferred the registration to my name, then put it away and forgot all about it."

WIK: I was holding the gun my mother had used to end her own life. WIDK: how she had gotten it back from Victor. I looked over at him with the question any former cop could read on my face.

"Yeah, that," he said, sagging in his chair. "The day before she did what she did, your mom called to ask if I still had John's Kimber. She *said* she had changed her mind, that she wanted to keep it for you."

Victor told me I had never wavered in my desire to grow up to be a cop during the three years following my father's death. No side trips into baseball player, fire fighter or super hero, so he didn't question my mother's claim she wanted to hold the gun for me till I was an adult. Twenty-four hours after he turned it back over to her, Zoë Valentine was dead.

Victor arrived only minutes after the event. She had called and asked him to stop by and help her move a couch, never indicating anything was wrong. "You were at Dodger Stadium that afternoon with a cop named Steiner and his three boys." When he found my mother's body, Victor called Sgt. Steiner and asked him to take me home with him for the night when the game was over. "Anyway, the Kimber was still registered in my name, so it came back to me once the investigation ended."

I thanked him for holding onto it and especially for returning it to me, then took a rain check on his lunch invitation. After he left, I returned the Kimber to its case, not sure how I felt about possessing the gun that had been in my father's hand the moment of his death and then, three years later, used by my mother to kill herself. Closing the burled wood box, I slipped it into the bottom drawer of my desk, categorizing it as an out-of-sight issue to consider at a later time. I reflected on what Victor had said, about how Zoë took steps to make sure I would not be the one to discover the atrocity she was leaving behind, a final maternal gesture before she abandoned me to the vagaries of chance.

Victor had reiterated his claim from Saturday, that I once dreamed of being a police officer, a statement supported by Gayle Chandler's recollection of a uniformed five year old solemnly saluting his brothers in blue, and I wondered why I had no memory of ever wanting to become a cop.

Lunch at Piper's didn't include any actual food, but was incredibly satisfying anyway. She had sacrificed several of the thirty-six roses so she could scatter pink and white petals on her bed, and their heady perfume contributed one more sensory ping as they were bruised and crushed under the rhythmic assault of elbows, knees, shoulders and spines.

By 2:00 P.M. we had worn ourselves out, leaving barely enough energy for talking as we lay tangled in the sheets. The standard, early-dating exchange of selectively chosen biographical information began, and within it I felt something more than the obvious sexual attraction. I watched for a sign she felt the same, but my phone interrupted too soon.

The call from Laurel, giving me a time and place for a meeting, required my leaving Piper's rose-petal-strewn bed, albeit reluctantly.

"Is it that case you're working on?" she asked, not bothering to cover any of her topographical attributes.

"Yes," I said searching the floor for my pants. "I have to arrange a funeral for a guy who isn't dead. At least not yet."

The delicate arches of her eyebrows lifted in question, so I clarified. "Don't worry. It won't be me who kills him."

Lubavitch's Funeral Home had a large parking lot, but only Laurel's car and Kitty's blue Chrysler were there when I pulled in a little after 3:00. I had carefully scanned my surroundings the last few blocks and detected no sign of surveillance. If Bobby Chalk and Zeke Martin were watching, maybe this would convince them of Dako's imminent demise.

Laurel, Rexanne and I took the morbid tour of coffin displays before asking Mr. Lubavitch if there was a place where we could discuss arrangements among ourselves. He showed us to the alcove where grieving families took respite during the stressful hours of a loved one's viewing and service, left us with a tasteful, if macabre, brochure of casket models and prices, then discreetly withdrew to give us privacy.

Along with coordinating final arrangements for Dako, Laurel had done research on the woman who worked as a part-time assistant for the iffy notary public in East LA that Grant Tenninger had visited a few days earlier.

"I plan on running into her tomorrow morning at her regular Zumba class and, since we share a deep, abiding interest in all things Elvis, we're going to hit if off immediately."

Smart. She would go through the back door to try and find out if a devil's covenant existed between Tenninger and Bledsoe. Laurel ducked out to ask a few questions about different coffins to keep up our facade as grievers, so I turned to Rexanne. She had been glaring at me since I walked through the door and I wondered what had bent her out of shape this time. Deciding I didn't care, I asked if she had set up the meeting with Bledsoe.

"We-l-l-l, not *exactly*," was her cryptic response.

She then explained, with feigned sincerity, that she was concerned by the idea of my meeting the developer alone at his office.

"We already know he has two psychopaths on his payroll. What if he has others? Once you're trapped in there, he could ice you in a New York minute."

Ice me? What vintage pulp was this kid reading? "So, you did *not* set up a meeting?"

"We-l-l-l, not exactly."

We were in the perfect place for me to strangle her, and I was pretty sure I could swing the payments on a base-model Slumberette, but I tamped down the urge and patiently asked her to explain.

"Bledsoe's hosting a black-tie fund raiser at the The Beverly Hilton on Saturday. Thousand-dollar-a-plate dinner and dance to rake in the cash for one last media blitz before the vote. And guess who's going?"

At one grand a pop, I sure as hell knew it wasn't me. "Who?"

"Us. You and me."

Rexanne claimed one of the advantages of being Harmon Richfield's only granddaughter was that his power position could open doors to everything from presidential inauguration balls to luxury sky boxes at

Cowboys Stadium. I could picture the bigger-than-life oil tycoon reduced to a size that would wrap nicely around Rexanne's little finger and had no doubt she had pulled it off, but I was reluctant to admit her plan was better than mine. Making my proposal to Hank Bledsoe in a crowd of glitterati guaranteed my safety and might be brazen enough to leave him rattled. Rattled men make mistakes, another pearl from Dako.

Still, there was potential danger, so I didn't want Rexanne anywhere near the Hilton come Saturday night. "I admire your ingenuity in persuading gramps to wangle us two tickets, but you're not going."

"Oh, I'm going."

"No, you're not."

"Yes, I am."

Why did everything between us come down to a childish stand-off? And why couldn't I be the sensible adult when that happened, instead of an immature adversary? I thought back to how Tommy Carmichael had dealt with one of us four boys when we tried to hang tough on some ridiculous notion. He had always forced us to defend our stupidity.

"Why?" I asked her in my most grown-up tone.

"Why what?"

"Why do *you* have to be at the fund raiser when it'll be *me* cornering Bledsoe?"

I saw her unnerving grin and once again felt like a spider about to meet its eight-legged deity.

"Because," Rexanne said, leaning deeply into my personal space, "*I'm* the attendee; you are merely my plus-one, so if *I* don't go, *you* don't go."

Laurel walked back in at that moment, telling us she had stalled Lubavitch on the contract signing, telling him we needed a day or two to analyze our financial situation before deciding on a funeral and casket price range, but assuring him there would be a contract, in case anyone came around with questions about the Farona services. "If we're done here, I need to have a Graceland tee-shirt made and memorize the lyrics to some Elvis Presley songs, so I'll see you both tomorrow."

After Laurel left, Rexanne turned my way, all sunshine and kittens now that she'd bested me. "Scuzi, but I have to go buy a dress and shoes. Make sure you order a tuxedo and puh-leeez get a decent haircut before Saturday."

Emasculating me is one thing, but when you insult the skills of Eduardo, who'd been cutting my hair since the Carmichael men and Shane and I got the five-for-twenty-bucks rate once a month in the back room of Eduardo's house on Vermont, you've crossed the line, dude.

"You're a total ball-buster, you know that?"

"You hurt me, Rick. You really do." Only she didn't look hurt. In fact, Rexanne appeared to be winding up to lob one more grenade at me.

"Oh, BTW," she said sweetly as she waltzed out the door. "There's a rose petal stuck to your fly."

I had four days to figure out every aspect of the Playa del Rey land deal if I hoped to convince Hank Bledsoe he and his partner needed to cut me in to buy my silence. Laurel might get a lead on any agreement between the two from the notary's assistant, but there was still the money angle to uncover.

According to the estimate stapled onto the architectural renderings of the mall and two high-rises, the construction project would cost almost two billion dollars to complete. Even a modest, Vegas-type skim would generate millions, but the new mayor would have to take a more public and ethical route to the money if he was going to use it to justify the initial twenty-million-dollar expenditure for the land.

Unable to figure out how LA County could legally siphon cash from the project, I turned to the next order of business. Piper's warm hello after the second ring conjured earthier words whispered in my ear only hours earlier. "Where do vain male actors get their hairs cut?" I asked, without identifying myself. She probably saw my name on her cell screen, although if she didn't recognize my voice after this afternoon's carnal marathon, I was overestimating our connection.

"That depends. Is the actor straight or gay?"

"Straight. And he plays the part of a dashing young private eye with mad sexual prowess."

I hoped the laugh I heard was *with* me, not *at* me.

"Then he'll want to book an appointment with The Bruce of Beverly Hills."

"*The* Bruce? Are you sure he's the one who cuts straight hair?"

"Straight, curly, plugged and combed-over. The Bruce will coax your wild, shaggy mane into razored, George Clooney perfection. Dare I hope the improvement is being made for a certain lady?"

The literal truth was yes—although Rexanne's behavior was rarely ladylike—but I'd already hedged honesty with Piper too often to risk it again. When in doubt, deflect. "How about I answer that by taking you out on a real date Friday night."

"I'm working."

That's when I remembered Lloyd saying the last performance of *Desire Trumps Will* would be the end of this week. I think he was hoping I loved it so much the first time that I might want to enjoy his five lines again. While I'd been thinking, Piper had spoken.

"I'm sorry, what did you say?"

"I asked if we could do it Saturday night instead."

Damn. The fund raiser. "I'm working."

"Oh." That single syllable conveyed genuine disappointment, and I flattered myself it was not the actress talking, but the woman. It seemed rude for me to suggest another "lunch" in her bed, when I hadn't yet taken her out in public, so I punted.

"I don't want you to see me before my upgrade from The Bruce. Why don't I call you at the end of the week and we can coordinate our social calendars." It was time for Piper to leave for the Tuesday evening performance, so we said our good-byes and promised to speak in a few days. Feeling like I was two-timing Eduardo, I dialed the number information gave me for The Bruce of Beverly Hills.

I stayed at the office, wanting to see if I could connect Bobby Chalk to the same janitorial service that paid so much money every week to Zeke Martin, wanting to think more on the profit angle of the land deal and *not* wanting to run into Rexanne if she had gone back to the Santa Monica house for the night.

As I worked at the computer to track Chalk along the same routes Cal Cooper had used for Martin, I listened to the radio, flipping around to catch as many political ads as possible. Up until then, the bashing had been nothing more than background chatter, but ever since Dako's envelope had been given to me for safekeeping, the content of those ads had indirectly affected the people around me, so I decided to listen a little more closely. Tenninger's faction and Bledsoe's supporters savaged each other the way they'd been doing for six weeks, but when I paid more attention to them I realized there was a second aspect of those commercials: the campaign promises.

We already suspected the attacks and accusations were only smoke screens to keep the voters from noticing any other candidates, so maybe we should be analyzing the rah-rah stuff, where each man might be laying subtle groundwork for his future dirty dealing. What better way to legitimize the land transaction than to tie it back to a lofty promise made long before the new mayor was supposedly aware of the acreage in Playa del Rey?

I heard no point of commonality between the candidates' ambitious guarantees over the following two hours, but I decided Rexanne's next assignment after buying her wardrobe for the fund raiser would be obtaining copies or transcripts of all prior campaign ads and scouring them for similar planks in disparate platforms.

And even if she turned up nothing, the busywork would keep the annoying young woman out of my soon-to-be Clooney-like hair. Every time we crossed paths we wound up sniping at each other and I was fed up with it. True, walking into that afternoon's meeting at the funeral home with a pink rose petal dangling from my zipper wasn't the classiest entrance I'd ever made, but Laurel had either not noticed or chosen to ignore the thing, while Rexanne used it to fuel a pissy attitude.

She was intelligent, she was pretty, and I saw something in those dark brown peepers of hers that had zapped a little shock to my heart the first time I gazed into them, something that continued to spark a flutter each time we made eye contact. It wasn't in the same solar system as my atavistic male response to Piper Lang, nor did it have that same magnitude, but a compelling force made me feel—at the very least—protective of The Lone Star State's seventh-richest twenty year old. Maybe it was because her father was sidelined and couldn't protect her himself.

Eventually finding what I needed to prove Bobby Chalk was being paid indirectly by Hank Bledsoe, I wondered if Tenninger had delegated the hiring of muscle to his business partner, the better to give him plausible deniability in the event the connection became public.

Or maybe Bledsoe had been a man of elastic moral fiber before Tenninger hooked up with him and they hatched their scheme. Deuce had a penchant for cozying up to badasses, as I had little doubt he'd had some dirty little arrangement with Hamid Khavazhi. The detective's presence at the warehouse the night my father died was neither coincidence nor a rogue sting by Tenninger and Det. Rowan, despite what Deuce had told Gayle and Victor.

Maybe Tenninger and Nostradamus had done the math and figured out a two-way split was twice as lucrative as a four-way, then chosen that night to kill off their respective partners. Maybe the unexpected appearance of a quartet of well-intentioned cops had dropped a rat in the gumbo, forcing Tenninger to improvise. By silencing Khavazhi with a bullet, he prevented the mobster from trading what he knew for a lesser sentence.

And maybe Dako was actually the stand-up guy Laurel said he was, waiting two decades to vindicate himself and bring Tenninger to justice, but I couldn't accept that interpretation until I finally knew what had transpired in Khavazhi's warehouse in the brief period between the first shot and Victor's discovery of that bloody scene with only two men left standing. Neither of those men was likely to volunteer details to the son of one of the victims.

There was also the unsettling issue of Dako's probable affair with my mother. The night before, I had slipped the incriminating snapshot between the pages of an Alexander Hamilton biography gathering dust on my night stand, but out of sight, at least in this case, was not out of mind and I wanted to confront him, beat the truth out of him, if necessary. My beach day of familial happiness had been sullied, one of my few childhood memories now compromised by the unwelcome presence of Dako Farona.

The Bruce more than lived up to his hype, so when I swaggered out of his Beverly Hills salon the next day, I had been transformed—at least according to him—from gawky sidekick to leading man. Le Bruce had insisted on throwing in a bit of eyebrow shaping at no extra charge, but his regular haircut fee was so inflated he could have high-lighted my pubes and chest hair and *still* come out ahead.

I shot up over the hill on Coldwater Canyon to a formalwear shop in Studio City, where I was fitted for a designer penguin suit for the Saturday fund raiser, then to offset the metrosexuality rays I'd been exposed to, I hit the Ventura Boulevard Fatburger location to reboot my butch. After scarfing down the meat and onion rings I had missed two days earlier, I drove to the Gingerbread House and made some calls.

Rexanne was leaving Saks when I reached her and she promised to get a jump on tracking down the transcripts as soon as she got home. I had expected her to protest being relegated to doing scut work, but the spending of large amounts of money seemed to have mellowed her. She reported no sightings of Zeke Martin or Bobby Chalk.

A quick call to the hospice confirmed no one had inquired about Dako's condition other than the three people on the list Laurel had given them. My plan to quiet Tenninger's and Bledsoe's fears of being outted was working.

Laurel had made progress with Ivy Crabbe, the notary's assistant. "One look at my Graceland tee-shirt and she forgot all about Zumba. We bonded over carrot and kale smoothies."

By exploiting Ivy's obsession with The King, Laurel had extracted enough information to know the woman had a key to the notary's office.

"She's one of those people who likes to impress you with her importance by dropping names and claiming she rubs shoulders with the rich and famous. I played giddily impressed, but didn't want to pump her too hard and arouse suspicion. Tomorrow night I'll ply her with champagne when we celebrate at her apartment, then I'll drill down a little deeper on anything she might know."

"What will you be celebrating?"

"Didn't you hear? I won a contest for a two-night sleepover at Graceland and a private dinner with Priscilla and Lisa-Marie."

"Let me guess. You get to bring along a friend."

Laurel would spend the afternoon creating the winner's notification papers—which, conveniently, would need to be notarized—and a handwritten letter of welcome from the former Mrs. Elvis, then she'd reveal her good fortune to Ivy in the morning.

"Can you be on stand-by to pick up the key once I get her sloshed?"

The plan was for me to let myself into the notary's office and search for anything connecting Tenninger and Bledsoe, while Laurel did the same at Ivy's place on her hunch the woman might bring home proof of her status in the world.

"I don't want Rexanne tagging along tomorrow night," I said. "Just in case things get all fighty and shooty. But with you and I both off her radar for the evening, she's bound to ask questions."

"Tell her you have a date with the Rose Parade Queen." Ah, so she *had* noticed the incriminating crotch petal the day before. "And I'll say I'm spending the evening keeping Dako company. The important thing is to make sure she has something to occupy her."

Lloyd had been away from his desk when I returned to the Gingerbread House earlier, but I went downstairs and found him reading *People Magazine* online. "Yo, Lloyd, any chance of getting three tickets for tomorrow's performance of *Desire Trumps Will?*"

I booked a limousine on Dako's account, then secured reservations at Spago before calling the Sutterman sisters to say I was treating them to an evening at the thee-a-tuh and a late Wolfgang Puck dinner. Kitty and Bitsy were not fooled, especially when I said they had to invite Rexanne to go with them and *not* mention I was sponsoring the outing.

"Can you afford this, Rick?" Kitty asked, already knowing the answer.

I assured them the expense was being covered by a client, but that it was imperative for Rexanne to believe they were taking her out, not me or the un-named client. They agreed to the terms, so I said I'd bring the tickets home with me.

That's when I remembered Bitsy's odd comment from the night before. I asked to speak privately with her, so Kitty got off the line. "You mentioned something last night about what a nice man Dako Farona is. Why would you say that, seeing as how you've never met him?"

"Well," Bitsy said, before clearing her throat for three or four seconds. "Rexanne is such a darling girl, I figured her father *must* be a nice person. Oops! There's the timer on my osso buco. Later, tater."

My ear canal filled with dial tone and two flat-out fibs.

Rexanne made a major deal over my new coif, stretching up to ruffle my hair before I could juke out of reach, then squealing with delight when it fell back in expertly-razored layers.

"Dude, you look awesome!"

Kitty and Bitsy entered and gave me the AARP version of Rexanne's enthusiasm, and I realized Eduardo and I would never meet again. Kitty looked at my manscaped eyebrows with professional interest, but discreetly kept her observations to herself as I'm sure she had done many times in a long career of making-up celebrities who denied their facelifts, nose jobs and wrinkle filler.

After the ladies returned to the kitchen, Rexanne showed me her many purchases for the fund raiser. Something she referred to as an "LBD," with a designer's name on the tag that looked like French alphabet soup complete with all the accent marks, a purse so small it would be hard-pressed to hold a field mouse and what looked to me like perfectly ordinary black high heels. When I failed to be suitably impressed by the shoes, Rexanne turned them over so I could see the blood-red soles.

"Cheese's crust! Did you walk them through a slaughterhouse?"

She shook her head and may have mumbled the word philistine, but right then Bitsy called us in to dinner and I made my getaway.

Over osso buco, Kitty invited Rexanne to the play and dinner the following night. After saying she was happy to go with them, she turned her eyes on me. "You coming, too?"

"Wish I could, but I've got something to do."

Her eyes narrowed, the shopping euphoria having worn off. "Something? Or some*one?*"

"Shut up and eat your beef," I said.

"Shut up and eat your *veal*," Bisty corrected.

Dako was sleeping when I arrived at his room in the hospice around 10:00 Wednesday morning, so I sat by his bed turning the snapshot over and over in my hand while waiting for him to wake.

Although his injuries had not been fatal, the grayish pallor and gaunt face proclaimed the toll two bullets and a three-hour operation had taken on him. I wasn't sure how old he was, but I guessed he must be coming up on fifty and, for the first time since I'd known him, he looked every year of his age.

Dako and I are the same height, six-two, but I'm usually described as lanky or rangy, while he has shoulders of bunched muscle and a chest like a gladiator's shield. I've never seen him eat a green vegetable and he doesn't work out, but he is naturally gifted with the solid, powerful body of a mountain gorilla. He uses that intimidating physique to his advantage, though not in the way you'd expect. Most people meet Dako, take one look at his manual-laborer/weight-lifter frame and assume he must not be very bright. By the time they figure out they're not playing checkers with a rube, but chess with a grand master, it's already too late.

Before his eyes opened, he coughed and licked his dry lips. I stood and filled a plastic cup with ice-water from the pitcher on the table by his bed, and if he was surprised to see it was me handing him the water, rather than Rexanne or Laurel, he never showed it. That's one more advantage Dako exploits in every professional battle of wills or wits: a complete lack of tells. His face gives away nothing unless he chooses for it to do so, and you have to work hard to earn any expression at all from him.

He cautiously propped himself up on his right elbow, reaching for the cup with his left hand and flinching when the stretch pulled something under his shoulder dressing.

"Damn it," he muttered, pulling his compromised wing to his side. I knew better than to offer help, so I merely held the cup and waited while Dako gingerly shifted himself into a half-seated position, using only his good arm for leverage. Once he'd settled against the stacked pillows, I extended the water so it was within his reach.

As he emptied the cup with steady, unrushed gulps, I sat back in my chair, the snapshot facedown on my thigh and covered with one hand.

After the last swallow, Dako tried to place the empty cup on the side table, but I realized the twisting movement couldn't be doing his abdominal incision any good, so I took the cup and put it alongside the pitcher.

"Why did you tell the police it was a random mugging?" I asked.

"I didn't want to reveal anything about the investigation. Better the cops think I was shot trying to keep some shit-weasel from ripping the Rolex off my wrist. Makes me look like an idiot, but keeps them from speculating about more."

"You don't own a Rolex."

"And now that shit-weasel's wearing my imaginary watch."

I wanted to catch him completely off guard with the picture, so I prolonged the general conversation. "I have the envelope."

"So Laurel told me. Are they going to find it?"

"No. But while you recuperate, we're continuing to gather everything you'll need for the pre-election bomb drop."

"We, meaning...?"

"Laurel and me."

He looked into my eyes as if he were mining them for more information, but I remained placid as a cow, emulating his own stoic refusal to give anything away. "I do *not* want Rexanne involved," Dako finally said, guessing when he couldn't find proof.

"With the case or with me?"

"Why would I want her endangered by either one?"

I assured him he could relax on both counts. Rexanne was content to fill her time shopping in Beverly Hills, and she disliked me almost as much as he did. That earned me a raised eyebrow and a suspicious smirk, a look I had seen on Rexanne's face more than once. That's when I realized his eyes were the same color as hers, too, deepest brown with a light scattering of golden flecks I hadn't noticed before.

I didn't like comparing them, as it required dragging her down to Dako's level, or lifting him up to Rexanne's, and I was loath to do either.

"I'm going to the notary's office tonight," I said. "If the mutual-destruction documents are there, I'll find them for you."

"The place has a state-of-the-art security system."

"So Laurel told me."

"Do you have the entry code?"

"No." *Now* I had his full attention.

"How are you going to override the alarm?"

"I'm not. I intend to set it off when I go through the front door."

He stared to see if I was joking. I wasn't.

"Well, that's plain stupid."

It was my turn to lift an eyebrow and smugly smile. I hope he felt like he was looking in a mirror, so he could see how annoying it was. "I have a plan."

"God help us all; Rick Valentine has a plan."

Locked and loaded, I turned over the snapshot, placing it on the bed close to his right hand, and never taking my eyes off Dako's face. He was good. Not a flicker of recognition, much less guilt or shame, even after he picked it up and brought it to within twelve inches of his face.

"You took this," he whispered, studying the photo, but I wasn't sure if he meant I had taken it from his wallet or that I had snapped the picture itself at the beach. It didn't matter, though, as both were true.

"Yes."

He laid the snapshot on the sheet and turned to look at me, once again probing for answers in my eyes. I returned the probe and Dako sighed. "What do you *think* you know?" he asked, as he had on my first stakeout with him years ago, when he began teaching me how to interpret my field observations, saying things are sometimes very different from how they first appear to be. Not this time, though. Things were *exactly* as they appeared to be.

"I know you slept with my mother."

I turned on my phone while walking out to the car, then sat behind the wheel with the A/C blasting and checked for messages that had come in during my hour with Dako. It felt like the old days, when my only office was my vehicle, so I settled comfortably in the ergonomic seat of the Corvette to return texts and calls.

Rexanne's text was just one word, but it conveyed the news that she had found something: *scor-r-r-r-re!!!*

Lloyd's officious voice said he had personally supervised the switching of my nameplate and that I was now good to go.

Laurel reported on her Zumba-launched morning with Ivy Crabbe. "She bought it all. When I told her I needed to notarize the prize certification before I could get our vouchers for two first-class tickets to Memphis, she offered the services of her boss."

In her excitement at the idea of a Graceland pilgrimage and dining with The King's close family members, Ivy had wanted to bring Laurel with her when she reported to the notary's office at 1:00 for her usual half-day, but Laurel claimed she had something to take care of and wouldn't be able to make it till late in the afternoon.

"She told me her boss leaves on the dot of 5:00 o'clock, so I plan to breeze in around 4:50 to make sure the guy's rushed and doesn't look too hard at my counterfeit paperwork. After he's gone I'll ask Ivy for a tour, then while she turns everything off for the night and closes up shop, I'll get the general lay of the land and distract her from locking things down."

We both knew it was a real long shot that she'd be able to get the security code for me, but with a little luck, Laurel could ensure every desk drawer and file cabinet was left unlocked without Ivy catching on.

Anything I had to break open would tip off the notary, and he would tell Hank Bledsoe and Grant Tenninger that Dako hadn't ended the search. I wanted both of them to think their hit man had solved the problem, the better to blindside Bledsoe at his little party.

"We'll go back to her place and get champagne-wasted. I'll text you the address when I have her key."

"Rexanne left me a message that she discovered something in the transcripts of the campaign ads," I told her. "So, we should all meet in the morning and see what we have so far."

"Let's not make it before 11:00. I'll fake the drinking as much as possible, but there's still a chance I'll be a little hung over."

"My office at 11:00. Will you let Rexanne know? I've got to hit some stores and put together my go-bag for tonight."

I had saved Piper's text for last, hoping for a jolt of sweetness to take the bad taste out of my mouth from the time with Dako.

"Lunch" 2day @ my apt?

I checked my watch. With so much riding on tonight's venture and not knowing how long it would take to gather what I needed, I couldn't risk losing any time, even time rolling in the arms of the lovely Piper Lang.

Starving 4 "lunch" but working 2day. 2moro?

I put away the phone and reached into my pocket for the snapshot, forgetting I had left it on Dako's bed after he fell asleep. I didn't want the ugly reminder anyway, so he might as well keep it. Dako hadn't denied the affair with my mother, but he hadn't been a gushing font of information either. "I fell in love with her," he had said in response to my statement that I knew about their cheating. "Your father was

putting in the kind of killer hours that fast-track you
to detective and your mother was alone too much."

"So you decided to take advantage of a vulnerable
young mom."

"That isn't what happened."

Only now can I look back and understand how
carefully Dako chose those words, keeping reality from
me without technically lying. In the moment I was too
fixated on blaming him and exonerating my mother to
parse his statement more doggedly.

"Are you implying she loved you, too? Because if
that were true my father's death would have cleared
the way for your happily-ever-after, and we both know
that didn't happen."

I was talking when I should have been listening,
shaping the past to meet my own requirements, and
Dako knew that and gave me what I needed, never
veering from the truth, but never presenting it in full.

"Yes, Zoë ended it. And, yes, I had hopes of being
with her after John's death. She wanted nothing to do
with me by then, and a year later I laid down my torch
and jumped into a rebound relationship."

"Rexanne's mother, Amanda."

He nodded. I could not change the fact that my
mother had cheated on my father, but at least she had
come to her senses, dumping Dako and breaking his
heart. It was everything I had wanted to hear and not
even close to what I needed to know.

He fell asleep before I could ask about the shoot-
out in Khavazhi's warehouse, but I had enough for one
day: his admission of adultery. The rest would have to
wait until he was well enough for me to beat the crap
out of him.

I purchased the 34-AA bra and sweat-stained

banger cap at a thrift shop right there in Canoga Park, then stopped at a run-down bodega to pick up a box of el cheapo condoms. A child's baseball bat from Dollar General and a small buy at a liquor store completed my shopping list.

I headed back to the Gingerbread House to wait for Laurel's call and to follow up on a few clients. Eventually this case would be done and I'd have to go back to earning a living.

Piper still hadn't texted me and it was getting close to time for her to leave for the theater, so I didn't expect to get an answer on tomorrow's get-together until morning.

I tried Rexanne, who breathlessly told me her findings. "Okay, they both spout a buttload of yap-yap-yap, but it only duplicates on one point." She explained there was a looming shortfall in the funds to pay out pensions for retired county workers. LA had ridden the boom and suffered from the crash like most other urban areas, and now the county's pension plan was down to only seventy-three percent funded.

"It's a polarizing issue," she said. "Lots of retired people and current employees are worried about their future financial security, but the lame ducks aren't inclined to pull money out of other areas of the budget to make up the difference."

"Bledsoe and Tenninger are saying they will?"

"Well, neither one is threatening to yank money out of school funding, law enforcement or any of the other allocations that could cost them votes, but they each promise to find a new revenue stream that will subsidize the pension plan without raising taxes."

Piece by piece we were putting it together. I did not know if I'd have it all by Saturday night, but I'd have enough to play mind games with Hank Bledsoe.

Justin knocked a few minutes before 5:00 and asked if I wanted to join him for a hump-day drink. I begged off and when his BMW started up and pulled out of the parking lot, quiet settled over the Gingerbread House. No flautist's keening, incense or ecstatic cries of release drifted up from the rub 'n' tug grotto directly below me, indicating either Moonbeam had no more clients that day or they were outcall.

I brooded over my strangely unsatisfying conversation with Dako until Piper's text came in. *Audition 4 soap opera 2moro. Fri?*

I texted back that a Friday lunch would work for me, then switched my waiting-time thoughts from Dako to Piper. That I had a ginormous case of the wants for the lady went without saying, but I knew there was more going on between us than physical attraction.

Piper earned her living playing different roles, making lies come alive you could say. But she held her personal life to a high standard of honesty and wanted the same from a partner. That was new for me, as dating had been a long run of mutual posing, positioning and little white lies since my awkward, virginy fumbling with sixteen-year-old Kylie Butler, the girl who dragged me to the Renaissance Faire when we were in high school. So eager was I to get at those maddening breasts of hers, I put in a torturous day of pretending jousters were cool, collecting my reward that night in the not-designed-for-lovers front seats of the Wrangler I had inherited when Sonny Carmichael joined the Navy.

My dealings with the fair sex had been a series of transactions along the lines of "I'll sit through a Bruce Willis boom!fest with you, and later you'll tell me you love me" or "I'll suffer a tour of Camelot if you'll let me put my hand up under your bra." No one ever came right out and admitted we were gliding over a möbius-strip surface of calculated trades, always angling to take more that we gave, but the understanding was ingrained.

For whatever reason, Piper liked the cut of my jib and wasn't afraid to let me know it. I felt as though I had dated a lot of real-life actresses for whom I had played a certain complementing character. Suddenly I found myself circling a professional actress who did not put up with role-playing fakery in her personal relationships. It was an adjustment for me.

The growling in my stomach threatened to drive me to the closest fast-food place, but then Laurel phoned. "Another flute of the bubbly and she'll pass out," she said. She was making the call from inside Ivy Crabbe's bathroom, so she had to give me the information I'd need to capitalize on my trip to the notary's location as quickly as possible, finishing up with: "Avoid the windows in the main office. They both open onto the street, but there's one facing the alley in the restroom. Police response time in that neighborhood averages about twelve minutes, so don't—"

"Hey, I have to tinky-winkle," a muffled voice interrupted.

"One sec, Ivy," Laurel called out. I heard a toilet flush, then a whisper. "I'll text her address and leave the door unlocked."

With that, Laurel was gone and the night's work had begun, so I hoisted my old camping backpack onto my shoulders and locked the office. On the drive to Ivy's apartment, I stopped to pick up a sandwich and a bottle of water, finishing both before passing under the freeway near the Universal Tower and cruising into a cul-de-sac rimmed with older, brick apartment buildings. Their combined underground garages had insufficient capacity to accommodate the hundreds of tenants, so cars were nose-to-tail curbside like a line of inquisitive dogs.

Circling twice with no luck, I was forced to park by a fire hydrant while I hustled up to Ivy's. The door was unlocked, as Laurel had said it would be. Inching it open I saw the keys on the floor and grabbed them, then closed the door on the sound of drunken female voices singing "Love Me Tender."

Cruising past the little strip mall where the notary's office occupied the northernmost slot, I carefully checked for lights and activity. Nothing. It was after 10:00 on a Wednesday in an area with no residences and no open business, so that was to be expected. There wasn't any reason to think Tenninger and Bledsoe still had the place under watch.

Satisfied I would be undisturbed, I parked the Corvette ten blocks away behind an auto body shop, shouldered the backpack, adjusted the hoodie to hide my face and loped through the shadows on my way to the strip mall. Once there I slowly walked past the other storefronts, checking for signs of activity on my way to the end. When I got to the window of my target I learned he was much more than a notary. If the words painted directly on the glass were to be believed, he also offered passport photos, copies, tax prep, bail bonds and payday check cashing. What, no tarot card readings?

Standing next to the window on the alley, I kept eyes on the street. I didn't know how often the area's routine patrols rode by, but I couldn't afford to set off the alarm with a cruiser only blocks away, so I waited.

Twenty minutes later a black-and-white rolled slowly down the street in front of the strip mall. I gave it fifteen minutes to move further along the looping route I guessed normally took around an hour, then swung the baseball bat hard, shattering the window, setting off the screaming alarm and firing the starter's pistol for my one-man race.

Sprinting around to the front, I keyed the lock and opened the door, entering, then securely locking it behind me. Unzipping my backpack as I ran to the broken window, I pulled out the banger cap and dropped it in the scattered glass on the floor. I popped the tops on two Colt 45 tallboys and poured half of each down the sink, running water for a few seconds to wash away the smell.

In the reception area I found the overstuffed couch Laurel had described, and set the cans of malt liquor on the floor alongside it. Prior to staging an interrupted sex romp, I unfolded a sheet of aluminum foil containing the three joints I had taken from Bitsy's not-so-secret stash in the canister labeled corn meal. After I set my pot bonfire ablaze, I dragged one end of the couch out from the wall, angling it enough for me to squeeze in when the time came, then tucked the bra behind the end cushion, leaving one strap and half a lacy cup exposed. To complete my tableau, I tore open one of the factory seconds' condom packets, pocketed the contents, and dropped the empty foil wrapper next to the couch.

Fanning my trio of toasting fatties, I waited until revolving blue lights lit up the night and siren whoops competed with the still-shrieking alarm. I folded one corner of the foil to snuff out the weed, crumpled it into a ball that joined the condom already in my pocket, then dived behind the couch and lugged it a few inches toward the wall. Using my backpack as a pillow, I settled as comfortably as I could in such a cramped space.

The two responding officers were not exactly *CSI: The Barrio* and they read the crime scene as simplistically as I'd intended them to. After shouting from both the broken window and locked front door that *"you fuckheads better come out right goddamn now,"* they waited for the business owner to arrive, and I'm sure their fingers were twitchy on the trigger the whole time.

Mr. Notary-slash-bail-bondsman-slash-etcetera unlocked the front door so Turner and Hooch could storm through yelling *"clear!"* every time they spun through an opening with weapons drawn. Given the size of the suite, that burned about six seconds before they joined the notary in evaluating my trompe l'oeil.

I could see six shoes from my floor-level vantage point behind the couch, two pairs of black leather police-issues and a scuffed and broken-in set of tan loafers. The shoes had a conversation in front of the couch.

"What'cha got here, Mr. Arroyo, is a coupla kids lookin' for a quiet place to play hide-the-weenie," the first cop feet said.

"You notice anything missing?" This from the second pair of regulation shoes.

The loafers turned and walked away, while a reedy voice said, "I don't know. Let me check."

As the loafers left, a hand picked up one of the cans from the floor. "Half empty and warm. They musta been here awhile before the alarm kicked in."

"Yeah, and it looks like at least one rubber got a test drive." The foil wrapper on the floor was nudged by the toe of a shoe.

"We better tell the beaner his security ain't worth shit."

"What'cha get when you drive down to TJ and buy a system from your cousin Pedro."

"Oh, hey, look what we got here."

I could feel vibrations as black-shoe's fingers probed the couch cushion only inches from my face.

"Double A," he said, followed by a snort.

"Itty bitty titty committee." Their chuckling was cut short by the return of the tan loafers.

"Everything seems to be okay, but I found this on the floor under the broken window."

The banger cap put a final punctuation mark on the obvious tale, so Rizzoli and Isles verbally walked Arroyo through the scene's timeline, warning him the half-empty malt liquor cans and residual weed reek indicated the kids had been settled in for some time before the alarm tripped.

"Musta been some kinda short in the system, 'cuz that siren shoulda gone off as soon as they smashed the window."

Apparently used to break-ins of that sort, Cagney helpfully carried in a sheet of plywood from the trunk of the squad car and Lacey nailed it over the point of entry.

"But now I won't be able to reset the alarm," Mr. Notary's voice said with some concern.

"Oh, those kids won't be coming back tonight, Mr. Arroyo."

"Yeah, they prob'ly shit themselves when the alarm went off before *he* did."

Their chuckles reassured the notary it had been less crime than prank, so five minutes later the lights went out and three pairs of shoes took a hike.

And I had all night to comb through every file there.

The notary wouldn't dare call Tenninger or Bledsoe and risk revealing a weakness in his ability to protect their secrets. As long as he was convinced the break-in was *not* connected with his powerful customers, he'd keep his own secret and take it up with the alarm company the next day.

Laurel had done a good job. All file cabinets were unlocked, as were the drawers in the notary's desk, so I had unlimited access to everything. Unfortunately, everything turned out to be ordinary paperwork relating to the many trades of Mr. Arroyo, and a substantial collection of ponygirl porn. Abandoning the file cabinets, I did a narc-search of the premises.

Without having to resort to the deeper, trickier skills taught me by Dako, I found a small metal box securely sealed in a heavy-duty plastic bag at the bottom of the toilet tank. While it *could* have been merely a jerry-rigged water-saver, I assumed it was what the notary had gone to check on while the two cops cracked wise over a teen girl's brassiere. With all the equipment and files in the suite, it was the bathroom he checked, which is why he found the planted cap.

A sturdy combination lock secured the lid, and breaking it was not an option if I wanted to keep from alerting anyone that the land scam was still being investigated. I went searching for the combination.

In less than ten minutes I found the opening sequence for the lock, computer passwords, user names, ATM pins, the toll-free number 1-800-RIDE-HER and pretty much every other piece of sensitive personal information Mr. Arroyo thought he'd hidden securely. All of it was neatly printed on a sheet of paper taped to the flip side of the desk blotter. What an idiot. Dako believed ninety percent of people opt for convenience when hiding information, and warned about ever considering a desk a safe repository. I photographed the secrets cache before flipping the blotter over and repositioning the desktop items exactly as they appeared in the cell phone picture I'd taken before moving them, then opened the lock on the metal box.

Two sheets of paper had been folded in half and rolled up to fit inside. I slipped the rubber band off the short paper tube, unrolled and unfolded the nearly identical documents, then laid them side by side, a matched pair of smoking guns.

It took the copy machine a few minutes to warm up, during which time I located the notary's official seal. Once I was done, the copies had the same raised imprint as the originals and would pass muster with everyone but an expert capable of differentiating ink signatures from Xerox imitators.

I put everything back in the commode vault the way it had been when Arroyo left with the cops, locked up the drawers and file cabinets to cover Laurel's ass (she had helpfully offered to make sure they were all secure while Ivy washed the coffee pot and turned off the copier), then I locked the front door behind me before trotting back to the car a little after 3:00, a phantom who had never been there.

My tap on Ivy Crabbe's door brought a quick response from Laurel, who had been dozing next to it while she waited. I handed in the keys and gave a thumbs-up. "Ivy?" I whispered.

"Passed out after I played drunk enough for her to insist I spend the night on her couch."

"You are *very*, very good," I said, with genuine admiration.

Before quietly closing the door, she whispered in Elvis's distinctive style, "Thenk you. Thenk you very much."

When Rexanne banged on my door at 7:30 I pulled the covers over my head. "Go away," I groaned, knowing she wouldn't.

"Get up; we've got work to do," she announced, rudely barging in to invade my privacy. Next she invaded my personal space by flopping down on the bed right next to blanket-shrouded me. Rexanne grabbed the most accessible upwardly pointing protrusion—my shoulder, thank God, as I had been dreaming of Piper before the interruption—and roughly shook it.

"Crimes to solve, desperados to catch," she insisted. "Wakie, wakie."

I sat up and thrust my face at hers, forcing her to pull away as I growled, "Get. Out. Of. Here."

"Whoa! *Somebody* needs a Xanax and a mint."

When I continued to glare, she rolled her eyes and left, but I was unable to go back to sleep. I had gotten in at 5:00, after leaving Ivy's and going to the Gingerbread House to hide the poison-pill proof with the other evidence against Bledsoe and Tenninger, so I had been asleep only two hours when Rexanne's pounding disturbed me. Tired as I was, I should have dropped off again immediately, but the arms of Morpheus refused to embrace me for the hour I tossed and turned before finally giving up.

Rexanne lacked the capacity to look chastened, but she *was* conciliatory when I trudged into the kitchen, hurrying to pour me a cup of coffee before I could do it myself. Accepting her caffeinated apology, I sat at the table and slid two pages across to her.

While I transitioned from Mr. Hyde to Dr. Jekyll on the regenerative power of coffee, Rexanne read the statements. "Wow, they *really* must not trust each other to put these into the mix."

"I suspect trust diminishes in direct proportion to the amount at stake, and the money involved here is apparently staggering." Plus, neither of them believed one of these documents would ever surface. As long as everyone played nice, their insurance policies would stay hidden and no one would be forced to make a kamikaze sacrifice.

"It's pretty smart what they've done, though," observed Rexanne.

She was referring to the opening paragraph of each document, where the author admitted to being coerced by the other man into participating in the scam. The word blackmail wasn't mentioned, but that was the obvious inference.

"People automatically side with the underdog," I said. "So, admitting to having done something that had been used against him, each man's petty crime will pale in comparison to the larger violation of public trust by the other."

I had no doubt Tenninger and Bledsoe could choose from a large inventory if either one was ever compelled to expose some past illegal or immoral behavior in order to indict the other for wider-reaching criminal behavior, but with too much at risk on both sides, the pact would never see the light of day. It would keep both men honest—at least with each other—and they could rake in their millions without fear of a partner hamstrung by the poison pill.

"My guess," I said, mostly recovered from my

sleep-deprived crankiness, "is that once everything's working for them, once the partner who's no longer linked to the off-shore selling the land gets his half of the profits, a simultaneous destruction of the documents will be triggered."

"Leaving no loose ends to trip them up," added Rexanne.

We agreed it was too bad the main body of the insurance policies didn't spell out the specifics of the plan, only referring to it as a way to bilk millions out of LA county, but if one of them ever came to light, the signator would already be more than willing to fill in the details in order to bring down his former partner. The real strength of each document was the author's claim he had been forced to participate by the other man, but could no longer carry the shame and guilt of his actions. Nice touch.

I had barely enough time to swing by the tuxedo place for a fitting before my meeting with Laurel at the Gingerbread House, so Rexanne maturely said she'd hold off telling her own findings until all three of us were together.

On my way to Studio City I texted Piper to wish her luck on the audition.

While a gnarled hand fiddled in my groin, I looked in the full-length mirror and had to admit the screen idol haircut and designer tuxedo were major improvements, though I was a little disappointed Piper wouldn't see me in all my black-tie Clooneyness. But maybe if things kept going well with her, we'd get a chance to walk the red carpet as a couple one day. That thought warmed me until a bony knuckle got a bit *too* familiar with my junk.

"Everything okay down there, dude?"

The aged tailor creaked himself vertical, a tape measure hanging around his neck like a stethoscope and a line of pins fanning out from between his lips. He spoke around the spikes.

"My nephew did not follow the chalk marks on the inseam. I'll have to redo it myself. Kids," he said dismissively. "No respect for the craft."

"But it'll be ready tomorrow, right?"

"Pick it up any time after 10:00 A.M." How he hit those p's and t's without blow-darting me, I'll never know.

The three of us gathered in my office to share intel and finalize Saturday night's approach to Hank Bledsoe. Laurel reported Dako was getting restless at the hospice, but that she had convinced him to stay at least until Sunday morning, when we'd have our final information before setting up Hank and Deuce for public exposure.

"Of course, he'd kill me if he knew how much you're involved in all this," Laurel said to Rexanne.

"It can't be helped. There's too much of a chance Hank will recognize you on sight and Rick won't be able to get in as close to him as I can."

"Did you find what we need?" I asked Laurel.

She produced a piece of spyware the size of a flattened contact lens. It looked transparent until you held it up to strong light and saw the threads of micro-circuitry.

"That's three grand's worth of technology there, and I'd like to amortize the cost over a few more investigations, so don't lose it." She called it a 'button' and explained it had recording capability, but could not transmit. "It would bulk it up too much, so you need to access Hank's phone twice, Rexanne," Laurel said. "Because if this doesn't get retrieved, you may as well not have planted it."

We worked on the theory that Bledsoe would call Tenninger as soon as I made my threat. If we could record that call, we might get the final details of the land scam before exposing the two perpetrators.

The button was even thinner once Laurel peeled it from its adhesive backing, and Hank would be very unlikely to notice it sticking to his phone in the busy party atmosphere. After Laurel walked Rexanne through a series of practice peel-stick-and-retrieves, we moved to other business. I showed my copies of the poison-pill documents, assuring Laurel the originals were safe in the www.2regni.net envelope, and that the fakes I'd left at the notary's would pass the smell test.

Rexanne reported the only point of commonality in the two sets of campaign promises was the issue of the under-funded pension plan and each candidate's commitment to sourcing new revenue to make up the difference. After claiming she needed to get to an appointment, Rexanne left, although once she was gone, Laurel clued me in that Manny Petty is not a guy's name. She also said if all went as planned Saturday night, we'd go public the Thursday before the election.

"That won't give their legal sharks enough time to mitigate the charges," Laurel said. "But you know they'll try like hell. And all the while Hank and Deuce will deny everything."

"I don't think they'll be doing that."

She gave me a questioning look which I answered with sphinx-like inscrutability. "At least not if *they're* the ones who go public and reveal the scam."

"Are you mental? Why would they do that?"

"I have a plan."

As if she were channeling Dako, she said, "God help us. Rick Valentine has a plan."

Justin had been after me to have lunch with him ever since the break-in that wrongly targeted his office instead of mine, so I tapped on his open door after Laurel left to visit Dako, and asked if he'd like to grab some Thai food.

Over mouth-searing panang and slithery rice noodles, we talked about criminal cases—his, fictional and riveting from his former TV series, and mine, true-to-life, but duller than C-SPAN. He found it hard to believe that in three years of working for a top LA investigator I'd only seen a few cases rise above the level of mundane, but I assured him it was fact.

I saw his disappointment, confirming my theory that at least *some* writers live their lives in secret frustration because nothing ever happens to them as interesting as the stories they create for books and scripts. That achieved, I set my lure and dangled it in front of him. "Of course, there's this one case I'm working on right now...." I didn't offer details, but I said it related to the trashing of his office and directly linked to some powerful, well-known people.

"The kind of people who have you bumped off if you cross them?" he asked, eyes bright with interest and the caffeine from two Thai iced teas.

I nodded. "They've already tried with one of my colleagues."

I never revealed names, and I swore Justin to secrecy, but I was certain the thrill of danger and mystery would be too much for him to keep to himself. I counted on his sharing the story with Jason and Pat, so the three would already be primed when I needed their help.

After a gentlemanly fight over the check, we each threw down a twenty onto the paper slip filled with unreadable chicken scratches and a clearly written amount under thirty bucks. Justin went back to the Gingerbread House and I left to buy ammunition. My father's Kimber was about to come out of retirement.

The rest of Thursday afternoon was filled with welcome distractions, preventing my brooding over the situation with Dako and my mother, and his possible role in my father's death. I wanted the truth, no matter how harsh, but I knew it might have to wait until after Tenninger and Bledsoe had been nailed. I needed a clear head to make sure Laurel and Rexanne stayed out of range once I drew fire down on myself.

Piper called to say her audition had gone well and that she could hardly wait to see me the next day. I then surprised myself by telling her I had missed her during our three days apart and how much I wanted to be with her again. Her purring promise to make my wait worthwhile erased any lingering doubts I had about saying too much too soon.

I realized it was time to turn in the Corvette, although I had really come to love driving it. With my Wrangler no longer a vehicle of interest, and Rexanne using Kitty's Chrysler, there was no justification for keeping the primo wheels.

I telephoned Rexanne to set up a time the next morning for her to follow me in the Jeep to the rental place.

"No can do, chief," was her immediate response.

"Why not?"

"It's in the shop getting the door fixed from when I accidentally bashed into a concrete pillar in that parking structure across the street from Dad's office."

"I thought that happened when Zeke and Bobby ran you off the road."

"Who said they ran me off the road?"

I had worried over her near-death experience, when it turned out she was only a careless driver and the two heavies had accosted her on foot at a mall food court.

"Why do *you* care? I'm paying for the Corvette and you get to look semi-cool for a little longer."

When she reported her Twitter following was up to eleven hundred forty-nine, but that May-Ann Harris was closing in on account of her posting sideboob, I pretended I had another call coming in and hung up.

I phoned Bitsy Sutterman to tell her to forget about making dinner, that I'd bring take-out from their favorite place, the last surviving open-pit barbecue in Los Angeles. Foley's Pit Stop was a relic grandfathered in under the anti-smog regulations, and it emitted towering clouds of porky flavor from its location not far from Baldwin Hills. The fifteen miles the detour would add to my drive home was worth it, as the favor I intended to ask was huge.

My last call before leaving for the day was to Babs and Tommy Carmichael in Boston. We usually speak a few times every month, with Tommy and me arguing over the strengths, weaknesses and bonehead mistakes of the Celtics, Red Sox and Bruins, as compared with the Lakers, Dodgers and Kings. It ended as it always did, when Tommy evaluated my contribution to the conversation with his standard dismissal—"You're so full of beans."—and handed the phone to Babs, who caught me up on the non-sports aspects of their world.

"Sonny's out on that nuclear submarine for a few months." The youngest of my three faux siblings had made a good career out of the Navy, steadily moving up through the ranks, despite his lack of a college education.

Babs told me Ruthie would go into labor with her first baby any time now. "A girl, in case you want to make sure your gift is the right color."

I'd known Ruthie was pregnant, but had not understood that I was expected to send a gift. Thus do mothers (even pretend ones) guide their sons to do the right thing. I dutifully asked for ideas, then made a mental note to stop by the baby store in Studio City the next day before going to Piper's.

Shane, the foster boy who had been a year older than me was in trouble with the law again. Minor league stuff, as always, but a reminder that not all alumni of CPS and foster care were as lucky as I had been.

Flossing pork shreds out of my teeth before bed, I looked in the bathroom mirror and wondered if I was up to the challenge of checkmating two men as powerful as Grant Tenninger and Hank Bledsoe. Dako had given me the lead on only a few cases when I worked for him and they were of the smaller, less dangerous kind—the ones unlikely to result in a death. Except for my first solo case, in which Marie Winters had been murdered, I'd handled only routine investigations, so I mentally went over my plan. It seemed solid, as long as everyone did exactly as I asked, but you never really know when the wild card will be thrown.

Dako would have to participate for it to work, but his recuperation necessitated limiting his role to a passive one: bait. I remembered observing him as he pulled all the elements of a case together with skill and patience, allowing me to see the cat's cradle as it was strung, not recognizable while it lay slack on his fingers. But when he finally yanked those strings, the intricate web snapped, trapping his prey.

Could I do that on my own? It wasn't as though Dako had so much faith in me he had chosen me for this case. I just happened to be the guy conveniently standing in the lobby after Laurel got his call saying he was being followed by two of Bledsoe's men. She had told me as much when I asked her. I was only an inadvertent proxy fighter in Dako's war.

I *did* have a dog in the race, though, as the only two people who could give me answers about John Valentine's murder were right at the heart of it. I intended to grill Tenninger about that night in Khavazhi's warehouse before I yanked the strings of my own cat's cradle and wrapped up his political ambitions for good.

Dako would still be around when the case was over, so I'd have all the information I'd gathered from the police report, Uncle Victor, Gayle Chandler and Deuce Tenninger before I confronted him. If he lied to me, I would know.

Rexanne stayed at Laurel's again that night, so the Sutterman sisters and I enjoyed a quiet, albeit messy, dinner of babyback ribs, barbequed pork sandwiches, corn on the cob and cole slaw. They had always been so good to me, treating me more like a grandson than a boarder, and I was ambivalent about possibly endangering them by asking for their help.

I should have remembered what hell-raisers the two had been when they were younger. Both jumped onboard as soon as I laid out my idea to them, a far cry from the skepticism I'd gotten from Laurel and Dako when I told them I had a plan.

Over blueberry cobbler, Kitty offered suggestions and improvements, and it touched me to realize how willing they were to come to my aid. I sharply felt the responsibility of their safety. "Are you *sure* you don't mind doing this?'

"Rick," Bitsy said, laying a fragile-looking hand on my arm. "Once a woman passes seventy she becomes invisible. Everyone ignores her except when she's slow writing a check at the grocery store cash register."

Kitty snorted. "Yeah, *then* they're all over you like stink on shit!"

"A poet, my sister," commented Bitsy dryly. Kitty was busy sketching on an unlined pad, however, and didn't fire back with her usual, charming: *up your nookie with a Girl Scout cookie.*

Somehow they had convinced me I was doing *them* the favor by allowing them to feel useful.

I drifted off to sleep with warm thoughts of Piper Lang, hoping she would slip into my dreams and play a preview of tomorrow's lunch date.

I fired the Kimber Custom again and again, familiarizing myself with my father's weapon as I holed-up paper targets at the range. Victor had been right; it was an impressive handgun. I modified my trigger-squeeze to match a tighter pull than the one on my Sigma until I could put every round in the kill-zone.

If we made it past the following night's fund raiser with the rest of the information we needed to put away Tenninger and Bledsoe, I'd bring the Kimber to my meeting with them. My Smith & Wesson would

be in Rexanne's hand and, although that would be
mostly for show, I intended to drive her to the range
first thing Monday morning and work with her until
I was sure she wouldn't shoot her own foot if things
went sideways in our face-off with the bad guys.
Laurel's obvious skill with a handgun made her the
better choice for that part of my plan, but I needed
those skills elsewhere. Besides, there were other
things Rexanne had proven she could do that Laurel
might have trouble with.

By 9:30 I had wiped out an entire gang of two-
dimensional criminals and the Kimber felt natural in
my grasp. I picked up the tuxedo, purchased a pink
blanket and a newborn-sized sleeper set, then drove to
Santa Monica to take a quick shower before I left for
Piper's. Drying off, I heard Cyndi Lauper in the bedroom, so I hurried to check my phone and saw it was
Piper calling.

"Couldn't wait till I got there to hear my sexy
voice, huh?" I teased.

"Rick, I have a callback!"

It didn't sound to me like an illness and she was
obviously excited, so I asked what that meant.

"The people I auditioned for yesterday want me
to read with one of the stars of the show who's in town
for the weekend."

"That's great! Congratulations. Want me to pick
up some vino on the way over so we can toast your
good news?"

"Well, uh, that's the thing. The casting director
scheduled the reading for an hour from now. I have to
cancel our lunch."

I was disappointed, but tried to make my voice
sound more hopeful than needy when I asked, "What
about afterwards?"

"There's no telling how long it will take. If I'm the only callback, I could be in and out of there in fifteen minutes, but if I have competition, they might read us in rounds, eliminating actresses one at a time all afternoon."

Landing the job was important to Piper, a big opportunity, and I did not want my own selfish disappointment to dampen her enthusiasm. "Listen, you go kick some callback ass, and we'll celebrate tonight." Only when the words flew out of my mouth did I remember the final performance of *Desire Trumps Will* was that night. Her silence told me I had put her on the spot, so I regrouped fast. "Well, not *tonight*, of course, but—"

"I'm working," she overlapped. "Maybe we can do it tomorrow night." Now it was Piper who had spoken before thinking. "Oh, wait—"

"I'm working."

They had told her to be in costume and makeup as the character she was reading for, so she said, "Gotta run. In a half hour I need to be an Alabama Kardashian, so I have to go kill some brain cells."

After we disconnected I realized I should have suggested something. Dinner on Sunday, a movie, anything. But she had been rushed and I had been too slow recovering from my disappointment.

With the middle of my day suddenly open, I drove to the office to follow up on any client inquiries. When I stopped at Lloyd's desk to get my mail, he was chirping into the phone about the wrap party after the performance that evening.

I wondered why Piper hadn't invited me, and my puzzled look prompted Jason to ask what was wrong when I met him on the landing on my way up to my office. Once I told him, he assured me there were a dozen reasons for an actress not to want a date hanging around at a wrap party.

"Wrap's the final chance interested producers, casting directors and agents can freely mingle with the whole cast, so actors are under pressure to 'work the room.' Plus, it'll be late and she'll be too tired to do a young stud like you justice," he joked, punching my arm.

Piper and I had done all right by each other on our first date, and that had been late at night after a performance, so I was not as reassured by Jason's words as he probably intended. I did take his advice, though, and ordered flowers to be delivered to the dressing room she shared with Lord Larkwhit's dowager mother and the tavern maid who nightly captured the heart of Master Will.

I went with what the florist assured me was his most dramatic spray of white orchids and wrote on the card: *Rare, special and beautiful to look at—much like you*. I signed with my first name only, because *fondly* sounded stiff, *yours* was presumptuous and *love* was not yet on the radar.

Rexanne called shortly after 5:00 to tell me she'd spent the afternoon with her dad at the hospice center and that he was grumpy and stomping around, but still willing to acquiesce to Laurel's preference that he stay put till Sunday. "Oh, and I'll be sleeping at Laurel's again tonight. She's been a wreck since Dad got shot and I think she needs me to be there."

Dako must have put that suggestion in Rexanne's head to keep her away from me, as I had seen little in Laurel's behavior since the shooting to indicate she was other than her normal, in-command self. I should have been relieved Rexanne wouldn't be around all evening to annoy me, but I resented the idea of Dako manipulating her that blatantly. "Anybody would be worried if their employer was almost killed," I said. "Good jobs are hard to find these days."

It was a rude and thoughtless thing to say, but if dealing with Rexanne had taught me anything, it was that I could wear rude and thoughtless like a comfortable old sweatshirt. She made a derisive snort into the phone. 'Wait, you think Laurel works for my father? It's the other way around, dilbert."

"Bullshit." My sharp-witted response provoked a weary sigh from Rexanne, a sigh that belonged to a much older, much more jaded person.

"Can you meet me somewhere for a drink?" she asked.

"You're not old enough to drink."

"Jeez, Rick, how many bowls of literal do you eat in a day? Drink means liquid, but it doesn't have to mean alcoholic liquid."

The Starbucks on Ventura in Studio City is less crowded at 6:30 P.M. than it is at 6:30 A.M., so we were able to commandeer one of the tiny tables along the wall. I stirred my coffee and Rexanne repeatedly poked a straw through something that appeared to consist solely of froth and sprinkles.

"Laurel was my mother's best friend in high school. In fact, she's the one my grandfather sent to LA to try to talk Mom into coming back to Dallas after she dumped her husband and left. Instead, Laurel was the one familiar face at Mom and Dad's quickie nups at the courthouse. She held my father's hand in the waiting room the night I was born, and a couple months after the divorce was final she followed him to California.

"My dad was apparently a real mess in those days. He was broke. He had gotten married on a whim to a girl pulling the exact same stunt. And for reasons I've never understood, he wouldn't go back to doing what he loved, which was being a cop."

Couldn't go back, I thought, but didn't verbalize. Rexanne was spinning a tale I had never suspected and I wanted her to continue uninterrupted, hoping I would learn something about Dako which tied into my father's murder.

She explained that Laurel had come from money. Banking wealth, not oil money, so her father's fortune was never as large as Harmon Richfield's, but she inherited half of it on her father's death when she was twenty-five.

Buying the successful investigative agency from a retiring PI who had worked many of the high-profile celebrity cases from the 1960s through the 1990s, Laurel hired Dako to run it and put the name Farona on the front door. "I think she did that in hope Farona would eventually be her last name, too, but my dad wouldn't marry her." Rexanne stirred and poked at her venti cup of sugar and spice, but it was clear she had lost interest in it.

"Did she love him?" I asked.

"Did. Does. And he loves her."

"Then what's the problem?"

A slump of the shoulders and another old-person sigh prefaced her response. "Money. He's never had any and his pride will not let him be the guy people think conned two different heiresses into marrying him."

"That doesn't any make sense. He's the heart of the agency. He's known and respected all over Los Angeles, which is why the biggest cases always go to him." I couldn't believe I was hearing myself defend Dako, but that wouldn't be the last surprise to come out of the conversation. "Even if he's only on salary, he's got to be doing okay financially."

"Oh, Laurel pays him as much as he'll let her, but he still never seems to have any cash. My mom used to joke that you could give him a thousand dollars at breakfast and by noon he'd have turned it into twenty bucks. He's one of those people who's not very good at managing money."

I had a different take on why Dako might never have gotten ahead financially, but I kept it to myself, instead asking Rexanne what time I should pick her up the following night.

"Laurel already booked a limo for us. She says it will stand out less than the Corvette." It made sense. We didn't want to call attention to ourselves and it might be harder to tail us if we were in one of a fleet of black Lincolns departing from the Beverly Hilton after the fund raiser.

A call came through from Piper as I was pulling into the Sutterman's driveway. I noticed the time and realized the curtain was about to go up, making me wonder if the orchids had inspired a last-minute proffering of an invitation to the wrap party. "Rick Valentine, swashbuckler for hire," I answered.

"Thank you for the orchids. They are perfectly lovely."

"As are you."

"So-o-o...I know you're working tomorrow night, but I hoped you'd be available to join me for a run at the reservoir in the morning."

The path around the Hollywood reservoir is a rigorous one and I didn't relish her seeing me dripping sweat, but I didn't want to wait until the following week to connect with her. Plus, an early morning run might lead back to her place. We set a 7:00 A.M. meet time at the head of the path.

The play's first-act music started up in the background, but I hated to let her go. "Hey, how'd your callback turn out?"

"It's down to two of us, but I think I have the edge. I invited the star and the producer to the show tonight, so I should get the part unless I trip over a firkin." A disturbing picture popped into my head, but then I realized I was confusing firkin with merkin. "I have to go, Rick. See you in the morning."

"Mañana, then."

Jason had been right. Being a civilian, I looked at the play as entertainment. For Piper it was a job she wanted to do well enough to land *more* work.

The good feeling about meeting her the next day lasted until the conversation with Rexanne replayed in my head and I wondered where all of Dako's money went. I had never seen him purchase a lottery ticket or bet so much as a dollar on a football game, he disdained drug use as much as I did, and his feelings for Laurel ruled out spending a bundle on ladies of the evening. When I originally took possession of the envelope, I theorized he was blackmailing someone, but Laurel had since persuaded me otherwise. Now I had to consider the possibility that *he* was the one being blackmailed all these years.

I hadn't found anything to indicate animosity between Dako and Tenninger prior to the night my father died, but there was a chance what happened in Khavazhi's warehouse was bad enough that Grant Tenninger could use it first to force Dako out of the LAPD, and then extort money from him long term. That possibility would explain Dako's single-minded drive to bring down the former chief of police, and it made me even more determined to get the truth from Deuce once I had the advantage in our upcoming showdown.

If my plan worked, that is.

On my way out to the car I realized the early morning air was colder than I had anticipated when I chose a short-sleeved tee-shirt to go with my sweat pants, so I returned to the house to snatch my gray hoodie from the back of a chair. Still shivering as I zipped it and slid behind wheel of the Corvette, I put the heat on low.

Piper was already stretching when I found her, one leg extended out, heel braced on the low log fence as she bent forward with her arms reaching for her propped-up foot. Even in the baggy track suit she looked good, but I knew not to interrupt a runner's warm-up with an uninvited hug. She gave me a quick smile, then straightened, bouncing lightly on her toes a few times before stretching her arms up over her head and leaning deeply, first to one side, then the other. I was mesmerized.

"Aren't you going to stretch?"

"Nah, I'm good."

She stepped close enough to touch her fingertips to my chest and said in her deep purr, "Yes, you are." Then she was off like a shot and I followed, hound pursuing fox, but with much more benign intentions if I caught her.

After the initial sprint, we settled into an easy pace and despite the fact that Piper was five inches shorter, her long legs matched my stride. Without the imminent probability of either one of us jumping the other's bones, our conversation remained relaxed, even as our muscles and lungs took on the challenge of the reservoir's track, which we would circle twice before coming back to the car park, a long run in which to learn more about each other.

At Piper's request for details about my family, I gave her a fast parental recap, leaving out that whole murder/suicide angle and only stating they had died when I was a kid. I didn't give her time to express sympathy, launching immediately into a description of the Carmichael family and how they had made me one of their own.

Her childhood was more the classic American story: blue-collar mom and dad, two brothers and a Golden Retriever named Peabo. Born and raised in Cincinnati, she left Ohio the week she turned eighteen to take a shot at Hollywood. "Between commercials, TV parts and the occasional modeling gig or boat-show hostess job, I've managed to eke out a living so far, but if I don't score something major in the next four years, I'll have to accept that it ain't gonna happen."

"Do you have a plan B?"

She smiled mischievously as she turned to me and said, "Yes. The same one every failed actress falls back on when she hits thirty. Bag a rich guy before your looks go."

We were walking the final quarter-mile by then, letting our heart rates come down as our breathing slowed. Impulsively, I stopped and grabbed her wrists, pulling her in closer. "That doesn't give me a lot of time to make my fortune," I said, understanding I had upped the ante. The moment was heavy with promise, with intimacy beyond what we'd already found in bed, so I wrapped my arms around her. She snuggled against my chest and pressed her face close enough to the side of my neck to deliver a series of soft kisses.

Piper shivered—maybe from the perspiration on her skin evaporating in the chill air or maybe from the emotional ledge on which we were both hesitantly balancing—and she slipped her hands into the pockets of my hoodie for warmth.

Almost instantly she leaned away from me. "And what is *this*?" she asked playfully, withdrawing something from my pocket and stepping back.

As soon as I saw she was holding the crumpled sheet of foil used to wrap the joints I'd fired at the notary's office, I tried to take it from her, but Piper danced out of my reach with a laugh, holding her prize aloft. To my horror, I saw the discarded condom was stuck to it.

Spinning to block my second lunge, she looked at her find, shrieking and dropping it when she, too, noticed the latex tube dangling like a dead possum's limp tail. "Eeuww!!" Her recoil from the disgusting object brought her up against me, her back connecting with my chest for only a second before she jerked away, looking first at me, then at the ground.

"It is not what you think," I said, but the loosely wadded foil had opened enough on contact with the dirt to spill out three half-burned joints, compounding what was already a crap situation.

"Must've been *some* party," she said coldly, then turned to run toward the parking area.

I picked up the obscene litter, jamming it into my pocket before taking off after her, but when I caught up, Piper wouldn't look me in the eye. I heard myself stumbling over an explanation that hardly made sense to me, so I understood when it failed to move her.

As she unlocked the door of her little white KIA, she gave me a last tearful glance and I hated myself for having made her feel used. She slammed the door while I stood helplessly, then she zoomed away as fast as four cylinders of Korean technology could go.

In the limousine on the drive to Laurel's house I checked my phone one final time, but my texts and voicemails to Piper throughout the day had gone unanswered and remained so now. I turned off the phone, knowing I'd need to pay full attention to the task at hand for the rest of the evening. Settling back against the soft leather seats, I considered what was about to happen.

I doubted there was a possibility of danger at the fund raiser itself, as Hank Bledsoe surely wouldn't want two apes like Zeke Martin and Bobby Chalk at his upscale function. But if I didn't handle my contact with him exactly right, there was no way to stop an ambush of the limo on the way home or retaliation over the next couple days. A lot hinged on my being able to play the right kind of sleaze. I had to come across as knowledgeable enough to be afraid of, but too dangerous to go after.

The rest of the scheme was up to Rexanne, and she had been annoyingly close-mouthed about how she would put the button on Hank's phone without his knowing it, much less how she would successfully retrieve it once it had served its purpose. I intended to use the short drive from Laurel's to the Beverly Hilton to take another run at Rexanne. Maybe this time I'd get more than, "Hey, trust me, dude."

She must have been watching from the window, because she was out of the house and walking to the curb before the driver had come to a full stop. I barely had time to open the door and scramble out before she paused and posed. "What do you think? Texas cleans up real good, huh?"

It was the understatement of the year. She was breathtaking. As she did a slow spin to give me the three-sixty view I was put in mind of a jewelry box Ruthie Carmichael had in her room. When I came to live with her family, the three boys had welcomed me with tours of their rooms and belongings—all of which they let it be known would be shared with me. The toys and games, trucks and Super Soakers made me feel at home in their boyworld, but it was Ruthie's jewelry box that touched the heart of the shell-shocked eight year old who had lost his mother less than two months earlier.

Taking me by the hand, she pulled me from the rough-and-tumble, walking me to her room. With a finger to her lips, she showed me her treasure. Ruthie lifted the lid, and a dainty ballerina rose to spin on a mirror pedestal to the tinkly notes of a piece of music I would much later come to recognize as Beethoven's "Für Elise." With both arms arced above her head and one slippered toe touching the knee of her supporting leg, the dancer spun gracefully in a tutu of periwinkle blue. All at once I had no use for squirt guns and trucks or any of the other macho toys down the hall. I needed my mother.

When I burst into tears, twelve-year-old Ruthie instinctively put her arms around me, shushing me gently until I recovered. She threatened hell-fire and a plague of cooties if any of the other boys even looked at her jewelry box, but I was allowed to enter her room, lift the lid and watch the twirling ballerina whenever I needed comfort.

Rexanne wore her LBD—which I had learned from Bitsy meant little black dress—rather than a tutu, but as she made her graceful turn, I once again felt the surge of emotion. Not the feeling of comfort I had taken from watching the little plastic dancer twirl to Bagatelle No. 25 in A minor, but a powerful caring instinct. I knew she had chosen black to appear older and more sophisticated, but Rexanne suddenly looked like a girl dressed in a woman's clothes, a vulnerable creature in need of my protection.

"You look beautiful," I managed to say, suddenly worried I was bringing a child into a battle she was too young for.

"Thanks. Fly cummerbund," she said, smacking my midsection with the back of her hand, breaking the spell before clambering into the limo.

Rexanne needed protection like a Great White needs soft food. We split up once we were inside the ballroom so Hank would not associate her with me after the fact, but I smiled and fake-listened to other guests near enough to her to step in if I had to.

She made her move after Bledsoe shook hands with a new arrival and pointed him toward the open bar. As the man walked away, Rexanne pushed in close to Hank. "Mr. Bledsoe? I'm Rexanne, Harmon Richfield's granddaughter? He's so sorry he couldn't be here tonight, but he gave me a check with a one on it and told me I could add as many zeros as my little heart desires!"

The name Harmon Richfield registered first on Hank's face, turning it into a doughy welcome mat. His second reaction was to the obvious charms of the perky dazzler with the Dallas twang she ladled on for his benefit. Mention of a check rounded out the trifecta, so there was no one in the room he wanted to focus on at that moment more than Rexanne.

"Well, aren't you the sweetest little Texas belle,"

he said, smoothly taking her hand in his. "How does a man as important as Harmon Richfield even know about an obscure LA construction guy like me?"

With her free hand Rexanne tapped his arm in coquettish admonishment, then left it there when she spoke. "Oh, don't you try any of that false modesty on me, Mr. Bledsoe—"

"Call me Hank. Please," he smarmed, releasing her other hand so he could cover the hand on his arm with his own in a manner halfway between avuncular and pervy.

"Granddaddy Harmon says you are a mover and shaker...Hank." Rexanne beamed up at him. "Why only last week he said to me, *mark my words, that man's going to be governor of California one day.*"

Basking in her attention, surfing the waves of his ocean-size ego, Hank Bledsoe was getting the socks charmed right off him. "Oh, I don't know about *that*," he said, obviously pleased, but with a self-deprecating laugh that sent a ripple through his spare chin.

Rexanne pulled away, putting her hands on her hips and speaking sternly. "What did I just say about false modesty, Hank? I find that a *very* unattractive quality in a man." She pouted her reprimand, but kept her sparkling eyes lasered in on him.

"Hank, could I introduce you to—"

That was as far as the distinguished gentleman with the silver mustache got before Bledsoe blew him off. "Later, Jim, I'm busy right now."

He turned his toad-like head back to Rexanne, who gave him a look of fascinated approval. "Now, *that's* the kind of confidence we Dallas girls like to see in our menfolk."

It was hard to guess which the old lecher wanted more, Harmon Richfield's check of many zeros or his granddaughter, and I tensed, thinking Rexanne had gotten in over her head.

Before Hank could suggest anything unseemly to his admirer, Rexanne squealed like a teenager. "Oooh! You know what we should do, Hank?" I had a pretty good idea what *he* thought they should do, but her idea was better. "We should take a selfie and send it to my grandfather!"

Opening her purse Rexanne prattled on. "Oh, crap on a cracker! I had to leave my phone in the limo 'cause this purse is so gosh-darn teensy. Is it okay if I use yours to send him a picture of us, Hank? Please, *please?*"

Beguiled, he fumbled the cell out of his jacket, but before he could hold it out to snap the selfie, Rexanne took it from him, cuddling against his side to distract him. "In real close, darlin'. I want grampa Harmon to see how political I'm getting to be."

Hank slipped his arm around Rexanne's waist, strategically sliding his sausage fingers up until they grazed the underside of her left breast. It took all my restraint to keep from stepping over and laying him out. Rexanne dealt with it much better. Rather than gagging or slapping his roaming hand, she leaned her head on his shoulder for the picture, then instantly stepped away from his repulsive touch, making it seem as if she only wanted to check the screen.

"Oh, you look so handsome! I'm going to shoot this to my phone so I can send it to my grandfather on the limo ride back to my hotel," she chirped, diddling the phone as if dialing. When Rexanne handed back the cell, she said, "You mind if I hit the buffet and grab a pound of your shrimp? I'm so hungry I could eat the ass-end out of a rabid squirrel and all these other nice folks are just dying to talk to you."

I could see he was trying to think of a way to keep her there, but Rexanne cute-handled the situation by raising up on tiptoes and whispering into Hank's ear, then giggling. He grinned like a besotted suitor as Rexanne gave his arm a quick squeeze and took off. I caught her eye, then ducked into an alcove. She headed toward the buffet, but soon as she saw Bledsoe engaged with other guests, she changed course and joined me.

"The button's in place, but I feel like I've been slimed. Ick, yuck and patooey!"

"What did you whisper in his ear?"

Rexanne slitted her eyes at me. "Why, Rick," she said, troweling on her over-the-top drawl. "Are you jealous?" And there she was, right back to her usual annoying self.

"I like to have all the pertinent data before I go in, that's all," I said like the stiff straight man in a comedy duo.

"The pertinent data is Hank will by *very* happy to see me when I return. Or did you forget I still have to retrieve the button? Now, if you'll excuse me, I wasn't kidding about starving, and that buffet has a half-cord of crustaceans with my name on it."

She walked away and it became my turn to watch for the chance to catch Hank alone. With Rexanne's departure, he had once again been swarmed by well-wishers and sycophants, so it was another ten minutes before I saw my opportunity. "Hey, Mr. Bledsoe, good to meet you," I said heartily, pushing in to extend my hand for a vigorous pump job. "My name is Sam and I'm close friends with two of your biggest supporters!" He flashed me his politician's smile until I leaned in and said, "Zeke Martin and Bobby Chalk."

I hadn't spoken loudly, but Hank's eyes darted

around to make sure no one had overheard. "Maybe we could speak privately," I suggested, steering him toward the alcove Rexanne and I had recently vacated.

"What do you want?" he asked, yanking his arm from my grip once we were hidden from view.

"A taste of that Playa del Rey land action."

His eyes betrayed guilt, while his lips sputtered protest. "I don't know what you're talking about!"

"No? Not even about those three off-shores? One in your name, one in Grant Tenninger's and the one you two hold jointly?" The mention of his partner's name and the secret accounts shocked him, I could tell. Hank was maybe sixty pounds overweight and had been glistening with sweat *before* I'd confronted him. Now moist beads stood out on his forehead like frog spawn.

"I'm going to call security," he bluffed.

"You do *not* want to do that, Hanky, because I know everything. Including the location of those two little insurance policies you and your buddy signed. Spoiler alert: they're in a notary's office in East LA."

He went all shaky on hearing that, putting one hand against the wall for stability. In a subdued, frightened voice, he asked, "What is it you want?"

"A meeting. You, me and Tenninger. I'll give you my terms, then you can decide if you want to do business with me or not." I took out a piece of paper on which I'd written the number of the disposable cell phone I'd picked up that afternoon. Hank took it, but stared daggers at me.

Slinging my arm around his shoulders familiarly, I led Bledsoe back out to the ballroom, chatting as though we were the best of friends. "I know you sent Zeke and Bobby to kill Farona, but they really porked the poodle on that one. Tell Tenninger I can take care of the Dako problem as part of the deal if you like."

"For Christ's sake, keep your voice down," Hank pleaded, as we ventured among the guests.

"See, Dako fancies himself some kind of white knight, looking to expose you two. Me, I'm only an enterprising lad who wants a modest piece of the action, so I'm rooting for you to pull this thing off." People were converging on him, so I pumped his hand and smiled like a bible salesman.

"You have a great night, Mr. B. And good luck at the polls."

Disappearing back into the crowd, I positioned myself to watch Bledsoe. As expected, he soon began working his way to the main doorway of the ballroom, always smiling, shaking every hand, but moving along smartly. A matron who looked like the test dummy for a Bulgari Bedazzler latched onto his arm and bent his ear at the entranceway, giving me the chance to observe his extrication and the direction of his escape. I got to the doorway in time to see Hank repeatedly hit the call button on one of the hotel elevators.

I'd checked earlier and knew he had taken a room at the Hilton for the night—the better to entertain any sweet young things he met, I assumed—so that is where he would seek privacy to call Tenninger. As soon as he ducked into the elevator, I went looking for Rexanne.

She stood in a small pod of people, holding a plate and nodding while a good-looking man around thirty spoke animatedly, but when I waved at her, she broke away from the group and came to me. "He's making the call," I said.

"How did it go?"

"Perfecto."

We had nothing to do until Hank returned and Rexanne could go back in for the button, so we tried to look like we belonged. Which meant engaging in party chat. I'm not good at party chat. Rexanne nattered about now having six more Twitter followers than her competition, despite May-Ann's desperate sideboob ploy, but then she shut up and it was apparently my turn to talk.

"Anyone punch you in the face while I was with Bledsoe?" I asked.

"What? No."

"Ah, then that must be cocktail sauce at the corner of your mouth." Like I said, not good at party talk.

She scowled at me, then dabbed at her lips with a cocktail napkin, giving up her plastic plate full of shrimp tails when the next busboy passed by. While I watched the doorway for Bledsoe's return, Rexanne scanned the room for celebrities.

"Hey, look," she said, tugging on my tux sleeve. "There's that actress from the play Kitty and Bitsy took me to."

I automatically turned to where Rexanne pointed, not registering her words until I saw Piper Lang. It felt as though I'd taken a kick to the gut, not because she looked like Aphrodite rocking a liquid gold gown, but because her arm linked casually through that of another man. Thirteen hours earlier she had walked out on me when she thought I'd been with someone else, but girls who look like her have always been able to replace guys like me with a snap of their fingers. Through the surge of anger, I realized Rexanne had spoken again. "I'm sorry, what did you say?"

"I said the man she's with looks familiar, but I can't place him."

I'd never seen the jerk before, but his type was familiar to me, too. Smug, successful businessman, the kind who can easily afford exquisite things. And in her shimmering golden dress, with a tumble of blonde hair grazing her bare shoulders, Piper was, indeed, an exquisite thing. She clung to the arm of the man, who had to be at least two decades older, and I wondered if she had decided to go after a rich husband four years ahead of schedule.

"Wait! I know who he is," Rexanne said excitedly. "He's that actor in the soap opera my mom watches. The billionaire industrialist who sold his trophy wife into slavery after she miscarried his brother's child. I wish I had my cell phone so I could tweet this. My followers would love it."

"Quick, look at me," I said, as I had seen Piper turning our way, almost as if she sensed my hostile glare. "Smile like you would at George Clooney."

Rexanne didn't even ask why. She immediately slipped her arm through mine and turned her eyes up to me, hitting the high beams as she did. Through lips frozen into a worshipful smile, she spoke stiltedly, swapping consonants like a sucky ventriloquist. "He's tretty old. Could I tretend you're Dradley Coot-ther instead? And why exactly an I suddenly your date?"

Sliding a hand over hers on my arm, I glanced up and saw the satisfyingly stricken look on Piper's face.

"I'll be back," I told Rexanne, pulling away and turning toward the bar. Piper had let go of her date's arm, but he was regaling a crowd of admirers and hadn't noticed. When Piper saw where I was heading, she whispered something in loverboy's ear, then began easing through the clots of people on a path parallel to mine.

We kept eye contact as best we could, although

waiters, guests and inconvenient columns interrupted often. I made it to the bar before her and asked for a Budweiser. A few seconds later I felt her presence next to me, but didn't turn to look.

"White zinfandel, please," she said softly to the bartender, as he set a foamy pilsner glass down in front of me. We both stared straight ahead, neither one of us having arrived with a plan. I breathed in her perfume, a fragrance laden with arousal power not derived from Calvin Klein's chemical artistry, but from my association of that scent with multiple rounds of unforgettable sex.

Piper whispered a thank-you when the glass of blush wine was set down on the bar napkin in front of her. Slender fingers grasped the stem of the glass, but didn't lift it to her lips. "I thought you were working tonight," she finally said. I heard neither accusation or apology in her tone, although I felt she owed me one or the other.

"And I thought *you* weren't," I shot back, meeting her eyes for the first time since we had gotten to the bar. For a second she looked as though she had been slapped, but then a weary resignation settled on her face.

Without rancor, merely stating it as fact, she quietly said, "You're a real asshole."

"Part of my charm, babe." Whether it was the dismissive *babe* or my unsubtle inference that she was sleeping with someone to get a job, Piper decided she had taken enough shit from me. She picked up her glass and walked away.

I had hoped for more when I came to the bar. A fight, maybe. Or a drink thrown in my face. Attacks and defenses on both sides that would have landed us in bed again. Make-up sex.

All I got was a beer.

And then, since I wasn't driving, a second one. I'm not really sure how much time passed or how many brews came aboard before Rexanne poked my arm and said, "I have the button."

"Huh?"

"The button. I got it back from Hank's phone." She gave me a close look. "What's wrong with you?"

I looked at her and, because she had made the mistake of not being Piper returning to apologize and say she loved me, I fell right back into rude and thoughtless. "You have a piece of shrimp between your front teeth." I said, none too soberly.

The second woman I'd verbally slapped that night hit back without hesitation. "Asshole!" she spat at me.

Yeah, that seemed to be the consensus.

"Rick, your pants are ringing."

Kitty's non sequitur dragged me up through an alcoholic miasma. My eyelids unstuck after a heroic upward tug of my eyebrows and the rippling clock face on my night stand coalesced into the numbers eight, four and five.

The rapping on my door sharpened, as Kitty tried again. "Did you hear me, Rick?" Your pants have gone off every few minutes since 8:00 and I think you should answer them."

Pants? I rolled onto one elbow and scanned the room. No pants. Then I heard a muffled ring-tone: *girls just wanna have fuh-uhn*.... It was coming from beyond the door, so I swung my legs free of the covers and tried to stand. Tried and failed. I sat down hard, hands gripping the mattress edge to steady me.

"I'll be right out," I croaked, the effort bringing up a sour, belching invoice for multiple beers on an empty stomach.

Cyndi Lauper had shut the hell up by the time I was vertical and had pulled on sweatpants, but if Kitty was right, she'd be warbling her brains out again any time, so I padded out to the hallway in bare feet, wincing at the retina-stab of morning light.

Kitty was gone, but Bitsy greeted me with a tall glass of something that looked like it had been wrung out of a loaded Pamper's.

"Drink this. It'll make you feel better."

"What is it?" I managed, taking the glass.

"Probably better you don't know. But I watched it raise Richard Burton from the dead after many a bender, so I'm sure it will help."

Cyndi started nagging again, so I followed her voice to the dismembered tuxedo scattered across the living room floor. While crossing to the singing pants, I read the crime scene. Jacket, bow tie, pleated shirt, cummerbund, shoes, pants and socks, in that order triggering the vaguest recall of a staggering strip-down last night as I made my way from the front door to my room. I had no memory of the ride home.

Careful not to spill Bitsy's hangover helper, I bent to retrieve my cell phone.

"Good morning, sunshine," Laurel's voice trilled.

I grunted in response. It was as eloquent as I could be at that moment.

"Yeah, Rexanne told me you got shit-faced last night."

With a giant word piñata I only broke open and parsed after hanging up, she congratulated me on a successful mission, informed me the button was downloading onto a flash drive, said she was on her way to fetch Dako from the hospice, and that the four of us were meeting at 11:00 to listen to the playback.

I had only two hours to resume human form, so I held my nose and downed the diapertini.

When I rang Laurel's doorbell a few minutes before 11:00 A.M., I was ninety-five percent, thanks to a shower, shave and the Huggies highball. The remaining five percent belonged to the throbbing, never-do-that-again lobe of my brain, and time alone would ease that.

Laurel was the only one firing on all cylinders that Sunday morning. Dako still moved stiffly, although his pallor had diminished, and Rexanne held tightly to the snit she'd taken on the night before.

I couldn't blame her. A pretty girl all dressed up for a party and feeling good about herself wants to be told there's food stuck in her teeth about as much as a guy who has stayed erect through thirty minutes of sexual acrobatics wants to hear his performance rated "fine." I would try to work in an apology before I left, although I wasn't sure anything short of groveling would satisfy her.

We gathered around Laurel's laptop to hear what the button had recorded. She was ready to fast-forward through Rexanne's initial charm offensive and my blackmail gambit, but Dako insisted on hearing it all.

"You don't get the true lay of the land by looking at only one hill," he pontificated. "And I want to know how you two did on your own before I put my life in your hands."

I couldn't fault him for wanting to evaluate his daughter's ability to operate well in a challenging situation, but I resented the implication that he still didn't trust *my* judgment after our three years of working together. Still, if my plan went kablooey,

Dako would be the recipient of Tenninger's first bullet, so I cut him some slack.

The button had begun picking up sound as soon as Rexanne peeled away its flexible port, so every twang-laced word of her conquest was heard by us. When other voices replaced hers, Dako signaled for Laurel to pause the playback.

"You did good, kiddo, but let me give you a tip." Instead of bristling the way she would have done had I been the one offering suggestions, Rexanne listened closely.

"Bledsoe's a moron, which is why he bought what you were selling, no matter how over the top it got. But, if it had been a savvier guy, let's say a snake like Tenninger, you would have been made in a flash. He may not have called you out on it at the time, but for damn sure he would have sent a couple clowns to kick the cute out of you before you had a chance to do him any damage."

"So, more subtlety, you're saying?"   Rexanne asked this without even a hint of the snottiness she invariably aimed my way.

"Yeah.   Try more Jessica Fletcher, less Jessica Rabbit.   Because unless you're trying to fool a 'toon, real is better."

He nodded at Laurel to restart the playback, so we heard a few minutes of cacophonous party patter and political blah-blah before my voice entered the audio scene.

I covertly kept my eyes on Dako as he listened, evaluating his nearly imperceptible nods of approval and the smile that made the Mona Lisa look like she was laughing her ass off.

When I spoke my departure line and party voices converged on Hank, Dako once again asked Laurel to pause. I braced myself for whatever criticism he was about to level at me, while Rexanne hung ready to enjoy watching me get schooled.

"You did good, kid," Dako said, looking me in the eye. Laurel tensed, and I assumed she also expected a lesson to follow. When it didn't come immediately, I prompted him, unwilling to let him extend the moment for drama.

"But?"

"But nothing. I couldn't have done better myself."

I felt my face burn. It was the most committed compliment Dako had ever given me, but instead of feeling pleased, I was embarrassed by my need to hear it. And humiliated knowing he could read every bit of that on my face.

Laurel diffused tension when she restarted the button's audio. More voices, including the cultured, high-pitched one I recognized as belonging to the jewel-encrusted matron who had waylaid Hank right before his exit.

Rexanne made gagging gestures on hearing Diamond Lil's impassioned pitch for the cause she hoped the future mayor would see fit to support.

"That sounds like it would cost a lot of money, Mrs. Boatwright," Bledsoe said.

"Oh, not really. My friends and I figure a mere fifty thousand dollars could put better clothes, shoes and accessories on every homeless person in Beverly Hills," the woman gushed. *"Maybe not Versace and Laboutin, but some of the lesser lights in design. My lord, even high-end Macy's would bestow a more prestigious profile on those unfortunates. Really, Mr. Bledsoe, do you think rags reflect well on our city?"*

"You have certainly given me something to think about, Mrs. Boatwright. Let me have my people get

back to you."

There was a thirty-second break before Hank's muttering voice said: *"Come on, come on, you worthless piece of shit."* Dako raised his eyebrow at me and I mouthed the word *elevator*.

Silence for another two minutes, then the beeps of a cell phone keypad. The third ring was interrupted by a voice I had been hearing for two months on the radio saying, "I'm Grant Tenninger and I damn well approve this message!"

We all leaned in, hoping to hear what we needed to make our case airtight.

  *—**Tenninger.***
  —Grant, Hank. We have a problem.
  —Yes?
  —Some little prick just absconded me at my fund raiser and—
  —Accosted.
  —What?
  —Unless the little prick threw you over his shoulder and carried you off, you mean accosted, not absconded.
  —You want to play thesaurus right now?!? That cocksucker knows everything about the Playa del Rey deal! And I mean fucking everything!
  —Not possible. Who was he?
  —Tall, skinny kid named Sam something. And I don't give a bat's butt-hole how impossible you think it is, he knew it all. The off-shores, our little shell game with the property taxes—
  —Jesus!
  —Fuckin' A. The kid even knew about those "special" documents we signed. Knows right where they are.

—*Well, Farona's the only one who figured out something was up at Arroyo's place, so he must've passed the information on before he croaked.*

—*Uh, yeah, about Farona. My boys may have fucked up on that.*

—*Shit, he's still alive?*

—*Yes, but he's circling the drain at a hospice out in Canoga Park*

—*I don't care if St. Peter's dragging him through the pearly gates by his dick, get somebody in there to step on his fucking air hose.*

—*Been there, tried that, but he's guarded twenty-four-seven. Look, if it makes you feel any better, this guy Sam offered to do Farona as part of the deal.*

—*And what kind of deal does is he asking for?*

—*A cut. He couldn't give a shit we screw LA out of a hundred mil, he just wants a taste of the action. Gave me a number where to reach him and says he wants a meeting.*

—*Okay, here's what we're going to do. Let him sweat it out a couple days, then set it up. All friendly and businesslike. He comes alone, we come alone.*

—*Is that smart?*

—*Fuck, no. We'll show up with guns and your two enforcers. If he's got any proof, we confiscate it and subtract him from the equation. So make nice on the call, let him believe we're squirting in our shorts and willing to make a deal.*

—*Okay. What are you going to do?*

—*Call that dumb bastard Arroyo and have him destroy those two statements.*

—*But then I got no insurance if I'm elected and you shaft me on the deal.*

—*Yeah? Well, neither do I if I'm the mayor and it's you who decides to go off the reservation.*

—So...uh, how do we handle this? I mean, to cover ourselves in case somebody sprouts a wild hair up his ass?

—Tell you what, Hank. One of us fucks the other one, let's agree the fuck-ee puts a bullet in the fuck-er and be fucking done with it!

"He eats with that potty mouth?" Rexanne broke the silence after the two men concluded their heart-to-heart.

"Let's ignore their fucking language and look at what they handed us on a platter," Laurel said. "Rick? Did you spot it?"

"Property taxes. I never mentioned them."

"Didn't I tell you he was a moron?" Dako said to her, and it took me a second to realize he was talking about Hank.

"What else?" Laurel asked me. I quickly went through everything I had heard, seeking another piece of the puzzle.

"Shell-game. Hank used the word shell-game."

"The moving around of something so quickly and so smoothly that the eye can't follow," said Dako.

"Now you see it, now you don't," I responded. Laurel was smiling proudly at me, but Rexanne looked back and forth from her father to me, a confused observer at Wimbledon.

"So, a little sleight of hand with the property taxes on the future development in Playa del Rey," Dako said. "Money to be used to prop up the pension plan and make the new mayor look like such a hero no one will ever dare question his decision to buy the property."

"I get that it has something to do with property tax," Rexanne interjected. "But what? We don't have any way to figure that out." Dako smiled. Laurel smiled. I was in the dark, but smiled so as not to reveal that fact. "Do we?" Rexanne asked, not so sure of herself anymore.

"Actually, we do," said Dako, immediately putting his hand up practically in my face. "No, Rick, let me tell her."

I shrugged my assent. Although I had no idea where he was going, I was happy he thought I did.

"Hank mentioned a figure—one hundred million dollars—and I doubt it was arbitrary. We research the tax rate on developed property in PdR, then play with time and numbers to see if we can figure out their scheme."

"You and I can do that," Laurel said. "While Rick waits for Hank's call and puts the finishing touches on his plan."

"Yeah, the plan," Dako said, and I braced myself for criticism. I knew he wasn't thrilled to let me take the lead on this, but he was enough of a pragmatist to know he wasn't yet back to full capacity. He had no choice but to take second chair. He also hated that Rexanne would be at risk during the showdown. Dark eyes boring into me, Dako finally spoke. "Do me one favor. Don't get my kid killed."

"Lunch!" Laurel called out. "Rexanne, come help me throw together some sandwiches."

Things went quiet once the women left the room. It was the first time Dako and I had been alone since I'd confronted him with the snapshot, and we didn't have much to say to each other until I decided to capitalize on the private moment to ferret out more information about my parents. "Did my father know?"

"About Zoë and me?"

"No, the Superbowl over-and-under that year." I

was poking the bear, but the bear didn't seem to want a fight.

Very softly, he said, "In the end, yes; he knew."

Dako's pallor returned after lunch. Moving from the hospice and participating in the long work session had worn him out more than he would admit, but all of us could see he needed rest. He wanted to be driven to his own apartment, but both Laurel and Rexanne insisted he stay at home with them.

When I saw how slowly he got up from the table, the way he leaned on Laurel as she walked him to the bedroom, I reminded myself that only seven days had passed since he'd been shot and undergone abdominal surgery. Most guys would still be in the hospital begging for pain meds.

"Hey, Rick?" Rexanne said.

"Yeah."

"I know who Jessica Rabbit is, but who's Jessica Fletcher?"

"Google her." That must have deflected the fact that I didn't know either, because she moved on to her next question.

"Are you sure you need my dad for your plan?" I could tell she didn't think her father was ready to dive back into regular PI work, much less the risky LARP I was about to stage.

"All he has to do is sit in a chair. No fighting, no shooting, I promise."

She had apparently moved beyond my boorish behavior of the night before, so I thought I'd use our few minutes alone to talk about her own part in upcoming events. I needed her ready, since Bledsoe's call could come through any time and I would have only so much say in scheduling the meeting. If she made one mistake, I'd end up in a grave next to John and Zoë, not exactly the family reunion of my dreams.

"Have you ever fired a gun?" I asked Rexanne. She looked at me like I was seriously impaired.

"I'm from Texas, dude. I carried concealed to my prom."

I checked my phone before driving home to Santa Monica, but there wasn't anything from Piper. Pushing all the confusing thoughts about her out of my mind, I carefully went over my to-do list. First on it was setting up a lunch with Justin, Jason and Pat. I made three calls as I drove, and when I was done they had all agreed to meet me at 12:30 the following day at Casa Vega, a Mexican restaurant on Ventura that's been around since The Bronze Age. The calls to Cal Cooper and Moonbeam Fink would have to wait until the meeting was scheduled.

Rexanne had said she would go with me to the firing range the next morning, after I assured her I was not challenging her skills, but only wanted to familiarize her with my Smith & Wesson Sigma. Gun snobs often refer to the SW40 as a Glock-wannabe, sneering at its polymer frame, but the grip is comfortable in my hand, and the slightly shorter-than-average barrel gives it an edge on staying hidden when it needs to be. Plus, the weight is only a skosh over one and a half pounds, so I knew it would be easy for Rexanne to handle.

I would be bringing my father's blue-steel Kimber to the party.

I put in a call to Bitsy to ask what she needed picked up for dinner. With halibut filets, two lemons and a bouquet of parsley in my hands, I headed to the fifteen-items-or-less line, where I saw a familiar face. Normally my eyes skip right past that rack of small-format periodicals offering one hundred slow-cooker recipes or foolproof ways to get a bikini body by summer, but the insolent face displacing a third of the cover on one of the soap opera mags belonged to Piper's date from the night before.

I understood that punching a magazine in a grocery store would be childish, but his dignified, silver sideburns and snow-bright teeth pissed me off bigly. The former put me in mind of The Bruce's handiwork, the latter the skill of some Hollywood dentist a guy like me would never be able to afford. After we tried to stare each other down for a minute, I yanked his smarmy face from the rack and shoved it up against the paper-wrapped fish.

Whiff *that* you smirking jackass.

As I set my five items on the conveyor belt, I saw the man in line ahead of me take notice of the soap magazine, then glance over at me with what I interpreted as judgmental amusement.

"For my grandmother," I said, nodding toward the publication. "Can you believe women read that garbage?"

The guy gave me a whaddya-gonna-do shrug of commiseration, but I was still relieved when Smirky McShowbiz went head first into a plastic grocery bag.

After dropping off the other items in the kitchen, I took the magazine to my room to read about the man Piper had slept with to land a part on his show.

Examining his face more closely, I upped my age assessment. Factoring in makeup, flattering lighting, Photoshop and probable surgical tweaking, that mug belonged on someone closer to sixty than my previous estimation of mid-to-late forties. The headline read:

Will Damian's Past Come Back To Haunt Him?

Before opening to the article, I grabbed a marker, blacking-out those two, too-perfect front teeth. The hillbilly touch leveled the field of competition a bit, so I added a couple horns at the top of his flawless hair. Satisfied I had reduced my rival to a caricature, I opened the rag and found the article on him.

There was almost nothing in it about the actor, whose name was Dylan Rainer, but lots of dirt on Damian Caldwell, the rich fiend who twenty years ago discovered the baby his third wife carried belonged to his brother, Carson.

After staging the hot air balloon accident which caused Samantha to miscarry, Damian bided his time for seven months before surprising his wife with a trip to the Middle East, a vacation from which she never returned. Unbeknownst to Damian, Samantha was already two months preggers with his *own* child when he sold her to a swarthy man in a filthy burnoose for the price of a Grand Slam breakfast at Denny's.

As Damian reeled from the news that somewhere in the UAE he had a grown son, my stomach rumbled. I carried the magazine to the kitchen to get something to eat.

Laying the thing open and face-down on the counter, I went to the refrigerator. As I poked among the Tupperware containers for a snack to hold me till dinner, I heard Kitty's voice.

"Who put horns on the faygeleh?"

I turned from the fridge and found her looking at my cover art.

"On the what?" I asked.

"Faygeleh. Yiddish word for poofter."

Kitty misread my shocked expression as one of incomprehension, so she clarified further. "You know, gay. In his case, DC gay."

"DC?" I repeated stupidly, as the god-awful realization descended on me.

"Deeply closeted."

Appetite suddenly gone, I closed the refrigerator door and asked, "Are you sure?"

"Oh, yeah. Back in '79 or '80 I did makeup on the miniseries that gave Dylan Rainer his first major role as a heart-throb." She told me about the young male lead horning after the wardrobe master, while pretending interest in his female co-star for the benefit of the tabloids. My mind was elsewhere.

I knew the term *beard*, although it was becoming less relevant in a society where out-and-proud was now more ho-and-hum than holy-and-shit. Nobody aside from the decidedly un-Christlike Christians of the extreme religious fringe gave a flip anymore about other people's sexual orientation, but I could see how an older actor who had made his living embodying female fantasies might choose to keep his privates' prefs private.

Piper hadn't slept with him, she had provided camouflage. My mistake was reading the picture in front of me exactly as presented, instead of doing what Dako always advised: reserving judgment until the brush strokes and signature have been authenticated.

Why hadn't she said something at the bar the night before, I wondered. Maybe because I had made Rexanne give me a lovestruck gaze while I held her hand possessively.

I did the math. Condom plus weed added to hot younger date totaled up to the kind of man you don't waste your time on.

I had faulted Piper for interpreting the contents of my hoodie pocket as prima facie evidence of a crime—against the heart, if not the law—then done exactly the same thing to her when I saw her with Dylan Rainer. Given time, maybe we could laugh at our misreads and move on.

The only problem? I now understood Piper was innocent, so I could hope for a reconciliation. But as far as she knew, I was screwing around with another woman, which might make her less receptive to a kiss-and-make-up. Not sure how to put things right and assuming any flowers I sent would wind up in a trash can, I focused on my plan instead, falling asleep as I went over details in my mind.

The burner rang Monday morning on the dot of 7:00 and I picked it up without speaking. After a few seconds I heard Hank Bledsoe's voice.

"Sam?

"Yeah."

"My associate and I are willing to discuss your preposition. Come alone to my office tomorrow night. The address is—"

"No can do, Hanky," I interrupted.

"I thought you wanted this."

"What, a trap? A couple'a mooks jumping me when I step over the threshold?"

A nervous chuckle preceded his next statement. "Why would he and I do something like that? We're businessmen, not *gangstas*."

"And you two have a hundred million reasons to cut me out of your deal in the most permanent way possible."

It was risky, naming the amount, but it worked. After a mental scramble in which Hank probably tried to figure out how I could know that particular factoid, he realized he wasn't the one calling the shots. His attitude suddenly became conciliatory.

"Sam, you're reading me all wrong. We *want* to do business with you, especially if you were being straight when you said you could take care of that little problem of ours."

He meant, of course, the Dako Farona problem. "Good, then we're all on the same papyrus," I said. He had suggested a meeting the following night, but I wanted to give Dako another few days' recovery time. Plus, Laurel had been concerned about detonating our bomb too early and having the fallout settling before next Tuesday's election.

Bledsoe wanted tomorrow, so I countered with Thursday; we compromised on Wednesday. Midnight suited both of us, as nobody in this gavotte wanted outside eyes witnessing our dance moves. I insisted on naming the venue.

"That's bullshit."

"I'm outnumbered dos to uno at the get-go, and I'm guessing you and your partner will be bringing dates, so I name the place."

"Oh, like you're gonna show up all by your lonesome?"

"My plus-one will be Farona, trussed up like a Christmas turkey."

A dismissive snort. "Yeah? I heard he was as good as dead anyway."

"You heard wrong. And if you want to check it out, call that hospice in Canoga Park you're so interested in. As of yesterday morning Dako Farona is no longer partaking of their pureed food and lime Jell-O hospitality."

"You're saying you've got him?" Alert, hopeful.

"I'm saying I can *get* him. Along with a certain envelope you've been chasing."

Silence while Bledsoe weighed his options and realized he didn t have any. "All right, Sam, you win. Midnight on Wednesday my associate and I show up alone—"

"And unarmed."

"And unarmed," he echoed. "What's the address?"

I laughed. "Get serious, Hanky. I'm not giving you time to post your gunsels on the perimeter. I intend to walk out of the that meeting a rich man with no more metal in me than the fillings in my molars."

I told him I would text the address at 8:00 P.M. on Wednesday and, after some grumbling, he caved and hung up.

I assumed it would take them less than an hour to put eyes on the Gingerbread House after I texted Hank, so by the time they saw me arrive with Dako around 10:00, they'd feel confident I really was naive enough show up alone. If the eyes belonged to Zeke Martin and Bobby Chalk, they might remember the address from their futile search for the incriminating envelope and tell their boss my real name. I'd let that work for me, too. The greener they thought I was, the more likely they were to get sloppy.

I got out of bed feeling good. Ever since I had heard Dako growl the Mickey Spillane terms years earlier, I had wanted to work mooks and gunsels into a conversation.

I told Kitty and Bitsy the when and where of our proposed op over breakfast. Laurel had given me two grand in cash on Sunday to pre-pay expenses, but the Suttermans insisted on bankrolling their own necessities. The excitement of participating in a sting had taken twenty years off each of them and I had another glimpse of how cool they must have been as two young, single women in Hollywood's heyday.

"We need to go shopping," Kitty told me. "But Rexanne still has my hooptie."

I had too much to do that day to chauffeur them. Plus, the 'Vette was a two-seater, so I called the shop where Rexanne had left my Wrangler and was told I could pick it up anytime.

"Can either of you drive a stick?" I asked.

Bitsy aimed a confident smile my way and said, "Sweetheart, when I was on location for *The Bridge on The River Kwai*, I took Sessue Hayakawa joyriding in a goddamn Sherman tank. I think I can handle your itty-bitty Jeep."

While the twins got dressed, I called Laurel to tell her the meeting was set and to ask if she and Dako were making progress on the hundred-million dollar question. She told me she was waiting for the tax assessor's office to open so she could confirm rates for Playa del Rey to factor into the rest of what she and Dako had.

"Oh, and Rexanne did some background on that organization that certified the sixty acres of wetlands were dead."

"Does it look hinky?" I asked.

"Like Trump's forehead pelt."

She wanted me to come over and work with Dako, but I had a busy morning ahead of me, so I told her I would swing by late in the afternoon.

Once I'd driven Kitty and Bitsy to the body shop and left them with the Wrangler, I took off for the Gingerbread House. I didn't need to meet Justin, Jason and Pat at Casa Vega until 12:30, so I would have plenty of time to take advantage of that gift certificate for a massage from Moonbeam Fink.

I tipped her a hundred bucks, as the "extras" I requested went beyond the parameters of the one-hour incall Rexanne had paid for, and the Moonster was beaming when she opened the door to let me leave. The money came out of Laurel's advance on expenses, so it hadn't cost me a dime to feel the kind of relief I did at that moment.

Turned out to be short-lived.

Moonbeam leaned back seductively against the door frame, forcing me to angle sideways to avoid brushing her substantial breasts with my shoulder as I passed by.

"It's been a pleasure doing business with you," she murmured, before slinking back into her lair and closing the door.

When I turned, I saw Lloyd staring at me with a pained look. But it didn't come close to the look of pain on the face of Piper Lang as her eyes went from mine to the sign on the door behind me.

"I'm sorry, Mr. Valentine," Lloyd whined. "I didn't know what to tell her."

Her was already out the front door by the time I recovered enough to call out her name and give chase.

She was fumbling with her car keys when I caught up with her in the lot. "Piper, wait!" I made the mistake of putting my hands on her shoulders to bring her around to face me. She jerked away as though she had received an electric shock, and I held up both hands in capitulation.

"Don't you touch me!" she hissed.

"I know that looked bad, but—"

"Ya *think!?*"

"Please, Piper, let me expl—"

"Exactly how many women are you currently screwing, Rick?"

"Only you!" Epic fail, born of frustration. "Wait, no, I didn't mean it like that."

She opened the car door, but I couldn't let her leave with everything so wrong between us. I pulled her to one side by her arm and closed the KIA door with my other hand. This time she didn't jerk away from me, but, with her back against the car, she raised her face defiantly and I unhanded her. There were tears in her eyes.

"Let me start with the obvious. I know you didn't sleep with Dylan Rainer."

"That makes two of us who know," she responded sarcastically. "Well, three, if you count Mr. Rainer."

"But I didn't know on Saturday night. And when I saw you with him, I went all direwolf and made my co-worker pretend she was my date."

Piper mulled over what I had revealed, then spoke softly—no purr, but no anger either. "Did it bother you to think I was with another man?"

No sense pretending. I had probably lost her anyway. "It hurt like hell squared."

She waited for me to put it together, but when I didn't, she spelled it out. "That's how *I* felt watching jailbait look at you like you were at the top of her dreamy list."

I was pretty sure each of us had just gone on record about our feelings for each other, so I explained who Rexanne was, then attempted to explain away Moonbeam. Piper listened without response, but the weary look of disappointment was on her again, although she didn't flinch or pull away when I brushed back a lock of blonde that didn't need brushing back.

"Anyway, I only came here today to say good-bye."

"Why? Am I kidding myself that this feels as important to you as it does to me?"

"No," she said softly, looking at the ground.

"Then why? Piper, tell me, please."

"Saturday afternoon I found out I got the part."

"That's great news, congratulations. Why don't we celebrate? I'll wrap this case on Wednesday night, and then—"

"They shoot in New York."

I must have looked stupified, or merely stupid, so she dumbed it down for me.

"I have to go to New York for the show."

The ground went earthquaky. "For how long?"

"It's an eight-week story arc, but the producer said it might turn into a regular role if things work out."

I said all the right words: how happy I was for her, how much she deserved the break, but there wasn't much heart in it. "When do you leave?"

"I have a flight out of Burbank at 7:30 Saturday morning."

She rose up on tiptoes to plant a chaste kiss on my cheek, and I watched the woman of my dreams get in her car and drive out of my life.

I waved off Lloyd's flustered apology when I entered the Gingerbread House. "I had no idea you and Piper—"

"Not your fault, Lloyd."

I trudged upstairs, trying to shake off a feeling of desolation. I may not be the most self-aware person on the planet, but I knew enough to realize I'd been struggling to feel part of something bigger ever since my happy childhood got rewritten by Charles Dickens.

Ergo, my attachment to the Carmichaels, who, by some miracle, still considered me one of their own almost a decade after any formal responsibility toward me had expired. And you didn't have to be Sigmund freakin' Freud to interpret my relationship with the Sutterman sisters as more than the kind dictated by living on opposite sides of a rental agreement.

Realistically, though, the only way I was ever going to be part of a genuine family was by making one of my own. Marriage, kids, the whole enchilada. And the only way I was ever going to experience the father/son time I had missed out on was to let go of the son fantasy and step up to the father role. For a twenty-seven year old who still got referred to as "kid" by the likes of Hank Bledsoe and Dako Farona, those were some heavy realizations.

My few months of professional independence had sharpened the awareness of my isolation, made me understand I didn't carry the lone-wolf gene that made fictional guys like Philip Marlowe and Jack Reacher so appealing. Embarrassing as it was to admit, I needed someone. And maybe more importantly, I needed someone to need me. Piper Lang had felt like that special person from almost the first moment I spoke with her.

Putting those unsettling thoughts aside, I looked around my office. Twelve feet by twelve feet didn't provide a lot of space and I'd be playing to an SRO crowd Wednesday night, so I did some rearranging. The spindly-legged sofa table I used as a credenza went out in the hall, flush to the wall between my office and Pat's small recording studio. I measured the top and called Rexanne.

"'Sup?" she answered.

"Do you have time to go get something for me today?"

"Abso-tootly. What do you need?"

Ever since Rexanne had found out she would be

packing hardware for the sting, she'd become less touchy. She no longer felt she was being relegated to a supporting role. Hell, for all I knew, she might've thought she was calling the shots.

"I need a quarter-inch thick piece of foam rubber, eighteen inches by four feet."

"Armholes? Or is this *not* for one of the fifty shades?"

"And some kind of narrow table cloth or runner to conceal it with a bit of overlap," I said, ignoring her jibe. Maybe I was maturing a little, too.

"Any particular pattern or design?"

"Nothing fussy, nothing that calls attention to itself."

"Got it. Bland as a virgin's rep." She said she would add it to her to-do list and we hung up. When I checked my watch I saw there was still time to make a short call to Cal Cooper before I had to leave for lunch at Casa Vega.

By 3:00 P.M. I felt like Santa Claus after he's emptied out his sack. Cal was delighted with his gift, Bitsy and Kitty were giddy as teenagers, and Jason, Justin and Pat were thrilled about their role in my plan.

As promised, I drove to Laurel's house after lunch to talk things over with Dako and her.

"Rick needs to wear a vest," she told him.

"They'll frisk him first thing. If he's sporting Kevlar, Deuce will smell a rodent and go postal. Same reason he isn't going to wear a wire."

"So, you don't care if he takes a bullet?" Laurel challenged.

"Uh, you two *do* remember I'm here in the room, right?"

"Sorry," Dako said. "She and I have been hashing out strategy by ourselves so many years I forgot you'll be waving from the vanguard float in this parade."

He looked better and was moving more like his old, grizzly-tough self, so I wasn't worried about his safety. Rexanne and Laurel, however, were still my concern. "Okay," I said. "I do want two KVs, but not for me. You have?"

"Not on hand," Laurel responded. "But I can get them tomorrow."

"I'll need your Colt Commander and, Dako, one of your ankle pieces. After Tenninger relieves me of those two, he should relax and assume he's golden."

"And you'll be bare-ass in a room full of vipers," observed Laurel.

"Nah, Rick's gonna feel-up Deuce's whole posse, aren't you, son?" Even while telling Laurel how savvy I was, he had to throw in that bunt of patronization.

"When I'm through patting them down, one or two of those ol' boys are going to think they're in love." Tough guy. Coming right back at you, Dako.

When I outlined for Laurel what her job was Wednesday night, she nodded approvingly. She would also be wheel man for the rented transport van I asked her to pick up, as Rexanne was too young for Avis and would be deployed elsewhere.

"Why do you need Laurel's Colt?" Dako asked. "I thought you bought yourself an SW-40."

How did he know what my carry weapon was? "Rexanne will have the Sigma. I'll get stripped of the Colt and whatever fun-size you supply me, but I have a hush-piece at the ready."

He grunted, whether from concern about Rexanne being pulled into the action or approval of my having an extra piece on hand, I couldn't tell. "So, while everyone else hustles their butt off, I sit like a lump?"

Accustomed to being the guy in charge, Dako wasn't loving the subordinate position and all I could think was *tough tater tots, pal.* Time to do a little patronizing of my own. "You're the hub of the whole ploy, pops. The central dude around whom all else revolves."

He must not have expected me to match his dismissive tone, because he winced when he heard "pops," a surprising tell on being reminded he was getting up in years. I half-expected him to retaliate with "whippersnapper," but he stayed silent.

Only now do I realize my failure to read the scene accurately, to remember how precise Dako's language was the whole time I worked for him.

That Monday afternoon, forty-eight hours before I was to command my first major operation, he hadn't been patronizing me; he'd been relinquishing power. Far from complaining about his reduced role, Dako was passing the baton in the most face-saving way he could.

I had not set him to shivering in his boots with my condescending attitude, but I had managed to hit him where he lived. It would have been a nice thing to realize *before* I shot him.

Bitsy told me on the phone to get my own dinner that night. She and her sister would be busy with prep, so I enjoyed my ten-thousandth Fatburger sitting in the Corvette in the shadow of the Beverly Center, trying to apply logic to the situation with Piper.

I'd known her less than two weeks. Realistically, how important could this connection between us be? Was I going to let a couple of rolls in the roses—

otherwordly good as they may have been—dictate my future? Cause me to make some irreversible decision?

I remembered Babs taking me to the dentist to have a wisdom tooth pulled when I was fifteen. Afterwards, I probed the socket with my tongue for a week, despite the pain it caused. Why? Because I was a jerky kid? Or because it is human nature to rake over our most uncomfortable issues again and again, to monitor the hurt so as to better appreciate its absence in the future.

Because I needed clear thinking over the next few days, I stopped mentally poking around in the pain of Piper's leaving. Without cheapening it to the level of 'there's plenty of other fish in the sea,' I did know I was still young. There would be others and, someday, one of them would be *the* one."

So, why was a voice in my skull taunting, "You keep telling yourself that, Jack."

Tuesday was a welcome blur, a diversion from any consideration of the almost gone girl. A dozen phone calls reassured me everyone involved in the plan knew what was at stake if he or she failed to follow protocol. I'd even come up with a trigger word in case things went sideways and I had to abort to keep someone alive. At least on my team. Deuce, Hank and the troglodytes were on their own.

Dako and Laurel came up with a theory on the hundred-million-dollar puzzle. They figured out what the savings would be if the builders of the ambitious development in Play del Rey weren't required to pay property taxes—a waiver that was within the power of the mayor's office, but only if the property was owned by the county, and for a period of no more than ten years.

"The mayor's initial sales pitch to the electorate will be that he's going to bring in ten million a year in lease revenue to shore-up the pension plan," Laurel explained. "What the voters won't know is the county will be losing twice that amount in tax revenue after he issues the waiver."

If Dako and Laurel were right, the big swindle would line the owners' pockets three ways. First, with the nearly twenty million bucks they'd make from the low buy price and high sale price of the original sixty acres; second, with a fat skim off the two billion in construction costs; and, third with a net savings of ten million a year after making a lease payment half the size of their legitimate tax bill.

If they sold the property to some unsuspecting billionaire before their decade of tax-coasting expired, they'd each walk away with more than Puerto Rico's annual GDP.

"There may be some tweaks and wrinkles we haven't grokked yet," Laurel said. "But those are the rough parameters."

Wednesday morning I woke up calm, which surprised me. I had expected either a case of the jitters or a rush of confidence, but what I had was stillness, the kind I had so often seen descend on Dako right before he went into a hot zone. A lot of people were depending on me, and I was counting on a few other people underestimating me.

I stayed away from the office, sat in my room cleaning a gun that didn't need cleaning—my father's Kimber. No calls came in and I sent nothing out. Maybe, if Piper had texted or phoned.... But she hadn't. No, everyone sank deeply into their individual pre-storm lulls, even her, packing and planning her splashy soap debut straight ahead.

I concentrated on the weapon that had killed my parents, my mother directly and my father indirectly when he took it off Hamid Khavazhi for that split-second. I broke it down, oiled it, put it back together, wondering what had fatally distracted my father in such a tense confrontation. Hoping Grant Tenninger would give me the answer. Dako had already given it to me, only I didn't realize it at the time.

I texted the address of the Gingerbread House to Hank Bledsoe's number at 8:00 P.M. Kitty and Bitsy were long gone by the time I left Santa Monica to pick up Dako in Beverly Hills. Big as he was, he had to stoop, twist and slide to get himself onto the leather seat, and I suddenly saw how uncomfortably close to each other we would be for the drive over the hill to Sherman Oaks.

Halfway up Coldwater Canyon Dako broke the silence. "Don't let Deuce get in your head."

"Not planning to."

"Yeah, nobody *plans* to," he muttered, more to the passenger-side window than to me.

Silence again until I crossed over Mullholland and nosed down toward The Valley.

"What I mean is you can't underestimate him. Deuce knows *exactly* where to aim for maximum damage."

Yeah, Dako, I'm thinking. *He's a real badass, but I'm ready for him.*

I hit the turn signal a half-block before Ventura Boulevard and Dako, like a kid who can't stop picking at a scab no matter how much it bleeds, comes at me one last time.

"The important thing, the *most* important thing is that you don't take your eyes off him when he runs his game-blade through your guts. Take the pain and stay focused." I suspected he was regretting his own past behavior more than worrying about my future actions.

Right before we turned onto the side street where the Gingerbread House perched thirty feet back from the curb like a Hobbit's cottage writ large, Dako unbuckled his seat belt and cuffed his hands behind himself.

"Make it real for the looky-loos," was his final piece of advice as I glided to a stop between white painted lines on the asphalt a couple minutes before 10:00 and brought out the Colt Commander. The Kimber at the small of my back would relocate when I got to my office.

After Dako swung his legs out the door and planted his feet on the ground, his rear end was still lower than his knees, and with his hands behind him he couldn't leverage himself up and over. Following his advice to be convincing, I grabbed a fistful of shirt-front and hauled him out.

He stumbled, whether for show or because he had grazed his head on the upper door frame when I jerked him up, I wasn't sure. I held the Colt on him while I closed the car door, then glanced around the lot and down the street, projecting normal caution, I hoped.

Dako slowed on approach to the front door as we had planned, so I gave him a shove forward with my free hand, causing him to stagger and me to drop the bulky manila envelope tucked under my arm. All the drama was caught in the light that filled the small porte cochere, the better to convince an audience I was in complete control of my captive and that I held the documentation they were after, a blackmailer as good as his word.

Snatching up the envelope, I unlocked the door and pushed Dako inside. As I closed the door behind us and clicked off the outside light, in order to make my guests feel less exposed when they showed up later, Dako slipped out of the cuffs he hadn't fully locked and made his way across the dark lobby and up the stairs to Pat's sound-proofed office. I ditched the newspaper-stuffed envelope in the restroom trash can, then went to my office and turned on the light my adversaries would be watching for from somewhere nearby.

I knew the dense branches of the avocado tree would prevent their seeing movement on the second floor, but they would watch and listen for any hint they were being set up. At 11:25 I opened the window and gave them what they needed to hear to be reassured.

I stood on the landing in total darkness as the front door of the Gingerbread House pushed open slowly at 11:51. A dim wash from the parking lot street lamp revealed two figures entering and pausing a few steps inside.

"Sam?" a familiar voice called softly.

"You're early." I hit the wall switch, flooding the lobby with light that revealed Zeke Martin and Bobby Chalk. They each brought up a gun, but mine was already aimed at them, and I was sure they'd been instructed to hold off on the homicidy stuff until after their bosses got what they needed. Well, *pretty* sure.

"Easy, boys," I heard, as Hank Bledsoe slipped in behind his crew. "We wouldn't want to intimidate our host." Their guns went down. Mine didn't.

"Should I have spelled out the meaning of alone

and unarmed, Hank?"

He put up his hands and chuckled. "You got me, Sam, but I always bring protection when I go into a dangerous neighborhood."

"And you think sleepy little Sherman Oaks is dangerous?"

"Yeah, I heard a guy on Fulton keeps a vicious pack of Chihuahuas and one of them killed a Rottweiler."

Los Angeles, where everybody thinks he's a stand-up comic. But playing dumb was my prime directive for the night, so I asked, "Really? How did a Chihuahua kill a dog that big?"

"The Rottweiler choked to death trying to swallow it."

"Enough!" A new voice cut off the forced laughter from Hank's henchmen as Grant Tenninger stepped through the door, tall, dignified, every inch the mayoral candidate of your dreams. He shut the door behind himself and locked it.

"Two more players and you guys could field a hockey team," I observed wryly.

"You must be Sam," Tenninger said. "Or should I call you Rick?"

Excellent. The troglodytes had remembered my name and ratted me out. Time for a look of surprise and a hasty recovery. "How did you...? Never mind. Are we going to do business or what?" Tough guy.

"We are. As soon as you put down that Colt."

I lowered the Commander and began backing up the stairs. "Fine, but I want no guns coming into my office."

"Including your own?" Tenninger asked.

"Point taken. So, why don't we *all* park our hard-ware on the table in the hall."

When we got near my closed office door, I slowly and cautiously laid Laurel's gun on the side table against the wall, indicating with a nod that Zeke and Bobby should do the same.

They both glanced at Hank for instructions, and I read the situation: Tenninger ran Bledsoe, but it was Bledsoe who ran the trogs. Tenninger had most likely set it up that way, keeping arm's length away from the muscle to maintain plausible deniability for any of their criminal actions. That explained why Zeke and Bobby didn't have the police connections to search DMV files for my home address.

Hank didn't notice them waiting for him to give an order. He was too busy staring at the nameplate on my door. Slowly he turned to them.

"How did you two dimwits *not* find his office?" he sneered. Bobby Chalk looked like he would happily put one between Hank's eyes, so I attempted to hurry along the mutual disarmament.

"Guns on the table," I barked, prompting Hank to give Zeke and Bobby the nod. Two more pistols joined the Colt on the plain white tablecloth Rexanne had purchased the day before to hide the thin layer of sound-muffling foam topping the table's surface. *"All* the guns," I snapped.

Tenninger opened his coat with an affable smile, attempting to convince the newbie he wasn't holding. Meanwhile, Hank elbowed Zeke, so a second pair of weapons emerged and found their way onto the cloud-soft surface of the table.

"Now *your* back-up piece," Tenninger demanded, looking at me.

"I don't have a—" Zeke, the ambulatory side of beef on the team, pinned my arms before I could finish the sentence, then Bobby groped me and came up with

Dako's compact Beretta and a smirk of triumph.

"You want Farona dead?" I shouted, sending a
fine spray of spittle at Bobby as he put the Beretta on
the table with the rest of the arsenal. "You want that
envelope? Then you'd better start showing me some
fucking respect!" Dako always said it helps to speak
their language.

"Let him go," Hank told Zeke. Then, to me, he
said, "No disrespect intended. We only act out of an
abeyance of caution."

"Abundance" I heard Tenninger mutter with a
shake of his head.

"What?" Hank asked.

"Nothing."

"Well, out of my *own* abundance of caution, how
about I frisk all of *you* now? It's four against one here,
and I'm not feeling the love."

Hank started to protest, but I put up a hand to
stop him. "If you decline, you'll never get your hands
on that envelope. Also, suck on this: I left it with a
friend and if he doesn't get a call from me telling him
to drive it over here tonight, tomorrow morning he
takes it to the press and the attorney general."

Tenninger knew I was lying, knew he had seen
the envelope walk in the door with me earlier. That
decided him on how to work me.

"You're right, Mr. Valentine. You're holding all
the cards, so let's play nice and everybody gets what
they want." As a gesture of his sincerity, he reached
under the back of his jacket and pulled a Glock 30
from his waistband, making a big point of setting it
with the other guns. When I lifted my eyebrows
skeptically, he raised the cuffs of his pants, revealing
nothing more than black socks. "You, too," he ordered
Hank, who then produced a sissy .22-cal Derringer

from his pocket.

With shrugs, Zeke and Bobby off-loaded another three pieces, making me wonder if the term 'pulling it out of your ass' might be literal in this case.

"Do you mind?" I asked Tenninger, pointing at Bobby Chalk.

"Fine, but hurry it up," he replied impatiently.

Tenninger was willing to indulge me despite his partner's indignant glare, so the more I looked like an amateur, the more rope he'd give me to hang myself. I frisked Bobby with the same roughness he had shown me, then did a lesser pat-down on the other three. When I was positive no orphan gun would materialize once we entered my office, I cleared my throat.

"Okay, shirts open so I can see if you're wearing a wire."

"Oh, for fuck's sake!" Tenninger bellowed, his patience exhausted. "This isn't a goddamn Leonardo di Caprio movie!"

"All right," I said. "But cell phones stay with the guns, so nothing gets recorded." I tossed my Smart Phone on the table and four other cells followed.

"Now that we're all unarmed," Hank said, "how do we know you don't have someone waiting to jump us on the other side of that door?"

I pulled out my key and tossed it to Zeke. "Here. You be the king's food taster." His expression darkened, but he obviously didn't get it.

Tenninger did. "Open the door."

Martin unlocked my office, while Chalk readied himself to snatch a weapon from the collection if his partner caught a bullet from inside. Zeke cautiously stuck his head through the opening.

"Ho-ly shit!" he exclaimed, stepping inside.

"What?" Tenninger asked, tensing.

"It's Farona."

"Is he armed?"

"No, I think he's dead."

I entered my office and the other three followed.

"Ho-ly shit," said Hank, unable to improve on Zeke's eloquence.

"He isn't dead. At least not yet," I assured them and, as if to confirm my words, Dako lifted his head and glared at me with eyes that were little more than swollen slits.

He was in a straight-back chair, duct tape at his ankles and around his chest, hands behind the chair back. His face looked like raw hamburger and flecks of blood dotted his shirt front. Hank looked at me with surprise. I smiled. "What? You didn't think I had it in me?" They had heard the beating through the open window, but up until then, I think they were skeptical.

Tenninger, a former cop and a more naturally suspicious person, glanced down at my hands, noting the raw, red scrapes across the knuckles, the small patches of drying blood.

"Close the door and let's do this," I said. Like a good boy, Zeke did as he was told. With the trap baited and set, everything was going according to my plan.

Once in high school English class we had to memorize a poem by that guy, what's-his-name with the club foot. It was something about a mouse, but all I remember is the one line that stuck out for me at the time.

The best laid schemes o' mice and men gang aft a-gley.

A-gley being Scottish for brick hitting you in the back of the head.

I had calculated everything down to the smallest detail. I knew who was where and what they were doing. My four targets were unarmed and ready to be manipulated, so I was sure I could call every beat of what was about to unspool.

I had no hint of the twist to come. Or how things would gang a-gley.

"The envelope!" Tenninger sharply demanded after Zeke shut the door.

"First, the deal."

"There is no deal," he said.

"Grant, we *have* to get our hands on that envelope," warned Hank.

"Oh, we'll get it."

"But, his friend."

"There *is* no friend. Junior brought the envelope with him tonight."

"What?" Hank apparently wasn't as observant as his partner in crime.

"And I'm guessing it's here in this room, right, boyo?"

"That's not true!" I yelled. "My guy doesn't get the call, you're shit outta luck, Deuce!"

At the mention of his old nickname, Tenninger stilled. He looked at Dako, then turned back to me, a cobra poised to spit and blind.

As Dako had said he would, Grant Tenninger proceeded to slither into my head.

"Farona share that little nugget while you were beating the fuck out of him, *Ricky?*" Venom-dripping fangs unsheathed themselves as he smoothly said, "Oh, yeah, I know your nickname, too. Little Ricky

Valentine, all dressed up in his cop suit, riding around on Daddy's shoulders."

He hadn't even struck yet, but I felt the poison burn as it entered my bloodstream. "Shut up right now or the deal is off."

"As I said earlier, there is no deal, Ricky. You are outnumbered, outflanked and outwitted."

"You don't know dick."

"Really? When Hank told me your name earlier tonight, I did a quick check on you. Learned you spent three years working for *that* coward." He jerked his head in Dako's direction, while I rested one hand on the edge of my desk, inches from where the Kimber was lightly taped to the underside of the wood.

"So? Big whoop. Everybody works for *some*-body," I bluffed.

"Leave it alone, Deuce." This came from Dako, a deadly warning.

Tenninger laughed. I felt the venom snaking through my veins, heading for the heart as I slid my hand closer to my father's gun.

"Jesus, Farona, didn't you tell the little shit you were doing his mom?"

"Don't listen to him, Rick!" Dako shouted.

Enjoying himself, focused on Dako, as were the other three, Tenninger didn't see my fingers slip under the desk top, didn't hear the light pop as I freed the Kimber from its tape cradle.

Tenninger taunted Dako. "What? You didn't tell him how you got his daddy killed?!"

Unlike instant pudding, instant enlightenment really does take no time. No box to open; no sugary dust to mix with milk. Instant enlightenment is a bolt from the blue, all made clear without a sliver of space or time separating the knowing from the not knowing. The mental images and revelations exploded and over-lapped, poisoning my thoughts in less time than it took one pulse of venom-laced blood to circuit my heart. Dako's words: *In the end,* yes. *He knew*.

There was the obvious key. My father would have never brought Dako with him to that warehouse if he had known about the affair. He went in ignorant, but learned the truth before dying.

When the snake needed my father dead—the straight-arrow cop who might *not* have been intimated enough to go along with the cover-up—he spat his venom, blinding my father long enough for Khavazhi to shoot. Then Tenninger shot Khavazhi, tying up every loose end except Dako Farona.

I did what John Valentine had done in that final moment of his life; I turned to Dako with the Kimber in my hand. This time there was no gangster with a weapon to interrupt, and I fired from five feet away.

"Oh, shit!" somebody else in the room yelled, as the thump to Dako's chest bounced him once before red bloomed around the duct tape over his heart.

Zeke and Bobby rushed me, as Tenninger yelled, "Don't touch his gun!"

Complying, Zeke twisted my left wrist until the Kimber dropped to the floor, while Bobby paid me back for earlier with a punch to the solar plexus that left me gasping for breath. I struggled, but between the gut slam and the fact that my shoulders were being wrenched half-out of their sockets, it was useless.

"Good work, Ricky. You, you," Tenninger said to Zeke and Bobby, "go bring in our weapons." They scrambled to do as he said, and a minute later I was the only vertical guy in the room without a gun. My eyes swept over the Kimber lying on the floor, but Tenninger saw the move. "Don't even think about it. Now, where's the envelope?"

"I told you, it's with a—"

The barrel of Deuce's Glock slammed into the side of my head and I staggered with pain and an instant wave of nausea.

"Wrong answer. Zeke, Bobby, Hank, tear this place apart." For a moment I thought Bledsoe was going to protest being lumped in with the hired hands, but a glance at Tenninger's face convinced him there was only one way out: Deuce's way. Once upon a time Victor, Gayle Chandler and Dako had learned that same lesson.

As Tenninger kept me Glock-blocked, my office came undone. The clipper ship paintings were ripped off the wall and, when they were found not to be hiding the envelope, went crashing to the floor. Uncle Victor's seascape met a similar fate, then my diploma, glass flying as it was smashed.

Next came the desk drawers, yanked out and turned over, spills of paper, pens, stapler, batteries and other miscellanea flowing floorward. The office was small to begin with, and I had removed all but my desk and the single chair in which Dako sat, slumped over and unmoving, so there wasn't much real estate left to search.

I could see Tenninger was about to send his guys through the rest of the Gingerbread House, but then he smiled, evidently remembering how inexperienced I was. "Turn it over," he said, nodding at the wooden desk.

"No!" I screamed, lunging for him.

Bobby Chalk clotheslined me with his right arm and I went down choking, sliding in broken glass. Bledsoe and Martin flipped the desk, revealing a fat envelope with a yellow label: www.2regni.net, held to the wood at the four corners by masking tape. I heard Tenninger's laugh as I struggled to get to my feet, glass shards porcupining both knees.

"Rookie mistake," Deuce crowed, as Sasquatch and Bluto grabbed me in a death grip.

"We had a deal!" I shouted, but Tenninger ignored me while he ripped the manila envelope from its moorings and tore open one end.

"Is it the real one this time?" Hank asked eagerly, as Deuce pulled out the top two sheets and studied them.

"Jesus Christ! I want Arroyo dead...tomorrow!" Tenninger's voice quivered with fury.

"What is it?"

He shoved the two pages at Hank. "It's the proof that could send us both to prison."

"That's not possible. Arroyo said they were still there and nobody could get to them. These have to be fakes!" Hank blurted out nervously.

"Run your fingers over the fucking notary seal. These are the ones we signed!"

Hank felt the raised imprints and then, because he apparently could come up with nothing original to say that night, whispered, "Jesus Christ!"

I thought it was a good time for me to chime in again, since my mouth was about the only thing I could move in the grasp of Thick and Thicker. "That's a duplicate! The real one isn't here! If you think—"

"Would you shut him up," Tenninger suggested to either or. Zeke punched me in the face and I stopped talking.

"Just let me think for a minute here," Tenninger said. "Okay, okay, this is going to be perfect. The schmuck is working alone and we have everything that could hurt us. To prove it, he picked up my metal wastepaper basket and held the envelope over it, dumping out a flash drive, a stack of 8x10 photos and fifty pages of transcripts and blueprints for the Playa del Rey development.

"But Farona's dead," Hank whined. "Won't that come back on us?"

"How? We didn't kill him, did we?"

"No."

"Ricky did. And Farona killed him."

Bledsoe looked confused, but Deuce was all over the situation. "You, is that unregistered?" he asked Bobby.

"Yes."

"Good. I want you to shoot our host, then wipe it down and put it in Farona's hand. Ricky was already helpful enough to kill Dako and leave his prints on the Kimber."

Before Bobby could move, Tenninger turned to Zeke. "Tomorrow, get to Arroyo's office and you make damn sure he's a corpse before you leave. No mistakes like when you 'supposedly' killed Farona. Understand? Now shoot him," he barked at Bobby. Zeke quickly let me go and stepped away. So, not as dumb as he looked.

Bobby Chalk raised the gun and aimed it at the middle of my face, pulling the trigger from only a few feet away.

Click!

"The fuck?" he eloquently stated, then checked the magazine. "Empty."

"You hired guys too stupid to bring their guns

loaded?" Tenninger snarled at Hank. "Get another one! Now!"

Without waiting for Bobby, Tenninger pulled out a lighter and took the empty manila envelope from my wastepaper basket. "At least *one* of us is prepared," he said, as the envelope caught fire and he tossed it in with the rest. Flames leapt a few inches over the top of the can, then subsided to less-dramatically burn up everything inside it.

Bobby returned with Laurel's Colt in his hand. "This is the one he had when we came in. It'll look like Dako took it off him," Bobby said helpfully.

"Fine. Now shoot the fucker!"

Again I stared into a barrel aimed at my face.

Click!

Tenninger stooped and grabbed the Kimber. "Well, I know *this* one is loaded!" He swung it at me and pulled the trigger.

Click!

A commotion at the window caught everyone's attention, as Rexanne scrambled over the sill and dropped into the room, cell phone in one hand, Smith & Wesson in the other. Brandishing my Sigma like she was dying to show off her skills, she said, "You boys chill, 'cuz I guarantee I'm the only one in this room whose gun is loaded. Hey, y'all ever hear of Meerkat?"

With seven people and a turned-over desk filling my small office, no one was very far from anyone else as everybody froze. Zeke and Bobby exchanged a panicked glance when they recognized Rexanne and made an eye-pact not to tell their boss how badly they'd screwed up by letting her go two weeks earlier.

Bledsoe's face registered shock and anger when he pointed a finger at Rexanne, saying, "You!"

Tenninger's head snapped around toward Hank. "You *know* this bitch?"

Hank ignored his partner and continued to glare at Rexanne. "You were supposed to write me a big campaign check " he said, apparently missing the gist of what was going on all around him.

But I had missed something, too. By taking premature pleasure in the befuddlement of Zeke, Bobby and Hank, I hadn't seen the snake coiling for a strike. I had thought the loaded Sigma and Kevlar vest would guarantee Rexanne's safety until the bad guys left the building, but Tenninger lunged, bringing the empty Kimber down hard on her wrist. She yelped and jumped back as the S&W hit the floor and Tenninger and I dived for it at the same time.

This woke up the meat puppets, so Bobby Chalk tackled me from behind, sending us both crashing to the parquet, as Tenninger came up with my Sigma and tossed the Kimber aside. Meanwhile, Zeke went to the window behind Rexanne, checking outside for additional tree dwellers before slamming it shut and locking it.

Rexanne rubbed at the wrist Deuce had chopped and there was fear and pain on her face, though she continued to subtly aim her cell phone. I'm sure she wondered why I hadn't called out the trigger word yet, but even with the side of my head jammed into the floor and Bobby Chalk's rank breath in my face, I hoped to get more evidence. While Tenninger held the fully loaded Sigma and tried to figure out what was happening, I taunted Bobby Chalk.

"Do you *ever* brush your teeth?" I snarled. "Your breath is like a skunk fart." A second later I mentally scratched off taking a kidney punch from my bucket list.

"Enough!" Tenninger shouted, before Bobby could do follow-up. "Get him on his feet!"

Chalk did as he was told, falling one twist short of adding a dislocated shoulder to my other injuries. Zeke hovered alongside Rexanne, waiting for orders.

"What do we do?" Bledsoe nervously asked his partner.

Tenninger ran a hand through his perfect hair, looking for the first time as though he did not feel in complete control. "Okay, okay, we can still make this work. We kill the girl, too, and it'll look like they were fighting over her. They shot each other and she was collateral damage."

"You can't kill her," Hank squeaked. "That's Harmon Richfield's granddaughter!"

"I don't care if she's Pope Frank's proctologist, she's a witness and we can't leave her alive."

"Excuse me, Deuce," I piped up, after seeing Rexanne's terrified reaction to his pronouncement of her death sentence. "I don't think you understand what has happened here." This inspired Pepé Le Pew to yank my arms even further behind me and I was really feeling the cumulative effects of the start and stop beating I had taken since Tenninger slammed the Glock into the side of my head. Still, I kept my voice matter-of-fact.

"First, from her vantage point outside the window and then inside, my associate, Svetlana,"—and here I gave a surreptitious wink to Rexanne—"has been capturing every word and action in this room the last twenty minutes and feeding it live to all her eleven hundred and forty-nine Twitter followers."

"Actually, I'm up to eleven fifty now," Rexanne

clarified. I shot her a silencing look and went on.

"And they have been retweeting it, and *their* followers have been retweeting, and down the line, someone *must* have sent it to an FBI agent, or a federal judge, or somebody somewhere with the power to bypass your local pet cops and put your ass in the slammer."

Rexanne had kept her cell phone down by her side, capturing and streaming without being noticed, but as Tenninger frantically tried to figure something out, she couldn't resist raising it and waggling it in the air. "Go, Meerkat!" she cheered, right before Zeke slapped the phone out of her hand and stomped it to bits when it hit the deck.

"If you think that solves your problem," she said to the room, "you guys seriously do *not* understand technology."

"Grab her!" Tenninger barked, and Zeke did, although Rexanne struggled like a marlin on a line when he wrapped both arms around her, pinning her arms to her side. "We take the girl with us."

"We're screwed, Grant," Hank whined.

"No, we're not. Think about it...even if she *did* record us, what do they actually have? A handful of moderately incriminating statements our lawyers can explain away."

"But—"

"We didn't say a fucking word about the Playa del Rey deal, and ashes in a trash can is all that's left of their proof. In fact, the only real crime she recorded was Valentine murdering Farona in cold blood. All we have to do is claim we feared for our lives and would have said anything to get away from a madman like him."

"If we kidnap the girl, aren't we—"

"What girl? There *was* no girl."

"But the recording, the polecat thing."

"Meerkat!" Rexanne yelled, still struggling in Zeke's iron grasp.

"If she was *shooting* the video, then she isn't *in* the video. For all anyone can prove, Valentine put the cell phone outside the window himself, and if he claims otherwise, who's going to take the word of a stone killer over two leading citizens like us? Now, let's move! You," he said, pointing at Bobby Chalk, while keeping the S&W on me. "Grab that trash can and bring it with us, in case anything survived."

And that's when I yelled the trigger word: "FATBURGER!!"

Deuce kept the Smith & Wesson aimed in my direction, knowing he couldn't shoot me now, but wanting to hold me at bay. Bobby delivered a farewell punch to my ribcage and Zeke lifted Rexanne up so her feet pedaled helplessly as he carried her around the fallen desk. Her colorful invective brought into question his IQ, penis size and mother's marital status at the time of his birth.

Hank Bledsoe, eager to exit the nightmare, was first to the door, first to see what waited on the other side when he swung it wide. He froze and Tenninger, who had been backing toward the door while providing cover for Bobby and Zeke, bumped into him.

"Damn it, Bledsoe!" Tenninger snarled as he turned around. But then he saw what had stopped his partner in his tracks.

"Because Sherman Oaks is such a hell-rowdy neighborhood," I said, "I thought I'd have my friends escort you safely to your vehicles."

The AK-47s aimed at the doorway were in the

hands of a band of the freakiest skinhead bikers imaginable. If The Three Musketeers had been into leather, nose chains, face tats, Mohawks and knuckle spikes, they would have *still* looked like pussies next to these guys. Well, two guys and what appeared to be a squarish woman with a chewed-off ear. They looked willing to rumble with the Jets *and* the sharks, meaning the NFL team and the ocean predators, not the dancing gangs of *West Side Story*.

Effectively de-fanged, Grant Tenninger lowered the impressively outgunned Sigma, while Zeke let go of Rexanne, who rushed to my side. Putting a protective arm around her, I spoke to Deuce as he glared at me with pure hatred in his eyes.

"Maybe your high-dollar attorneys can get you off the hook, Deuce, and maybe I'll go away for murder, but don't bet your rent money on either."

"You'll regret this," Tenninger breathed, loudly enough to be heard, but not confrontationally enough to inspire the bikers to forgo taking names and start kicking ass.

"We should be hearing police sirens any minute, so if you want to make your getaway, please allow the Skulls to escort you to your cars."

Dropping the Sigma to the floor so the crazy-eyed leather gang wouldn't misread his exit as a charge, Tenninger shouldered Hank aside and pushed through the door. Two of the Skulls turned their weapons with him as he passed, falling into line behind him, while the third indicated with a wave of her AK that the three stooges should follow their leader.

Before Blecsoe could clear the door, I called out, "Watch your back, Hank. Tenninger murdered his *last* partner in crime." I hoped that might spark an interesting conversation between the two.

Rexanne and I waited, her face still pressed against my chest, my arm around her, until we heard Justin's voice from below. "Clear!" he yelled up to us, slamming the door of the Gingerbread House behind him.

The slam's echo had not completely subsided when Dako came up off the chair, trailing duct tape and rushing straight at me.

"THE *DESK?!*" he roared, as Rexanne wisely stepped aside.

Laurel appeared in the doorway and snapped, "Dako!" as if calling off a mastiff before it ripped out someone's throat.

If he heard her, he did not acknowledge it, practically shoving his barrel chest into mine as he bellowed. "You left my evidence taped under your *DESK?!* I spent *months* tracking down what I needed to put that son of a bitch behind bars and you let him burn it! How could you be so stupid?"

Maybe it was the sudden vacuum inside me after a week of barbed-wire tension; maybe it was my anger at his automatic assumption I had screwed up; or maybe it was only the inevitable storm that had been brewing since I found that snapshot of my mother in his wallet. Whatever the reason, I totally lost it, going for him with no weapons other than righteousness and rage.

"You slept with my mother and got my father killed!!" I shouted, shoving him backwards with both hands. As Rexanne pulled away in shock and Laurel cried, "No!" I shot my fist forward with all my weight behind it, smashing it into Dako's jaw and sending him staggering.

As he went down I dived on top of him, slamming my fist into his face again, oblivious to Rexanne's screams and Laurel's attempts to grab my arm. Elbowing her out of the way, I kept attacking.

Dako didn't strike back, so my punches landed unimpeded, while shrieking police sirens neared the Gingerbread House, joining the shrieks of the two women trying to stop me. When I broke his nose, real blood mixed with the counterfeit stuff Kitty had applied earlier, and the makeup on my knuckles gave way to genuine bruises and abrasions.

Rexanne climbed onto my back, slapping at my head and screaming for me to stop hitting her father, while Laurel shouted my name and scrabbled at my arm more desperately, forcing me to shift to my less effective right fist to keep up the punishing barrage.

At least two of us were crying by then, Rexanne because she was afraid I would kill him, and me because nothing I did do to him would bring back my parents. "You bastard! If you hadn't slept with her Deuce couldn't have distracted my father long enough for Khavazhi to shoot him! And why didn't you draw your gun? Did you *want* him dead so you could take another run at my mother?!"

"Rick, stop!" Laurel screamed in my ear, now trying to block my fists with her own body. Rexanne hooked one forearm across the front of my throat, using her other hand to leverage her wrist inward, forcing my chin up and strangling me. Sirens wheeled into the parking lot.

And still I hit him. "You killed him! You killed my father!"

As one woman crushed my windpipe and the other grabbed my hair tightly enough to immobilize my head, I heard Laurel sobbing into my ear.

"Rick! Dako *is* your father!"

The pressure on my throat stopped when Rexanne fainted and rolled off me, slumping senseless onto the floor. Laurel's hands released my hair and I gaped at her with incomprehension, registering in the background that Justin, Jason and Pat had returned and that Kitty and Bitsy were looking on in horror. As a dozen why-didn't-I-see-its flashed through my reeling mind—including Laurel's harsh warning to stay away from Rexanne, and Dako's use of the word 'son'—I looked down and saw blood. Not the fake stuff from the squib Kitty had secured under the duct tape surrounding Dako's chest, but the genuine article oozing from the shoulder and abdominal sites of Bobby Chalk's gunshots, and flowing copiously from Dako's shattered nose.

The sirens had stopped, but shouted commands from a herd of cops storming the Gingerbread House accompanied the first touch I'd felt from a father's hand since I was five, as the bear beneath me rallied enough strength before passing out to launch a huge paw in my direction. It was like being smashed in the face with a HoneyBaked Ham. I heard my nose break, and the last conscious thought I had before joining my father and sister in oblivion, was: *what a way to start a family reunion.*

When I came to in the ambulance on the way to St. Joseph's Hospital, I saw Dako lying on a gurney parallel to mine. A paramedic worked to stanch the bleeding from the shoulder wound that had reopened during the one-sided fistfight, and gauze had already been taped over the torn-out stitches in Dako's gut. I looked at his wrecked face and saw that he was watching me.

"Are you all right?" he asked, the words ragged.

"Yes." a lie, but what the hell, I'd already blown the Fifth Commandment to smithereens.

"Good." He turned his head to stare at the roof of the ambulance, wincing when the paramedic pressed the shoulder packing so he could secure the tape to Dako's skin.

"Only a couple more minutes, guys," the paramedic said, squirting half a bottle of saline onto a thick gauze pad and pressing it against the worst of Dako's facial bleeding. "Then you'll be pumped full of happy juice and feeling no pain."

We three remained silent, until I finally turned to Dako and said, "You're lucky."

"Yeah, I'm *feeling* lucky," he said, the first hint of his old sarcasm creeping into his voice.

"If I'd had live ammunition in the Kimber, things would have gone very differently."

Unable to turn his head while his face was being treated, Dako cut his eyes at me. "I guess I'm not surprised you would have shot me."

"Not you. Deuce. Then I'd go to prison and you'd get screwed out of ten to fifteen Father's Day ties." It was the best I could do in the way of an olive branch.

"Yeah, that would truly stink," he said, his eyes returning to the roof of the rig, but not before I glimpsed them watering. From pain, for sure.

"I'm right about why my father died, aren't I?" Auto-correct. "Tenninger dropped the bomb about the affair, knowing John Valentine would turn to you, and giving Khavazhi his chance to shoot."

"Yes. And the reason I didn't kill both Deuce *and* Nostradamus was that I didn't have a weapon on me."

"Seriously?"

"It was a very different time. Cell phones and handguns weren't yet mandatory personal accessories for everyone over twelve. Besides, we were off duty, out of uniform, and Victor Ramirez had sold it to Gayle and me as nothing more than routine lookout duty. Easy peas and we'd each get a hundred bucks. Remember, I was even younger and dumber than you are now."

Okay, I deserved that. "Dako?"

"Yes?"

"Did you *really* think I learned so little from you that I would leave the envelope taped under my desk?"

"Tenninger told Hank the notary seal was—" He stopped, suddenly understanding how thorough I had been. "I'm impressed. Where's the real envelope?"

"Taped under the *receptionist's* desk, right out in the open where nobody would think to look. So you still have everything you need to make your case against Deuce."

"Unless his inside people at the LAPD roll on him first to cover their own asses and prevent him from throwing them to the wolves."

"Either way, it's a win."

"All right, guys, we're here," the paramedic said, as the ambulance came to a stop at the emergency entrance of St. Joe's. While he popped the rear doors and climbed out, I turned to Dako.

"There's one thing I don't understand."

"Only one?"

The driver had come around to the back of the rig, so he and the other paramedic unlocked the wheel brakes on Dako's gurney. "I never did figure out the importance of that website."

"What website?" he asked, as his gurney began its forward slide through the open doors.

"The one on the envelope, www.2regni.net."

The driver and paramedic grabbed the sides of

the gurney and lowered wheels to the ground as Dako laughed. I lifted up and craned my neck to hear his answer.

"Plain sight, son."

"I don't get it," I called out.

They were wheeling him away when I heard his answering words. "Read it backwards."

So I did in my mind. *Tenninger, Deuce.*

My phone was at the Gingerbread House and emergency room cubicles don't have TVs, so I didn't know what we had stirred up until Laurel walked in at 7:15 Thursday morning. By that time my nose had been reset, splinted and taped, my ribs pronounced bruised but unbroken, the glass had been picked from my knees, my concussion had been characterized as "mild," three broken fingers were set and plastered, and I'd been told I'd be peeing blood for a couple weeks while my healing kidneys bled off into my bladder.

"How is he?" I asked Laurel, when she entered with a grim lock on her face.

"You're an asshole," was her reply.

"And you're not the first woman to tell me that this week."

She tossed my cell phone onto the narrow bed, dropped a paper grocery bag on the floor and flopped down in the no-frills chair. Since she had been left behind to do mop-up with the police and the press, I assumed she hadn't slept.

"They restitched his gut and shoulder, but the plastic surgeon I lined up to work on his face can't be here until 1:30, so he's in a private room, drugged out of the pain zone and sleeping until then."

I naively thought a bit of levity might improve her mood. "Oh, he gets a plastic surgeon and all I got was a burly intern who gave my nose one cracking yank before pronouncing it 'close enough for rock 'n' roll.'"

I could tell it was a misfire even before she spoke.

"One of the *many* things you have yet to learn is how to throw a punch without trying to kill the other guy. When Dako popped you, he put out your lights and broke your shnozz, but he could have knocked your head off that pencil neck if he had wanted to." She then listed all his injuries. X-rays showed my repeated pounding had done much worse than I had realized and, along with rebuilding Dako's nose, the surgeon would be repairing one eye socket and a broken cheekbone.

"Jesus," was the best I could do on hearing how badly I had hurt him.

"Yeah. But in the two minutes of lucidity he had before the drugs kicked in, he told me it was worth it to finally bring down Tenninger."

"And did we?"

"Let's just say the snowball has started rolling down the hill and ain't *nobody* gonna stop it now."

It would be hours later, after the police had questioned me and I'd gone to the Gingerbread House, that I would learn the extent of our effectiveness in derailing the campaigns of Hank Bledsoe and Grant Tenninger, but right then I wanted to know if all our players were safe.

"I shuttled your three co-workers back to their cars, then drove your landladies to Santa Monica. Before they let me leave the house, they went in and packed a change of clothes for you." She picked up the paper bag to show me where to find it, then replaced it on the floor next to her chair.

"They're a couple of sweethearts," I said.

"Smart, too. I was worried I might make some noise taking the bullets out of all those guns. A click of shells hitting each other could've brought everyone rushing out of your office. Anyway, one of the sisters cut lengths of duct tape for me to lay on the table sticky-side-up, so every round I pulled could go on it like flypaper. When I was done, all I had to do was grab the ends of the tape and slip into the recording studio with all the brass secured."

I told her where to find the real envelope and she said she'd go get it, turn it over to the FBI, then come back in time to see Dako before he went into surgery.

"Why FBI instead of the DA or state police?"

"Those Playa del Rey wetlands were federally protected. One of the off-shore companies funded the phony environmental impact group that pronounced them dead, then Deuce used the information to purchase the supposedly worthless acreage for little more than pocket change and a bribe to a clueless flunky in the Bureau of Land Management. Funnily enough, it was Hank's off-shore that generated the fake tree-hugger petition to prove the land was worth twenty mil and give the new mayor a justification for the buy. They covered themselves on both ends of the transaction."

She and Dako had obviously continued their research while I was setting the trap, and it was good to know there would be federal charges against Tenninger, even if the state couldn't prosecute him for crimes he didn't get the chance to commit.

Laurel had mentioned Justin, Jason and Pat, as well as Kitty and Bitsy, but nothing about Rexanne, and I wondered how my instant sister felt about the previous night's revelation.

"Where's Rexanne?"

"I can't believe she's still awake after sitting in a tree for four hours last night, but she's at my house ratcheting up the buzz via social media. In addition to streaming your carnival sideshow while it was happening, she added a hashtag called Katch and converted it to a video that, as of an hour ago, was blowing up YouTube."

Even in a space as small as a curtained cubicle, there's room for an elephant. My mention of Dako's daughter invited the pachyderm onto the premises, so I asked Laurel to tell me the whole story. She said I would have to speak with my father to get details of his relationship with my mother, but was willing to talk about his relationship with me, which, though I had never known it, started before I was born.

When Dako Farona and Zoë Valentine began their affair, he was twenty-one and she was a year older. What had started out as heat, hormones and opportunity soon developed into deep feelings on both sides, bonds that were tested when Zoë became pregnant and wasn't sure if the father was her lover or her husband.

She chose to believe John Valentine was the father, shutting Dako down on his pleas for her to get a divorce and marry him. Still in love with the young officer, though, and left on her own while her husband worked nights and weekends of overtime to make a better life for his family, Zoë continued the affair through her pregnancy and beyond.

When the child was born, John Valentine gave up all those extra hours for a few months, spending more time with Zoë and the baby, unknowingly crowding Dako Farona out of the picture. But, when dealing with diapers, crying, 2:00 A.M feedings and a wife with post-partum depression wore thin, John resumed his former fast-track work schedule and Dako eased back into Zoë's life.

Officer Farona switched to the second shift so he could spend days with her and the baby, never tiring of reassuring the depressed young woman she was still attractive, dismissing her concerns about stretch marks, sagging and going from hottie to mommy. He bonded with the baby and uncomplainingly performed the less-appealing tasks of caring for an infant while Zoë napped or listlessly watched TV.

She slowly emerged from her insecure funk, in great part because of Dako's assurances of her desirability and his unflagging devotion to her son. The boy's first word was a six month old's interpretation of "daddy," spoken to Dako Farona, not John Valentine.

As Zoë stood by her claim that John was Ricky's father, Dako began to suspect it was based less in reality and more on her wish not to see herself in the unflattering light of cheating wife, a child by another man being the ultimate proof of betrayal.

By the time the boy was a year old, Zoë had recovered her former joie de vivre, no longer lounging around the house in a nightgown, living vicariously through the romantic diversions of soap opera divas. John was thrilled to have his wife back, looking sensational and stopping by the station once a week so she and Ricky could charm every cop in the squad.

Dako feared he was losing her, although he still spent most afternoons at the Valentine house with mother and child, still had Zoë's word that she loved him. Hoping to make a case for her to leave John, Dako took swabs from the toddler's cheek and his own, paying an independent lab to run DNA tests, so as not to draw attention by using the police facility.

Confronting Zoë with the truth did not go as he had hoped. Thinking she would see it as he had, a sign the three of them should officially become a family, Dako was blind-sided by her insistence the results must be wrong. He wasn't mature enough to understand he had backed her into a corner with the test results, pushed her to admit what she wasn't yet ready to face about herself, so he compounded the error by taking DNA from a coffee cup John Valentine had used and running a second test.

Although Zoë couldn't deny the fact of her son's paternity after the double proof, she asked Dako for time. She still cared for John, still relished her role as wife and mother, so she said she would have to find the right way to tell her husband she was leaving him and taking the boy he thought was his own.

Dako leveraged her request for more time into a promise he would have unlimited, albeit secret, access to his son until she felt ready to divorce John and go public about the boy's parentage.

For the next three years, Zoë stalled and Dako pressed for action. By then the child was a bright four year old who could differentiate between the policeman who took his mother and him to movies, the beach and baseball games, and the policeman who rarely made it home before his bedtime and was away most weekends.

It was only a matter of time before the boy would mention some activity he had done with "the other policeman," and John Valentine would figure out he wasn't talking about Victor Ramirez or any of the officers who sometimes took Ricky for play-dates with their own children while John worked.

On one of those afternoons when her son was

roller skating with another cop's two kids and she had spent hours in Dako's arms, Zoë finally agreed to leave her husband. It was the second week of May, 1994, and John had hardly been home long enough to do more than shower and change clothes for months. Although Zoë still loved him, she was *in* love with Dako, who was more of a father to Ricky and more of a husband to her than John Valentine had been for a long time. She promised she would talk to John about a divorce before the end of the week.

A few days later, Hamid Khavazhi murdered John Valentine and everything changed. As the widow of a well-liked, hero cop, Zoë found herself under constant, benign scrutiny by the numerous officers who had worked with her husband, men and women who pulled together, as cops always do, to help the family of a fallen comrade. The female officers brought casseroles and home-made cookies, tried to cheer the widow with manicures and lunches out, while the boys in blue treated Ricky to more manly outings.

Zoë's guilt caused her to push Dako away, as if by excluding him from her life she could rewrite six years of what she now told herself was an unforgivable betrayal, a giving-in to nothing more than lust.

"So, he walked away? The guy who supposedly loved her so much?"

Before Laurel could respond, the flimsy curtain enclosing the small space was pulled aside by a man in a suit who held up a badge. "Mr. Valentine? Det. Pierce. The resident on duty said you were being released this morning, and I'd like a few minutes of your time before you go."

"I was leaving anyway," Laurel said, standing.

"And Rick? I'll pick up that invoice from your office and make sure it gets into the right hands."

I understood her caution in not mentioning the envelope. Until we knew how deeply into the LAPD Deuce's tentacles reached, it was better to play safe. Pierce gave her a suspicious stare, but Laurel smiled her way through it.

"Hey, when a guy gets the snot kicked out of him, it doesn't mean his business comes to a halt."

She breezed out and I indicated the sole chair. "Please."

Det. Pierce sat down, pulled out a spiral notepad and spent ninety minutes questioning me about the wackadoo stunt—his words, not mine—I had played a part in the night before. When he finally flipped the pad shut he warned me not be shocked if the LAPD sent me a bill for the cost of deploying a dozen officers to the scene of a prank homicide.

After he left I asked for my discharge paperwork, then got dressed and turned on my phone. Thirty-two missed calls, many from unknown numbers which I presumed belonged to reporters. I quickly scrolled down to see if Piper had tried to reach me, but was more disappointed than surprised that she had not. She was flying to New York in two days and probably wasn't even aware of what had happened.

I returned Cal Cooper's call and once he heard my voice he started thanking me effusively. "Oh, my God, Rick! You're the best! And you can have three free hours of my hacking services any time you like."

"Good, huh?"

"Are you *kidding* me?! She was incredible! She looked *exactly* like Princess Leia, right down to the dualing-Cinnabons hair and that skimpy two-piece Jabba the Hutt made her wear when he had her chained up in his—"

"Okay, okay, I get it. You liked your masseuse.

"Oh, I *more* than liked her. In fact, I've already booked her to come back *next* Wednesday night as Xena, Warrior Princess."

I had only set up the late-night massage to make sure Moonbeam wouldn't be entertaining an incall client while the action went down in my office, but Cal had gone out on a limb for me, and I was glad he and Moonie had hit if off. The nurse entered with my paperwork, so I told Cal I'd talk to him soon and hung up. After I signed the release form and took my copy, the lady in white exited, pulling the privacy curtain wide open and revealing Rexanne Farona. I wasn't sure what to say to her, but, like a Hallmark card from annoying-little-sisterville, she had the perfect words.

"You look like turd salad, bro."

I waited for her to berate me for nearly killing Dako, but her opening shot was all the ordnance she had. Or was willing to use. Her eyes filled with tears as she rushed me, wrapping her arms around my chest and tucking her head under my chin. I winced.

"Ow! Ribs."

"Sorry." She slid down a few inches so her face was pressed against my sternum and her arms were tight around my waist.

"Ow! Kidneys."

Rexanne pulled away. "Well, that's as far down as I go, now that I know we're related." The smell of elephant filled the air and, after an awkward pause, she said, "Your mother is the one who broke my dad's heart before he met my mom?"

"So I'm told." I could sense the questions waiting to spill out of her, the same ones I had: Why didn't

Dako ever acknowledge me? Why hadn't she known of my existence? "I'm only hearing about all this today, Rexanne, so don't look to me for answers."

"You're right. The thing to do is speak with my dad...the guy you almost *killed* last night." Without warning, she raised a hand and whapped me in the side of the head.

"Ow! Concussion."

"Now you're just making stuff up," she snorted, walking out into the corridor, then turning back impatiently. "Well, shag your ass, dude. I'm your ride and I don't have all day."

God, she was annoying.

On the way to the Gingerbread House, where the Corvette was still parked, Rexanne reported on how much online exposure she'd been able to get for her Meerkat production and the audio of the phone call between Tenninger and Bledsoe from the night of the fund raiser.

"And guess how many Twitter followers I have as of this morning."

"How many?"

"Come on, guess."

"Two thousand."

"Try *forty* thousand and climbing. Turns out people like snuff tweets more than sideboob."

"They *do* know the murder was fake, don't they?"

"Who cares? But if May-Ann Harris goes all-out camel toe, we might have to show someone *really* getting killed."

"I nominate you."

Rexanne took her eyes off the road long enough to flash me a grin. "I always wanted a brother."

"And did you always want him to look like turd

salad?"

"Hey, you *did* almost kill my father." She went quiet, then a few seconds later murmured, "Our father."

Yeah, that was going to take some time for us both to get used to.

You would have thought I was a war hero from the reception I got when Rexanne dropped me off at the Gingerbread House. After briefly commiserating about my injuries, Justin, Jason and Pat told me how much they'd enjoyed playing the kind of thugs Joaquin Guzmán's HR guy would have rejected as "too rough," proving my theory—at least in the case of the two men—that most writers wish they could live out the fantasies they commit to paper.

Wielding the bogus AK-47s, walking Tenninger and crew to their cars two blocks away and giving statements to the police while still in costume and makeup had been a total high, so they wanted to take me out for a celebratory lunch. Given my physical state and the amount of follow-up I still had to do—mostly on the personal front—I begged off until the following week. The three left to celebrate without me and the building went silent. Our never-seen talent agent remained unseen, Ms. Moonbeam was probably home sleeping after her night with Cal, and Lloyd sat at his desk reading a script. He had been snippy when I came in, no doubt upset about having been left out of the action, what with him being a bona fide actor and all, but I was sure when the news broke about the evidence in the envelope and where it had been hidden for safekeeping, he'd be basking in media attention.

Someone had righted my desk, neatly piling the

contents on the surface for me to sort through and return to the proper drawers, mindless work that gave me time for reflection.

The odd response I'd had to Dako's daughter from the start made perfect sense in this new reality. My memory of Ruthie Carmichael's interaction with her two biological brothers was a telling template for my relationship with Rexanne. Chris and Sonny picked on Ruthie mercilessly, but would never let anyone else do that to her. And she referred to her brothers as insects or savages, but was always there with a hug, a band-aid or an encouraging word when one of the boys had been brought down by a bully, a fall or a bad report card.

I had been disconcerted about my feelings for Rexanne, both protective and combative. I saw her as a very attractive girl, but felt none of the sexual pull I'd had with Piper, or any woman before her, which made it strange that I resented Rexanne's flirting with the good-looking young officer who investigated the break-in at Justin's office. Without knowing it, I'd had nobody's-good-enough-for-my-little-sister syndrome. The thump I'd felt the first time I gazed into her gold-flecked brown eyes was one of recognition, as those were the same eyes that looked back at me when I shaved every day. Our father's eyes.

One of my many missed calls was from Babs Carmichael, but before I returned it I went online to research LAPD benefits for officers killed in the line duty. It took only minutes to learn money was never held in any kind of escrow account for children if there was a surviving parent. Zoë had received the full benefit on John Valentine's death and that was presumably what we lived on for the next three years. If my college tuition and stipend had not come from the LAPD, there was only one other possible source. The question was whether or not Babs and Tommy had known all along.

I dialed, thinking Babs must have called after hearing about the night before. I knew from Laurel and Rexanne we'd gone national and guessed my only mother figure wanted to make sure I was all right. But Babs hadn't seen the news and wasn't calling to check on me.

"Rick, you're an uncle!" was her joyful response to hearing my voice Ruthie had given birth to a seven-pound baby girl during the night, and I remembered the pink-on-pink gifts were still sitting in my room at the Sutterman house. I expressed all the appropriate enthusiasm, swore I'd call Ruthie later, and let Babs describe the high levels of cuteness and intelligence of her first grandchild.

When she finally wound down, I asked if she knew the source of the funding that had enabled me to go to UCLA.

"The lawyer told us the money was from your father's police death benefits. Why?" She sounded truthful, though wary.

"Are you absolutely sure it didn't come from a man named Dako Farona?"

There was a pause before she answered. "Well, I suppose it's *possible.*"

"So his name is familiar to you?"

I heard a sigh laced with resignation. "Yes, I know his name, but Tommy and I only met him the one time. It was a few months after you moved in with us."

"Do you know who he is?" By the time I'd gone to work for Dako, they had already moved back East and my employer was known to the family only as 'a big private investigator.'

"He *said* he was a close friend of your deceased father. He told us he had family money and wanted to use some of it to benefit his friend's only child."

No wonder Dako had always been broke. "How much?"

"Seven hundred a month."

So, my family had been bought and paid for. "Is that why you and Tommy kept me in your home till I was eighteen? The money?"

Raising three of her own and umpteen others, Babs Carmichael had developed a good ear for hurt feelings masquerading as an attack, and had yanked the chains of whinier jerks than I, including her own husband on occasion.

"Don't you dare question *his* motives or *our* love for you," she said unequivocally. "Mr. Farona made it crystal clear that money was to be spread out over *all* the children, not spent exclusively on extras for you. Tommy made a good salary as a plumber and the state modestly subsidized all the fosters, but with never fewer than five kids in the house, I wasn't able to take a job. Mr. Farona's financial support was almost as much of a godsend to us as you were."

I learned my Wrangler had also come from Dako, bought new, ostensibly for Sonny, but with the proviso it be handed down to me.

"Did you actually think we had the means to buy a brand-new Jeep for your brother?"

If it had been given directly to me, she explained, I would have suspected something. By giving it to Sonny, Dako gifted a sixteen year old he had never met with a sweet ride for two years before he joined the Navy. Because the car was a hand-me-down I never questioned its origins. Which is, of course, what

Dako had counted on. How had I not realized back then that Tommy's vehicle was an ancient Pontiac requiring constant tinkering to keep it running?

I was still rankled when I hung up. Was it from the irrational fear the Carmichaels had put up with me for ten years because they were being paid by Dako to do so? Or could it have been the disturbing memory that suddenly coalesced out of the Swiss-cheese images surviving from my first five years?

I now knew without a doubt that the man who had lifted and spun my laughing mother, the man who had tousled my hair and twirled *me* in a feet-flying circle, had never been John Valentine.

After checking in with Laurel and learning Dako was out of surgery and in recovery, I offered to spell her at the hospital so she could go home and get some sleep. She told me she and Rexanne wanted to stay with him through the night, but my presence would be welcome first thing in the morning.

I was relieved. Although I needed to talk to him, Dako would be out cold for a while and, except for my post-fight blackout, I hadn't slept in a day and a half.

Luckily, the Corvette was automatic, because my bulky, right-hand cast banged awkwardly on the steering wheel and would have been useless trying to operate a stick shift. Made me wonder how I would get around once the rental was returned.

Having slept most of the day, Kitty and Bitsy were refreshed and perky when I walked in the door. The smell of grilling steak woke my stomach, so, despite the weariness and aches, I sat down with the twins for my first meal since dinner the night before, soon realizing what a total pain in the butt the cast would be for the next six weeks, when Bitsy had to cut my rib-eye for me.

"Thank you for everything you did last night," I said, after I'd quieted my gnawing hunger. "And where in the world did you get those guns?"

"The Fakays?" Kitty asked. "Same place we got your dummy ammo."

"This prop guy we used to know, Eddie Chang," volunteered Bitsy. "He retired twenty years ago, but he still has connections in the business."

"Well, let me know what he charged so I can reimburse you."

The Suttermans exchanged a glance I couldn't interpret. "You don't have to do that," Bitsy said dismissively.

I assured them the money wouldn't be coming out of my pocket, that it was a legitimate business expense, reimbursable from my advance.

Again, a look passed between them, then Bitsy cleared her throat. "Uh, Rick? Eddie doesn't want to be paid in currency."

"Then what?"

"Suffice to say you need to make yourself scarce this coming Saturday night."

The fork slipped from my hand and clattered onto the plate, as her meaning became abundantly clear. "You've *got* to be kidding!"

"Oh, please," snapped Kitty. "Are you going to tell us you're the *only* man on earth who never wanted to do it with twins?"

The soothing oblivion of a Vicodin, along with the shock of learning I had, in effect, pimped for a couple eighty-two year olds, put me to sleep right after dinner. I had intended to ask about my free-rent situation, suspecting Dako's hand behind that, too, but I knew the question would be better tackled when I was rested.

Twelve unbroken hours of drugged sleep left me feeling better, though when I looked in the mirror it was like staring at a page in Kitty's portfolio of horror makeup. Blue-black bruises covered the swollen skin surrounding my bloodshot eyes. The strips of tape holding the splint on my nose stretched halfway across each side of my face, and a crusted-blood mustache covered my upper lip.

After deciding a shave wouldn't improve the situation enough to bother, I blotted away the scab-stache with a wet washcloth, got dressed and joined the Suttermans in the kitchen for some desperately needed coffee. Over breakfast the topic was still Wednesday night's caper, though we steered clear of their "arrangement" with the old prop guy.

During the four hours they'd been holed-up in Pat's studio, Kitty had made up our three cheato-banditos and Bitsy had made panini for everyone. Kitty had shown Laurel the duct tape trick to prevent the bullets from clacking together as they were being emptied out of the various weapons, but Jason had made it look like Dako was firmly secured to the chair.

"It's ingenious, really," said Bitsy. "You wind the duct tape around the actor's wrists, chest and ankles, then do the same thing to the arm rests, legs and back of the chair. When he sits down, all you have to do is wrap one more piece of tape around each area, leaving a gap at the ends which you cover with a small strip of silver masking tape."

"Jason came up with the technique when his star complained about having to sit tight for hours playing hostage while the director dicked around with retakes and artsy-fartsy angles," Kitty added.

I had missed seeing the duct-taping of Dako, as I had been in Pat's studio helping her select the right sound effects to broadcast out my open window when the time was right. We edited together a ten-minute recording to convince Tenninger and his posse that someone was being beaten to a pulp.

I steered the topic around to my rent situation and they admitted Dako had approached them shortly after I moved in, offering to pay my rent and asking them to keep it secret.

Again I faced the fear that people had been paid to put up with me, to pretend to be family or friend, but that notion was quickly dispelled when Bitsy said, "We started mailing back his checks years ago."

"He still sends one every month, but we haven't cashed any since we started thinking of you more as a grandson than a tenant," said Kitty.

That made me realize the Carmichaels hadn't gotten a subsidy from Dako since I turned eighteen and moved into a UCLA dorm, but they had never let go of the ties that bind. Babs still fussed at me and worried about me the same motherly way she did with Chris, Ruthie, Sonny and even poor, screwed-up Shane. Tommy disparaged my opinions on sports like he did with his other sons. I truly was a member of their family, and I should be grateful Dako's money had made all our lives a little easier.

I didn't hear any campaign ads on my drive to Burbank, although in the aftermath of the explosive allegations, talk radio was alive with speculation. Some thought the mayoral vote should be postponed and others were happy the demolition of the two frontrunners' credibility would open the way for the less-monied—but much more principled—distant third in the race, a former city councilwoman who had worked tirelessly to better the plight of disadvantaged children, homeless veterans and the working poor. Sounded to me as though for once the system might function as originally intended.

Laurel dozed in the chair next to Dako's bed, her hand loosely holding one of his. She woke on hearing the door close, and when I noticed how drained she looked, I regretted not having manned up and insisted on taking the overnight watch.

"How is he?"

"Godzilla? Don't worry, he's bounced back from much worse." She stood, stretching. "Oh, for a week of sleep."

"I'll stay here all day."

"Good. You should have a conversation with your father."

"I know about the money, Laurel. Tuition, rent, the Jeep."

"Yeah? Well, maybe you'll turn out to be a half-way decent investigator after all."

I asked about those stakeouts we'd done together, when I was supposedly checking out her potential for Dako, and she confirmed it was the other way around.

"Mostly, though, he was trying to protect you. He knew he couldn't keep dragging you with him every time he testified in court or did surveillance, but he was reluctant to put you in harm's way on your own. He needed to be reassured you could take care of yourself if things ever got hairy."

Sending me out with Laurel had accomplished two important things. Dako bolstered my confidence by entrusting me with the "training" of another investigator, while covertly providing a replacement bodyguard. That and everything else I had recently learned about Dako Farona pointed to his being a caring, protective father, even if an unacknowledged one. So why hadn't he come to my rescue when my mother died? Why had he abandoned me to a foster care system that only by chance placed me with people as fine as the Carmichaels? Those are the questions I asked Laurel after she bent to kiss the unresponsive patient's forehead and prepared to leave.

"That all has to do with your mother, Rick," she said, patting my arm. "And it's not my story to tell."

Throughout the day as Dako slept, news trickled in via the TV in his hospital room, my laptop and Rexanne's frequent phone updates. I was certain she would have preferred to be at her father's bedside, but I suspected Laurel had persuaded her to give us some time together.

Rushed ballistics tests linked several of the guns owned by Zeke Martin and Bobby Chalk to a backlog of unsolveds, ranging from home invasion robberies to attempted homicide, so the two were being held in custody without bond. And singing like Josh Groban was my guess.

The separate attorney-bots for Tenninger and Bledsoe dismissively downplayed the implications of the inflammatory YouTube video that had already been seen by everyone in America except babies under a year old and Amish hard-liners. Like residents of a monkey house, the two lawyers slung poop at each other, hoping some of it would stick so their own client would come out smelling marginally better.

The FBI, having looked through the contents of the manila envelope, made the first of several announcements about lines of inquiry they were pursuing: the illegal purchase of federally protected wetlands by an off-shore company owned jointly by Grant Tenninger and Hank Bledsoe.

Mr. Arroyc also made news, coming forward to reveal the details of the poison-pill documents even before the state authenticated them and made them public. He'd probably seen the video and not taken it well when Tenninger ordered Zeke Martin to kill him, so throwing his former customers under the election-fraud-bus was sweet, sweet revenge.

It was only the beginning of the long, slow slide toward prison for Hank Bledsoe and the man Dako had waited more than two decades to bring down.

Every hour or so, a doctor or nurse would pop in to check Dako's vital signs, then at noon, the iv that had been hydrating and medicating him was removed and I was told he should wake any time.

When he opened his eyes I wasn't sure how lucid he was, so I waited for him to speak. He took a look at my battered face, which wasn't half as jacked as his own, then noticed my cast. "What happened to your hand?" he asked, in a dry, raspy voice.

"Some dude slammed his face into it a few dozen times," I responded, standing to pour a glass of water and unwrap a flexible straw.

Dako started to lift himself up, but I stopped him with a sharp, "No." After bending the straw's built-in accordion, I slid my left arm under his shoulders to raise him slightly for a drink, then realized I couldn't grasp the cup with only the fingertips protruding from the plaster cast on my right hand.

Our eyes met as we both saw the ludicrousness of a situation in which neither of us could perform this simple task solo. I withdrew my supporting arm and used my left hand to pick up the water, while Dako gingerly rolled onto his side. By kneeling down and holding the cup below the level of the mattress top, I was able to get the end of the straw within reach of his mouth.

If either of us had been thinking clearly, we might have realized there was a control to raise and lower the head of the bed. But maybe one or both of us needed an excuse for no-fault physical contact.

After nearly finishing the water in thirsty gulps, Dako rolled back flat. "Teamwork," he said.

"You up for a conversation?"

"As long as you don't ask me to break your *other* hand with my face."

Officers Valentine, Ramirez, Chandler and Farona parked at the rendezvous point not far from Khavazhi's warehouse, then stealthily approached on foot. A block away they huddled at the entrance of an alley to observe the target for fifteen minutes, and when they saw no lights, movement or cars in that time, John Valentine signaled for everyone to move forward.

Pausing by the closed door of the windowless facade, they did a final visual sweep before Victor Ramirez peeled off to circle around to the loading dock, Gayle Chandler trailing him. After a couple minutes standing watch by the front door, John whispered for Farona to walk to the corner of the warehouse opposite the side where Victor and Gayle had disappeared and check the alleyway separating Khavazhi's building from the next one over. Gliding quietly to the corner, Dako looked around the edge, sweeping his eyes down the length of the narrow space, then turning and signing an all-clear. John waved him back to the door and, when Dako got there, indicated he would do the same visual on the other side.

John had walked thirty feet and was approaching the far corner of the warehouse when a single shot exploded from behind the front door. Fearing for his partner's safety, Dako automatically went for the door, surprised to find it unlocked. He barreled in through the opening, reaching for a gun he only then remembered wasn't on him.

"Det. Rowan was face down on the concrete with a hole in the back of his skull and blood pooling under what the exit wound had left of his face. Yusup Belkhan stood over him with a .45 in his hand, a piece he swung my way as I froze. Tenninger and Khavazhi pulled their own guns on seeing me, but in that moment before they did, I realized the two of them had been standing casually, as if engaged in relaxed conversation. Khavazhi shouted at Tenninger: *who is this?* Then John rushed in, gun drawn."

In a matter of seconds, Belkhan swung his gun toward the armed arrival, Officer Valentine took him out with two shots, and Officer Farona watched help-lessly as Khavazhi and John aimed at each other.

Instantly, Tenninger bellowed: "Valentine! Stand down!" But John didn't move a muscle. "Now! This isn't what it looks like."

"I think it's exactly what it looks like," Valentine replied.

"You know so much, how is it you *don't* know Farona's fucking your wife?"

In the heartbeat during which Officer Valentine cut his shocked eyes toward Dako Farona, Hamid Khavazhi fired his weapon. As the mortally wounded man fell at Dako's feet, a barrage of gunfire thundered from inside the warehouse and Khavazhi turned on Tenninger, screaming: *you set me up!!*

Tenninger was faster on the trigger, silencing Khavazhi with a head shot and one to the chest, before turning to the petrified young Officer Farona.

"Who's back there?" he barked.

"Vic Ramirez and my partner Gayle."

"Whether they come out of there alive or not, we keep this simple. Belkhan shot my partner, Valentine killed Belkhan, Khavazhi shot Valentine, and then I took down Khavazhi. You got it?"

When the twenty-six year old rookie wasn't able to bring words to his lips, Tenninger made the choice even simpler. If Dako told a story different from what had been laid out for him, the squad would find out he had slept with the dead hero's wife and that Zoë Valentine was a slut.

Tenninger told Dako to call in their location and, as he did, Victor Ramirez crashed onto the scene of carnage.

Dako fell asleep immediately after telling me the rest of it. His version matched those of Victor and Gayle, so I felt I finally had a clear picture of that fateful night so long in the past. The poison the snake had spat at John Valentine was the same used on me Wednesday night and, had I not already known about Dako and Zoë, venom 2.0 might have blinded me, too.

The young, unarmed cop could have done nothing to save his two fallen comrades, and a contradictory statement against the word of a veteran detective would have stood almost no chance of being believed. Tenninger had played his superior hand, forcing Dako Farona to fold in order to protect the woman he loved. And, by extension, her son.

Why, then, hadn't he claimed me? If not after John Valentine's death, then Zoë's? It was a question that would have to wait several hours until he woke again.

Late that afternoon the FBI picked up Hank Bledsoe as he attempted to board a flight to Geneva out of San Francisco, taking him in for questioning about the commissioning of the fake environmental report that certified the Playa del Rey wetlands were worthless and a second document from non-existent tree-huggers making it sound like it was worth twenty million dollars.

Amid the legal bluster and threatening bombast, Grant Tenninger was also hauled in for those reasons, although they were quickly overshadowed by far more serious crimes brought to light by the self-serving revelations of Zeke Martin, Bobby Chalk and two high-ranking members of the LAPD, after all four opted to cut their puppet strings and a deal.

By the time Dako woke, I was able to tell him Grant Tenninger would be brought to justice, maybe not for crimes long ago, or for those he had intended to commit after the election, but for contemporaneous behavior egregious enough to ensure long sentences from federal, state and local authorities.

The mood felt relaxed between Dako and me, maybe for the first time ever. Apparently, all we'd needed to access a state of mutual rationality was to pound the hell out of each other and siphon off the excess testosterone.

"I suppose you want to know why I didn't try to get custody."

"It had crossed my mind to ask."

After the funeral, he said, my mother wouldn't let him near either one of us. He had assumed it was to avoid gossip and to give her a chance to mourn the loss of a man she had genuinely cared for and thought she had treated shabbily, so Dako waited out the separation with understanding and patience.

"Seven months later she still kept me at arm's length, while things went bad for both of us. I was being undermined and sabotaged by Deuce, meaning cops who had known me and worked with me forever started wondering if so much smoke could really exist without the presence of fire."

By that time, Dako had waited more than six years to be with Zoë, but he was finally driven away when he realized she would rather be a dead hero's widow than a live failure's wife. While he was getting railroaded off the force, Zoë's shame had caused her to take up wine as a serious hobby, eventually parlaying it into full-time work. She stayed on that job two and a half years, then turned in her notice with a single shot from her husband's service weapon.

"I offered to take the two of you away somewhere to start fresh, but she was too heavily invested in punishing herself to abandon her penance. And as she pointed out, I was no prize: a semi-disgraced cop with no money, few prospects and a pretty regular drinking habit myself.

"She wanted you to grow up believing you were the son of a hero, not the result of adultery with a man like me, and the last time we spoke she made me swear I would never destroy that illusion for you."

Honoring her demand to the letter, if not the spirit, he had shadowed my life, telling himself I was better off with a loving family like the Carmichaels than with him, but sacrificing everything to optimize my survival chances.

His eyes closed and I wrestled with skepticism. Could my mother really have extracted such a life-changing promise from a man like Dako? And how could her will hold him to that agreement after she was dead?

I was eight years old and terrified. My mother, who had never touched me with anything other than gentleness and love, gripped my shoulders and shook me hard. "Promise!" she shouted.

"I promise," I mumbled, but she shook me more frantically. The by-then familiar smell of red wine soured her breath and we both cried, though for different reasons.

"Look at me! Swear you *will* keep your promise, no matter what happens! Swear!"

I sobbed pitifully, but understood she wouldn't stop unless I convinced her, so I fervently swore I would never become a policeman.

The doorbell rang and she eased her rough grasp, pulling me to her and hugging me. "I love you, Ricky," she whispered. "Always, *always* remember that." I stopped sniffling, still confused, but trying to be brave for her.

Sgt. Steiner's oldest son was at the door when my mother swiped a hand across her eyes, forced a smile and opened it. His father and brothers waved at us from the car. "Come on," he said. "We'll miss the first inning."

My mother gave me her usual peck on the top of my head, then waited at the open door while we two boys clambered into Sgt. Steiner's roomy Buick. I was relieved to flee from her inexplicable anger, but I still turned to wave at her through the rear window as we pulled away. Then, right before we turned the corner to head for Dodger stadium, she blew a good-bye kiss to me.

Would I have kept my promise if that *hadn't* been the last time I ever saw my mother? The startling, unearthed memory provided no answer, but all at once I felt empathy for the other person whose life had been irrevocably altered by an oath sworn to Zoë Valentine.

When he woke, Dako and I spent another hour in conversation and I told him about that afternoon I abandoned the dream of becoming a cop.

Shaking his head—though carefully—he said, "Your mother was a force of nature, Rick." There was no judgment in his words, merely an echo of regret for having been unable to hold her in his life. Or to life itself.

Laurel and Rexanne showed up to shoo me from the room at the end of the day and the drive to Santa Monica gave me time to think about the circumstances that had prevented my parents from being together, despite their profound love for one another. At first contact they had known they were star-crossed, but her marriage had been a formidable obstacle. And the mountain of guilt over John Valentine's murder turned out be impossible to scale.

Passing on dinner, I collapsed into disturbed sleep, waking Saturday morning at 6:00 with the realization I had let myself be daunted by a hill.

To save time at Burbank Airport I valet-parked, then raced into the terminal to look for Piper. Her flight was leaving in half an hour, so I knew she had already cleared security. After waiting agonizing minutes in the line inching toward the ticket counter, I asked a smartly turned-out young man for a seat on the New York flight about to leave, only to be told the last one available was in first-class. Praying my credit card could carry the freight, I held my breath until the computer burped out a ticket and boarding pass. Still holding my escape, the guy asked if I needed to check any luggage. I showed him my sole bag: the carry-on I had wisely snagged on my way out to avoid looking suspicious. It held nothing more than it usually did, a collection of ratty tee-shirts I like too much to part with, but it passed muster and I took off running toward security.

No random selection or terrorist vibe delayed me and I breezed through security, picking up speed as I heard a boarding call for the flight.

"Piper," I shouted, when I finally saw her in the crowd at the gate. She turned while I closed the gap between us.

Out of breath and unsure what I wanted to say, I grabbed her hand and pulled her from the shuffling flow. She gasped when she saw my hashed-up face.

"Rick—" she began, but I put a finger to her lips to stop her.

"I know you have to go and I hope the job turns out great, and yeah, I know this is crazy, but I'll be here when you get back no matter how long you're gone. If you swear you won't run off with some Wall Street hotshot or street mime, I promise I'll be a millionaire before your sell-by date. I love you and, let me reiterate, I *know* this is crazy." I finally shut up and took my finger away from her lips, as half the crowd milled forward and half stood and stared.

"Is it *my* turn to talk?" Piper asked.

I sheepishly nodded, although I dreaded hearing what she might say.

"Wait for me." Her hand darted to the back of my neck and she pulled my head toward her as she went up on tiptoes for a kiss, angling her face so as not to bang my nosial splint. It was over before I had even registered that it was happening, and she dashed through a much-thinned crowd to hand her boarding pass to the airline agent. Pausing at the gateway, Piper turned and mouthed the words *I love you*, not waiting to see my reaction before she disappeared inside.

It took an hour to get my ticket refunded and credit card charge reversed, but I grinned through that red tape like the village idiot.

CODA:

Much has happened in the five months since we brought down Tenninger and Bledsoe. Los Angeles elected the activist former city councilwoman by an unprecedented landslide and she is kicking ass and sweeping out the trash.

Piper perished in a fiery hot-air balloon accident last week after her gay husband found out she'd accidentally had sex with his estranged son, Abdul. We've Skyped, texted, called or emailed virtually every day she's been in New York, and she'll be coming home right after her funeral.

The seventh-richest twenty-one year old in Texas dropped out of TSU to join "the family business," and her father was so pissed he refused to hire her. When I told her she was welcome to take an office and join me at the Gingerbread House—which has become the unofficial San Fernando Valley branch of Farona Investigations—she bought the black Corvette for me and co-opted my Jeep. Rexanne is still annoying, but I finally gave in and joined the Twitter followers of *@Dallas_T_Rex.*

I've attended two weddings. Cal and Moonbeam tied the knot in a ceremony held aboard a replica Millennium Falcon, with an Ewok flower girl and a Wookiee best man—me, in a hairy costume even less comfortable than a suit of armor. Once I took over my student loans, Dako finally decided to buy a ring and make an honest woman out of Laurel. Ironically, Amanda Richfield, his bride the first time around, stood up as matron of honor.

And I have discovered that Dako (can't yet bring myself to call him anything else) kept his own version of my Wigmore's Wafers tin, so fragments of my childhood are coming back to me as I examine its contents, including a size 4-T LAPD uniform, the last of three he had made for me, the one Zoë threw at him the day after her husband died. Her instructions were to get rid of it, along with the little badge that says Officer Ricky in fading cartoon letters.

John Valentine's name will be carried on by me, even if I can't claim to carry his blood. And, because mythological heroes are loath to be separated from weapon and shield, I dug a hole at the base of his grave marker to return the Kimber and his badge.

WIK: the ultimate winner in all this is Holloway's Bellwort, a tiny, dicotyledonous plant believed to have been all but wiped out around the world. When a *genuine* environmental protection group examined the Playa del Rey acreage on behalf of the Bureau of Land Management, they found a single dormant taproot struggling to outlast the persistent California drought and that was sufficient for the land to be confiscated, reclassified and protected.

The specialness of Holloway's Bellwort lies in its amazing ability to hold on tenaciously for decades in a sort of suspended animation, existing, if not actually thriving. But then, when it finally gets what it needs, it not only revives, it flourishes.

I can totally relate.

Flight
Risk
Books

If you liked Rick Valentine...

...meet Blake Ervansky and Maureen O'Brien in the award-winning Hollywood murder series by April Kelly and Marsha Lyons that Kirkus Reviews called "tight and sharp-witted."

For a quick look at the first three books in the series, Murder In One Take, Murder: Take Two and Shamus Award Finalist Murder: Take Three, please turn the page. For outlines and sample chapters of all Flight Risk Books, visit flightriskbooks.com.

A preview of Not Funny, Valentine! the next entry in the Rick Valentine mystery series, due out December 2016, may be found at the end of this book and on our website.

MURDER IN ONE TAKE
FIRST PLACE WINNER · MYSTERY/SUSPENSE
Kindle Book Promos' 2014 International Contest

MURDER IN ONE TAKE
"This perfectly crafted Hollywood murder peels back the curtain on not one, but two worlds, giving the reader a glimpse into the glamour of show business and the slow grind of down-and-dirty police work, blending the two domains in clever metatextual ways. Plenty of snappy banter and clenched-jaw exposition...all the intrigue of Hollywood's big-budget blockbusters."

— Kirkus Reviews

MURDER: TAKE TWO
"Kelly and Lyons return to their distinctive brand of mystery starring the LA-based duo (Maureen O'Brien and Blake Ervansky) who combine traditional investigation with the Hollywood perspective. Darker than its predecessor, this installment doesn't sacrifice the humor or turns of phrase that were the hallmarks of the first. Tight and sharp-witted."

— *Kirkus Reviews*

MURDER: TAKE THREE
2014 SHAMUS AWARD FINALIST
Best Indie PI Novel

SHELF UNBOUND'S 2014 TOP 100
Included all three Ervansky/O'Brien
detective novels

MURDER IN ONE TAKE
by
Marsha Lyons and April Kelly

Det. Blake Ervansky is first on the scene when an Oscar-winning star is shot by his ex-lover. As lead cop on the case, Ervansky has everything he needs to put away Ali Garland: motive, weapon, videos of the murder and a dozen eyewitnesses, one of whom is his partner of less than 24 hours, Sgt. Maureen O'Brien.

This is LA, the beating heart of show biz, though, so nothing is as it seems, even Ervansky's new partner. Ali Garland appears to have been justified in defending herself with lethal force, but could this wide-eyed ingénue be the architect of an airtight double fake? Has she really pulled off the perfect murder?

Ervansky and O'Brien will only unravel her skein of deceit when they turn to the same Hollywood magic that convinces audiences aliens can phone home, talking clown fish do search and rescue, and every hooker is just a nice girl waiting for the right millionaire.

———⟨≡⟩———

"The writing is intelligent and excellently paced, the dialogue believable—and humorous. I highly recommend it to all mystery lovers."
—*The Pulp Den*

Florida Authors and Publishers Association
First Place Gold Medal winner

MURDER: TAKE TWO
by
Marsha Lyons and April Kelly

What has six legs, black stripes and kills people?
A homicidal magician and the biggest tiger in his
world-famous show. Murder will be hard to prove,
though, because the dead guy never existed, all the
evidence seems to have been eaten, and the victim's
corpse isn't the only thing that has disappeared.

When Maureen O'Brien suddenly vanishes, PI
Blake Ervansky learns about her shocking former
life, a past he doesn't think he can live with. Then,
before he can tell her their partnership is over, a
call from a client in hysterics reveals that a recently
solved case has come messily unsolved.

Putting aside their own difference, Maureen and
Blake circumvent a corrupt sheriff and draw closer
to the truth, until Blake winds up in a deadly game
of cat-and-mouse in which he's the mouse, and the
cat outweighs him by 400 pounds. It's a cage match
he won't survive unless the skills Maureen acquired
in her dark past can neutralize the killer before
Blake becomes cat chow.

*"...doesn't sacrifice the humor or turns of phrase that
were the hallmarks of the first. Tight and sharp-
witted."*

—*Kirkus Reviews*

A Shelf Unbound Top 100 book - 2014

MURDER: TAKE THREE
by
Marsha Lyons and April Kelly

When movie action hero Micah Deifenschlictor is accused of murdering his longtime agent, private investigators Maureen O'Brien and Blake Ervansky are offered a small fortune by Micah's attorney to prove her client's innocence.

Blake and Maureen uncover evidence that eliminates Micah as a suspect in less than a day, earning the huge paycheck for very little work. When the case boomerangs back to them, however, the detectives realize they may have been duped into participating in a cover-up.

After secretly reopening their investigation, Ervansky and O'Brien are drawn into something much larger and darker than mere homicide, something that will bring unimaginable grief to Blake's life, not only changing him as a man, but irrevocably altering his relationship with Maureen.

2014 Shamus Award Finalist
Best Indie PI Novel

"Wow! This series just keeps getting better."
—The Pulp Den

He's back!

Rick Valentine, PI, MI and good guy,
returns in:

NOT FUNNY,
VALENTINE!

Due out December 2016

CNN Headlines News:
LA stops laughing as killer stalks stand-up comics.

Not Funny, Valentine!
by
April Kelly

In LA's competitive comedy scene, every stand-up knows the golden passkey to the lead in a sitcom, an HBO special or a headlining gig in Las Vegas is an appearance on one of the late-night Jimmys—Kimmel, Fallon or Crockett. But when rising-star comic Paulie Villanova is murdered with one of his own props in the Green Room of James "Jiminy" Crockett's program minutes after his debut on *Every Night,* competitive turns cutthroat and comedians begin dropping like pregnant pole-vaulters.

Rick Valentine still has that new-detective smell when he's hired by the mother of one of the dead comics to find her son's killer after the coroner rules the death a suicide. If Rick can prove murder and track the perp, he may be able to link all the dead stand-ups to a single killer. The one thing they all had in common? Recent performances on *Every Night with Jiminy Crockett.*

While Rick goes about sleuthing the traditional way, his sister Rexanne, wannabe PI and annoying pain in Rick's neck, tries out on open-mike night at The Comedy Cave, hoping to get an inside track on the string of unfunny deaths. With better-known comics understandably reluctant to book gigs on *Every Night,* Crockett is forced to mine the second-tier of funny and, while scraping the bottom of that barrel, he "discovers" Rexanne.

When Rick learns his sister has set herself up as bait for the killer, he tries to prevent her from going on the show, but Rexanne is as stubborn as she is beautiful, and she ignores Rick's brotherly advice. Despite the fact that her jokes stink, her timing sucks and she knows Crockett is only booking her to try to break the curse of what is being called the "ha-ha-homicides," Rexanne prepares for her national debut as a stand-up comic.

Rick has seen her act and knows it's a forgone conclusion she will die onstage, so it's up to him to ensure that death is figurative, rather than literal.

Is Jiminy Crockett trying to bump the ratings on his third-place show by actively sustaining the curse? Is a once-famous comedian, now reduced to being the singing hemorrhoid in a Preparation H commercial, taking revenge on the generation of funny guys who replaced him? Can Rexanne remember the set-up goes *before* the punchline?

It will be up to Rick Valentine to answer those questions and bring a killer to justice.

WINGED
by
April Kelly

FIRST PLACE WINNER - GENERAL FICTION
Kindle Book Promos' 2014 International Contest

"Kelly's fast-paced novel takes the reader on a flight of fancy couched in realistic, straightforward and graceful prose that makes the fantastic utterly believable. It's hard to stop reading...fasten your seat belt for an enjoyable flight."

—Kirkus Reviews

"The strong voice speaking from the pages of WINGED, by April Kelly, immediately captures both interest and sympathy...with cliffhangers that keep the reader turning pages breathlessly. WINGED seizes the imagination because of its unusual premise, but it wins our hearts because it is, after all...the story of the universal need to pursue passions and dreams, often at a high cost."

—Southern Literary Review

WRITER'S DIGEST SELF-PUBLISHED BOOK AWARDS
Honorable Mention - 2013

WINGED
by
April Kelly

What if the cavalier decision you made about your child the day she was born had the power to reverberate for more than thirty years, dividing the nation, costing three people their lives, and destroying your family?

Homeless teen Allison Fitzgerald believes the two tiny membranes on her baby's back are not, as the doctors claim, a surgically correctable birth defect, but a pair of wings. And after having a vision of her child flying, she even names her Angel.

The "wings" will never lift the child off the ground, but they will engender in Angel a dangerous obsession with flying, an obsession that will one day drive her to attempt the impossible.

This darkly comic contemporary reframing of the Icarus and Daedalus myth explores the lengths to which a mother will go to protect her child, and ultimately offers a message of salvation, not only for the family involved, but for all mankind.

WINGED

Chapter One

Smile patronizingly at my naming her Angel, but remember I was only eighteen and my child *was* born with wings. Well, the doctor didn't call them wings. He called them a congenital anomaly and recommended they be surgically removed before we left the hospital.

I had never heard the word anomaly before, and I only recognized three syllables of congenital, the three that had gotten me in trouble nine months earlier when two other twelfth-grade girls and I had crashed a fraternity party where I downed about a dozen drinks that must have been ninety-nine percent wine and only one percent cooler.

The drugs they gave me during the birth— more to shut me up than to ease any pain, I suspect—impaired my ability to detect reactions from either doctor or nurses that would have indicated I had just expelled a freak. The words penetrating my mushy consciousness gave no clue there was a problem: *girl, umbilical, Apgar, turkey sub.* One of the nurses may have been placing her lunch order.

Three hours later I was stitched up, cleaned

up, and sitting up when a nurse brought me a pink wrappy thing with a tiny head sticking out one end. Immediately upon off-loading the bundle to me, she gave a tight smile and left. I had barely enough time to register the features of the squinched little face before the doctor approached my bed, his own face fixed in a squinch. It looked marginally better on the baby.

Once he had pulled the curtain around my ward bed—broke teenagers who can't even come up with a babydaddy name for the birth certificate don't rate the premium accommodations—the doc began a rambling tale about how some babies are born with webbing between their fingers or toes, and that it was customary to do the simple surgical repairs before they left the hospital.

"So what are you saying? She has duck feet?"

"No, no, no." He seemed panicked by my question. "Her fingers and toes are fine. But she has two very small membranous flaps on her back that we'd like to remove."

"I want to see them."

"I have to discourage that, Miss Fitzgerald. These congenital anomalies are routine for medical personnel, but for a new mother, especially one as young as...."

He might have said more, but I was already freeing my child from the pastel cotton burrito into which she had been stuffed. Once unswaddled, her little arms and legs did a bit of slow-motion waving, and her mouth opened in a gummy yawn, while the doctor held out a clipboard and asked me to sign the consent form.

I gently turned her over to place her on her stomach on my stomach and saw them for the first time: wings.

It wasn't much of an argument. I had only turned eighteen two months earlier, but I knew I was an adult in the eyes—if not the common sense—of the law, and that I had the right to say no to the mutilation of my child. Frustrated, the doctor left and I was finally alone with her.

Still facedown and sleeping on me, her tiny form rode the rise and fall of my belly as I breathed. One arm curved alongside her head, fist extended, and the rhythmic movement combined with the facedown, arm-out position made me think of Superman flying.

I wish I could say I had some warm and maternal feeling for that little stranger, but I didn't. There was a vague sense of obligation to handle her carefully, but no more than when I had held a puppy or a kitten as a child. No, the only feeling I had was a curiosity about her, an interest in this creature created solely by me. Well, by me and some unknown Sigma Tau Gamma.

The doc had been accurate in calling them membranous flaps. Though they matched the cream and pink mottle of her back, they looked more reptilian than human: two tiny triangles of skin which emerged from either side of the small knobs of her upper spine, then curved and hugged her shoulder blades. I gently stroked one with the tip of my index finger, Brailling the info to my brain. Not as soft as I thought they would be, and with the slightest of ridges along the sides, like piping under the skin. When I slipped my fingernail under the edge and lifted the flap, there was a small amount of tensile strength in it, enough to snug it back in place when I took my finger away.

I carefully turned her back over and her arms and legs began that slo-mo dog paddle again.

Cradling her against me, I took in the brownish fuzz that capped her head, one piece in front almost long enough for my licked fingertip to paste into a curl. I examined the minuscule diaper, deciding it looked like the one worn by the wetting doll I got for Christmas when I was five.

I leaned over to check out the itty-bitty eyelashes, so we were almost nose to nose when she opened her eyes. We both flinched, and I pulled back far enough to focus. The cliché caught me off guard, that intense rush of love that bonded me to her instantly. That alone would have been a powerful enough experience, albeit shared with virtually every other new mother since the beginning of time. But that was only the first jab of the one-two punch that changed my life forever; the tap that laid me out was looking into her eyes and seeing my own face—twice, tiny—reflected back. Not the face I had then, but my future face, the one that bends over a yellow pad tonight as I sit on this bunk and scribble out my life. Was that future me trying desperately to communicate answers to questions teen me had not yet begun to ask? Before I averted my eyes to break that frightening connection, three powerful thoughts surged into me: one, that this child would save me; two, that I would be willing to give up my own life for her; and three, that I would one day see her fly. All three have come true.

A tall, silver-haired priest was the next person to try to persuade me to have my daughter's wings removed. As I was in a Catholic hospital, I was not surprised to see a priest, but from the embarrassed look on Father Paul's face, he *was* surprised to see a female breast. Hey, what could I do? It was snack time for the kidlet, and an open ward doesn't offer a heck of a lot of privacy.

Father Paul was almost too easy a target. When he speculated that my daughter would be teased by her school chums—he actually used that word, chums—when they learned of her secret deformity, I countered by claiming to be reluctant to interfere with God's plan.

"If He created her this way, how can we mere mortals presume to improve on His plan? And she doesn't have a deformity; she has a pair of wings."

"Allison, you can't actually believe they're wings. That defies logic."

"Oh, right. But a pregnant virgin and a dead guy waking up after three days make perfect sense. Sorry, padre, but I'm sticking with the wings theory."

I'm not sure if it was my blasphemy or the sight of my swollen, blue-veined boob as the baby finished brunch and lolled away from it, but the good father stood quickly, scraping his chair back. I'm sure part of him wanted to stay and fight for the soul of a child born to so obviously a lost-cause mother, but I also sensed the larger part of him would be relieved to get back to the terminal patients who welcomed his comforting words. I decided to absolve him of my sins.

"I'm naming her Angel."

Camel's back, meet the straw. Father Paul didn't have much of a poker face and, looking appalled, he choked out a canned blessing, then exited ward left.

I had only said it to be a bitch, but when micro girl burped in her sleep and I looked down at the milk bubble inflating and deflating in the corner of her mouth, I figured Angel was as good a name as any. You don't have to believe in God to believe in angels.

I had three days in the hospital getting to know her, learning how to take care of her basic needs, and wondering where we could go when St. Luke's threw us out. Brian's mom and dad had been amazing, letting me stay at their house when I started looking like I was hiding a basketball under my shirt and my own parents ejected me from their vinyl-sided Eden (with detached garage), but Brian was taking early college entrance and I could hardly ask Mr. and Mrs. Haywood to let me stay on with the bambina. Nice as they were, I knew half the reason they invited me in the first place was their fervent, long shot hope that Bri was the father. They clung to the belief that being gay was a phase he would snap out of and that Greg was just his study buddy.

Brian came to the hospital the day after Angel was born, carrying a bouquet of daisies for me and a really inappropriate teddy bear in a black leather onesie for her. That was the day he told me he was leaving for Berkeley the following week. We had been good friends since the tenth grade, and his departure would bring me down to zero in the best-buds department, as Heather and Chelsea—my two partners in the great frat party debacle—had been forbidden to have any contact with me since our drunk and disorderly escapade. Most of the rest of my semifriends had pulled back when my pregnancy became obvious, with the few holdouts falling away when the principal told me I could no longer be a Gettysburg Cougar. (Go, silver and blue!) I think it was less that the other kids were judgmental and more that we didn't see each other every day at school anymore. Face it, the foundation for ninety-five percent of all high school friendships is proximity.

I bonded with Angel, ate instant oatmeal

and green Jell-O, and resisted two more attempts by the doctor to change my mind about removing the wings. On the fourth morning I was released. I stood on the steps of St. Luke's without a home, a job, a clue, a high school diploma, a family, or friends.

But I had my baby and, thanks to me, she still had her wings.

Jesus, I wish I had listened to that doctor.

About the author:

Emmy-nominated for both writing and producing, April Kelly spent more time in television than was sensible. She lives in Tennessee with her two dogs Titus and Ronicus.

For author biographies, sample chapters and a
complete list of our books, please visit
www.flightriskbooks.com